Look what people are saying about Leslie Kelly...

"*Don't Open Till Christmas* by Leslie Kelly is a present in itself where the humor and the sizzling sex never stop. Top Pick!"
—*Romantic Times BOOKreviews*

"Spend an evening of pleasure and fun, and treat yourself to an intensely emotional, funny, spine-tingling, and well-written book. A perfect 10!"
—*Romance Reviews Today* on *She Drives Me Crazy*

"Ms. Kelly has a delightful and engaging voice that had me laughing out loud and relentless in reading every delicious word."
—*The Romance Readers Connection*

"Leslie Kelly never fails to deliver a captivating story."
—*Romance Reviews Today*

"Leslie Kelly writes with a matchless combination of sexiness and sassiness that makes every story a keeper."
—*Fallen Angel Reviews*

"Leslie Kelly is a master of amusing contemporary romance."
—*WordWeaving*

Blaze™

Dear Reader,

It's been a couple of years since I first worked with Julie Elizabeth Leto and Tori Carrington on THE BAD GIRLS CLUB series for Harlequin Temptation. That book (*Wicked & Willing*) was one of my favorite-ever Temptation novels to write (I guess I just have a real soft spot for bad girls). So when Harlequin Blaze invited us to bring the miniseries over, I jumped at the chance, and was thrilled that Tori and Julie did, too!

Obviously, if you read all three of THE BAD GIRLS CLUB books, you will see a "shared" scene that appears in each. That was so much fun to write, and I have to tip my hat to Julie for creating it and including my heroine, even before I'd started on my own book!

I also took this opportunity to write the next-to-last installment in my Santoris of Chicago series. There was only one single brother left—ex-marine Nick— and I knew I wanted to write his story the moment I finished writing his twin brother Mark's. But the twins are quite different, as you will see, and I think pairing the serious military man with a supersexy, bad-girl stripper worked out beautifully.

I so hope you agree.

Happy reading!

Leslie Kelly

LESLIE KELLY
Overexposed

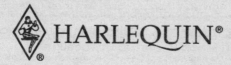

HARLEQUIN®

TORONTO • NEW YORK • LONDON
AMSTERDAM • PARIS • SYDNEY • HAMBURG
STOCKHOLM • ATHENS • TOKYO • MILAN • MADRID
PRAGUE • WARSAW • BUDAPEST • AUCKLAND

ISBN-13: 978-0-373-79351-8
ISBN-10:   0-373-79351-0

OVEREXPOSED

This edition published by arrangement with Harlequin Books S.A.

www.eHarlequin.com

Printed in U.S.A.

ABOUT THE AUTHOR

A two-time RWA RITA® Award nominee, eight-time *Romantic Times BOOKreviews* Award nominee and 2006 *Romantic Times BOOKreviews* Award winner, Leslie Kelly has become known for her delightful characters, sparkling dialogue and outrageous humor. All her previous Harlequin Blaze stand-alone titles have been nominated for the *Romantic Times BOOKreviews* Award for Best Blaze of the Year.

Honored with numerous other awards, including a National Readers' Choice Award, Leslie writes sexy novels for Harlequin Blaze, and single-title contemporaries for HQN Books. Keep up with her latest releases by visiting her Web site: www.lesliekelly.com, or her blog, www.plotmonkeys.com.

Books by Leslie Kelly

To a couple of my favorite "bad girls"—
Julie and Lori. And to one fun bad boy, Tony!
Let's be bad together again sometime!

Prologue

THEY CALLED HER the Crimson Rose.

As her name was announced in sultry, almost reverent tones at Leather and Lace, an exclusive men's club, an awed quiet began to slither through the crowd. The room stilled, noisy conversation giving way to quiet expectation.

Businessmen in open-collared shirts stopped their whispered flirtations with waitresses wearing tiny black skirts and skimpy tops. Attendees of an entire bachelor party returned to their table, elbowing the groom to watch and weep. Single men who came every week just to see *her* sat back in plush leather chairs and stared rapt at the stage through hooded eyes. The ice tinkling against their glasses was soon the only sound in the lushly appointed room, even the servers knew better than to interrupt the clientele when the Rose was on stage.

She danced only twice a week—on Saturdays and Sundays—and since the night she'd started, the Crimson Rose had become one of the hottest attractions in the Chicago club scene. Because while the jaded city had long been used to hard-looking dancers taking off their clothes and gyrating to the heavy beat of sexual music, they simply hadn't seen anything like *her.*

She wasn't hard-looking, she was elegant. Her delicate features and natural curves made every man who saw her wonder what it would feel like to touch her creamy skin.

She didn't strip…she undressed. Slowly. Seductively. As if she had all the time in the world to give a man pleasure.

She didn't gyrate, she swayed, moving with fluid grace. Every gesture, every turn an invitation to gaze at her.

Her sound wasn't sexual, it was sensual, erotic and soulful enough to make a man close his eyes and appreciate it. Though, of course, when she was onstage none ever would.

While her job might have diminished some women in the eyes of those around her, the Rose *owned* it, embraced it, lifted it up to a level of art rather than pure sexual titillation.

She liked what she did. And they liked watching her.

The low, sultry thrum of a smoky number began, but the stage remained dark as the workers put final placement on a portable red satin curtain, used only by her. It had been a recent addition by the management, who'd realized that the high-class, stage performer feel was part of the Crimson Rose's appeal. As was the mystery.

While most of the other dancers at the club performed under bright overhead light and full exposure, the Rose danced in shadow and pools of illumination provided by precisely timed spotlights. Her red velvet mask never came off. Most figured the management was playing upon the popularity of the aura of secrecy surrounding the Rose.

Finally the music grew louder, the gelled spotlights, ranging in color from soft pink to bloodred, illuminated the stage, dancing back and forth, each briefly touching on one spot: the seam of the closed satin curtain.

"Now, for your viewing delight," said a smooth male from the sound system, "Chicago's perfect bloom, the Crimson Rose."

No one clapped or whispered. No one *moved*. All eyes were on the center of the curtain, where a hand began to emerge.

It was pale. Delicate, with long fingers and slender wrists. A colorful design—painted-on body art—began at the tip of one finger, with a tiny leaf. It connected to a vine, which wound up her hand, around her wrist. As her arm emerged, more of the leafy vine, complete with sharp thorns, was revealed. It glittered, sensuous and wicked, alluring and dangerous.

Sinuous, slow, unhurried, she emerged from the drape, until she was fully revealed. But her head remained down, her long reddish-brown hair concealing her face.

The tempo throbbed. The dancer stayed still, as if completely oblivious to the crowd. Finally, the spotlights changed color, the vibrant reds giving way to a soft, morning yellow. And, as if she were a tightly wound blossom being awakened by a gentle dawn, the Rose began to move.

Her head slowly lifted, the delicate beauty of her pale throat emphasized by more body art. Her hair fell back as she turned toward the light, as if welcoming the morning.

Her full lips—red and wet—were parted, sending vivid images and erotic fantasies into the minds of every man close enough to see their glisteny sheen…. This was a woman made for the art of kissing. And sensual pleasure.

There the view of her face stopped. A soft red-velvet mask covered the rest. The mask glittered with green jewels like those in the vine, leaving her audience certain that the temptress's eyes must be a pure, vivid emerald. Most already knowing the mystery of her face would not be revealed, her admirers refocused their attention to the rest of her.

She wore layers of soft fabric, cut in petal shapes. Still like the flower being awakened by the sun, she began to indulge in the spotlight's warmth. Swaying, she stretched lazily like a cat in a puddle of light. Her movements were unhurried, revealing a length of thigh, a glimmer of hip.

Then the tempo picked up. So did her pace. She arched and swayed across the stage with feminine grace. But to most, she appeared lonely—removed from her surroundings—revealing a sensual want that begged for fulfillment that would never come.

Anyone in the audience would have fulfilled it for her.

Anyone.

Every move she made set the billowing layers of her costume in motion, until the petals nearly danced around her on their own. They parted to reveal her slender legs, providing a peek here and a glimpse there.

And then they started to disappear.

Every man in the place leaned forward. Wherever she turned, another bit of fabric hit the floor. Her hands moved so effortlessly that the layers seemed to fall by themselves. The light pinks and puffy outer veil went first, followed by the heavier satin pieces. Soon her long, perfectly toned legs were revealed up to the thigh. A drape of satin covering her stomach fell next, torn away from the strings of a bikini top.

She continued her siren's dance as the fabric fell away, the tempo pushing harder, her hips thrusting in response. Finally, when she wore nothing but a sparkly red G-string and two tiny, delicate pink petals on the tips of her breasts, she glanced at the audience, deigning to give them her attention. Normally, at this point, she would offer a saucy smile, pluck the petals off her nipples, then duck behind her curtains. She'd give them a glimpse—quick, heart-stoppingly sexy— then disappear into the dark recesses of the club until her second performance of the night. But tonight…tonight, she hesitated. No. Tonight, she *froze*.

Because as she cast a final glance at her audience, seeing a number of familiar faces in the crowd, her attention was captured by a shadowy figure standing in the back of the room, beside the bar. Ignoring the expectant hush from those familiar with her performance, all of whom were waiting for the payoff moment they'd come to see, she focused all her attention on *him*.

She couldn't see much at that distance, both because of the mask she wore and the spotlights still shining in her face. But she saw enough to send her heart—already beating frantically due to her performance—into hyperdrive.

From here, he appeared black-haired and black-eyed and black-clothed. She could make out none of his features, just that tall, dark presence—broad of shoulder, slim-hipped. He might be dangerous, given his size and the shadowy darkness swallowing him from her view—but now, at this moment, she felt lured by him. Entranced. Captivated.

Their eyes locked. He knew he had her attention. And in that moment, she desperately wanted to walk off the stage, across the room, close enough to see if his face was as handsome as his shadowy form hinted. Then closer—to see what truths lay in the mysterious depths of those inky black eyes.

But suddenly someone whistled…someone else catcalled. She realized she'd lost track of the music and the dance and the audience and her reasons for being here.

Titillation. Seduction. Those were her reasons for being here. Which made it that much more strange that, right now, the Rose was the one who felt seduced.

Enough. Time to finish.

Sweeping her gaze across the crowd, she gave them all a wickedly sexy look, as if her pause had been entirely purposeful. And entirely for their personal delight. In it, she invited them to imagine just who had her breathing hard—licking her lips in anticipation. Who had her skin flushed and her sex damp and her nipples rock hard.

She only wished she knew the answer.

With one more sidelong glance through half-lowered lashes, she reached for the tiny petals—pink, to match the tender skin of her taut nipples—and plucked them off.

The crowd was roaring as she disappeared behind the

curtain. They cheered for several long minutes during which she regained her breath and tried to force her pulse to return to its normal, measured beat.

When it did, she took a chance and peeked through the curtain, her stare zoning in on that dark place by the bar.

But the shadowy stranger was gone.

1

FOR THE FIRST TWO WEEKS after he'd returned from the Middle East, Nick Santori genuinely didn't mind the way his family fussed over him. There were big welcome home barbecues in the tiny backyard of the row house where he'd been raised. There were even bigger dinners at the family-owned pizzeria that had been his second home growing up.

He'd been dragged to family weddings by his mother and into the kitchen of the restaurant by his father. He'd had wet, sticky babies plopped in his lap by his sisters-in-law, and had been plied with beer by his brothers, who wanted details on everything he'd seen and done overseas. And he'd had rounds of drinks raised in his honor by near-strangers who, having suitably praised him as a patriot, wanted to go further and argue the politics of the whole mess.

That was where he drew the line. He didn't want to talk about it. After twelve years in the Corps, several of them on active duty in Iraq, he'd had enough. He didn't want to relive battles or wounds or glory days with even his brothers and he sure as hell wouldn't justify his choice to join the military to people he'd never even met.

At age eighteen, fresh out of high school with no interest in college and even less in the family business, entering the Marines had seemed like a kick-ass way to spend a few years.

What a dumb punk he'd been. Stupid. Unprepared. Green.

He'd quickly learned…and he'd grown up. And while he didn't regret the years he'd spent serving his country, he sometimes wished he could go back in time to smack that eighteen year old around and wake him up to the realities he'd be facing.

Realities like this one: coming home to a world he didn't recognize. To a family that had long since moved on without him.

"So you hanging in?" asked his twin, Mark, who sat across from him in a booth nursing a beer. His brothers had all gotten into the habit of stopping by the family-owned restaurant after work a few times a week.

"I'm doing okay."

"Feeling that marinara running through your veins again?"

Nick chuckled. "Do you think Pop has ever even realized there's any other kind of food?"

Mark shook his head. Reaching into a basket, he helped himself to a breadstick. "Do *you* think Mama has ever even tried to cook him any?"

"Good point." Their parents were well matched in their certainty that any food other than Italian was unfit to eat.

"Is she still griping because you wouldn't move back home?"

Nodding, Nick grabbed a breadstick of his own. For all his grumbling, he wouldn't trade his Pop's cooking for anything…especially not the never-ending MRE's he'd had to endure in the military. "She seems to think I'd be happy living in our old room with the Demi Moore *Indecent Proposal* poster on the wall. It's like walking into a frigging time warp."

"You always did prefer *G.I. Jane.*"

Nick just sighed. Mark seldom took anything seriously. In that respect, he hadn't changed. But everything else sure had.

During the years he'd been gone, the infrequent visits home hadn't allowed Nick to mentally keep up with his loved ones. In his mind, when he'd lain on a cot wondering if there would ever come a day when sand wouldn't infiltrate every surface of his clothes again, the Santoris were the same big, loud bunch he'd grown up with: two hard-working parents and a brood of kids.

They weren't kids anymore, though. And Mama and Pop had slowed down greatly over the years. His father had turned over the day-to-day management of Santori's to Nick's oldest brother, Tony, and stayed in the kitchen drinking chianti and cooking.

One of his brothers was a prosecutor. Another a successful contractor. Their only sister was a newlywed. And, most shocking of all to Nick, Mark, his twin, was about to become a father.

Married, domesticated and reproducing…that described the happy lives of the five other Santori kids. And every single one of them seemed to think he should do exactly the same thing.

Nick agreed with them. At least, he *had* agreed with them when living day-to-day in a place where nothing was guaranteed, not even his own life. It had seemed perfect. A dream he could strive for at the end of his service. Now it was within reach.

He just wasn't sure he still wanted it.

He didn't doubt his siblings were happy. Their conversations were full of banter and houses and SUVs and baby talk that they all seemed to love but Nick just didn't get. And wasn't sure he ever would…despite how much he knew he *should*.

I will.

At least, he *hoped* he would.

The fact that he was bored out of his mind helping out at Santori's and hadn't yet met a single *appropriate* woman who made his heart beat faster—much less one he wanted to pick out baby names with—was merely a product of his own re-adjustment to civilian life. He'd come around. Soon. No doubt about it.

As long as he avoided going after the one woman he'd seen recently who not only made his heart beat fast but had also given him a near-sexual experience from across a crowded room. Because she was in *no way* appropriate. She was a stripper. One he'd be working with very soon now that he'd agreed to take a job doing security at a club called Leather and Lace.

Forcibly thrusting the vision of the sultry dancer out of his brain, he focused on the type of *normal* woman he'd someday meet who might inspire a similar reaction.

He'd have help locating her. Everyone, it seemed, wanted him to find the "perfect" woman and they all just happened to know her. The next one of his sisters-in-law who asked him to come over for dinner and *coincidentally* asked her single best friend to come, too, would be staring at Nick's empty chair.

"Do you know how glad I am that your wife's knocked up?"

"Yeah, me too," Mark replied, wearing the same sappy look he'd had on his face since he'd started telling everyone Noelle was expecting. "But do I want to know why *you're* so happy?"

"Because it means she doesn't have time to try to set me up with her latest single friend/hair stylist/next-door-neighbor or just the next breathing woman who walks by."

Mark had the audacity to grin.

"It's not funny."

"Yeah, it is. I've seen the ones they've thrown at you."

"You seen me throw them back, too, then."

Nodding, Mark sipped his beer.

"Doesn't matter if she's a blonde, brunette, redhead or bald. Any single woman with a pulse gets shoved at me."

"And Catholic," Mark pointed out.

"Mama's picks, yeah. But *none* of them are my type."

Deadpan, his brother asked, "Women?"

"F-you," he replied. "I mean, I do have a few preferences."

"Big—"

"Beyond that," Nick snapped.

Mark relented. "Okay, I'm kidding. What *do* you want?"

That was the question of the hour, wasn't it? Nick had no idea what he wanted. It was *supposed* to be someone who'd make him want *this*. This sedate, small-town-in-a-big-city lifestyle.

"I don't know if I'm cut out for what all of you have."

When Mark's brow rose, Nick added, "I wasn't criticizing. You all seem happy. The couples in *this* family don't seem as…"

"Boring?"

"I guess."

"Thanks," his brother replied dryly.

"No offense. But you're all the exception, not the rule."

Mark murmured, "That's a lot of exceptions."

It was. Which meant Nick was out of luck. How many great, happy marriages could one family contain?

But damned if he wasn't going to give it a try. He'd been telling himself for the last three years of his active enlistment that once he was free—once he was home—he was going to have the kind of life the rest of his family had. The dreams of that normal, happy lifestyle had sustained him through some of the wickedest fighting he'd ever seen. He would not give them up now. Not even if they suddenly seemed a little sedate.

"Face it, they won't rest until you're 'settled down.'"

"Like *you?*" he asked, raising a brow. His twin was a hard-ass Chicago detective who could hardly be described as "settled down." The man was as tough as they came, despite his occasionally goofy sense of humor.

"Yeah. Like me."

Nick rolled his eyes. "You are in no way *settled down*." He glanced at the cuts on his twin's knuckles.

Mark smiled, a twinkle in his eyes. "Guy resisted."

"Does Noelle know?"

The smile faded. "No, and if you tell her I'll pound you."

"I'd like to see you try."

Leaning back in the booth and crossing his arms across his chest, Mark nodded. "I guess you might be able to hold your own now that the Marines toughened you up and filled you out."

It had long been a friendly argument between them that Nick had inherited their mother's lean, tall build like Luke and Joe. Mark and Tony resembled their barrel-chested father. But after many tough, physical years in the military, Nick was no longer anybody's "little" brother. "I think I could take you on."

"I think you could take *anybody* on. So why don't you come down to the station and talk to my lieutenant?"

"Not interested in your job, bro. I've had enough of rules and regulations for a while." They'd talked about the possibility a few times since Nick had returned home, but he wasn't about to relent on that issue. He'd done his time on the battlefields of Iraq, he didn't want to add to them in Chicago.

"Yeah, okay," Mark said, glancing around the crowded restaurant. "I can see why *this* is so much more up your alley."

Nick followed his glance and smothered a sigh. Because Mark was right. Helping at the pizzeria was no problem in the short term, heck he'd helped run the place when he was in high school, putting in more time than any of his siblings. But did he really want to become a partner in the business with his brother Tony, as he used to talk about…and as the family was hoping?

Seemed impossible. But Mark was the only one who would understand that. "I'm getting into protection," he admitted.

"You gonna mass-produce rubbers?" Mark sounded completely innocent, though his eyes sparkled with his usual good humor.

"I can't *wait* to tell your kid what a juvenile delinquent you were. Like when you put the Playboy magazine in Father Michael's desk drawer in sixth grade."

"Believe me, my kid will know Dad's on the job from the time he's old enough to even *think* about swiping candy bars. Now, what's with this protection business?"

"I'm going to work part-time as a bodyguard."

"No kidding?" Mark said, sounding surprised.

"Joe did some renovation work on a nightclub uptown and got friendly with the owner. Turns out they need extra security, so he set up a meeting. I went in Sunday night to talk to them."

"Bet Meg *loved* big brother Joe working in a nightclub."

Like the rest, their older brother Joe was happily married. Nick knew he'd never even *look* at another woman.

"So," Mark asked, "why does a club need a bodyguard?"

Nick knew *exactly* why this club needed a bodyguard after watching the erotic performance by a dancer called the Crimson Rose. The sultry stranger had inhabited his dreams and more than a few of his fantasies ever since he'd seen her on stage, revealing her incredible body while still remaining, somehow, so *above* it all. He imagined men with less control might try to do more than fantasize about the woman.

"The performers attract a lot of unwanted attention," he said, not wanting to get into details. Not because he was embarrassed about his job, but because he didn't want to start talking about the rose-draped dancer and her effect on *him*.

Nick didn't need that kind of distraction in his life. A hot stripper definitely did not fit in with the nice Santori lifestyle he kept telling himself he wanted. Not one bit. Which meant working with her was going to be a trick.

But he'd handled bigger challenges. Besides, meeting

her—talking to her—would take the bloom off that rose. Intense fantasies were meant for women who were untouchable, mysterious, unknown. It was, he'd come to believe while living in the Middle East, part of the allure of veiled women living in that culture. The unknown always built high expectations.

The Crimson Rose soon would *not* be an unknown. He'd see the face that had been hidden behind the mask and her secrets would be revealed. Which would make her much less intriguing.

Wanting his mind off *her* until it had to be when he started work, he changed the subject. "This place is hopping."

"So why aren't you out there taking orders from women who'd like to order a side of *you* with their thick crust?"

"Even the help gets an occasional night off."

He cast a bored glance around the room. A line of patrons stood near the counter, waiting for carry-out orders. Every table was full. Waitresses buzzed around in constant motion, all of them overseen by Mama. Nothing caught his attention…until he spotted *her*. And then he couldn't look away.

She stopped his heart, the way the dancer had, though the women couldn't be more dissimilar.

The stranger stood near the door, leaning against the wall. Looking at no one, her eyes remained focused on some spot outside the windows. Her posture spoke of weary disinterest, as if she'd zoned out on the chattering of customers all around her. She was separate, alone, lost in her own world of thought.

Not fitting in.

That, as much as her appearance, kept Nick's attention focused directly on her. Because he, too, knew what it was like to not fit in among this loud world of family and friends and neighbors who'd known one another for years.

She was solitary, self-contained, which interested him.

And her looks simply stole his breath.

From where he sat, he had a perfect view of her profile. Her thick, dark brown hair hung from a haphazard ponytail, emphasizing her high cheekbones and delicate jaw. Her face appeared soft, her skin creamy and smooth. Though her lips were parted, she didn't appear to be smiling. He suspected she was sighing from her open mouth every once in a while, though out of unhappiness or of boredom, he couldn't say.

Dressed casually in jeans and a T-shirt, she also wore a large baker's type apron over her clothes. That made it impossible to check out her figure. But judging by the length of those legs, shrunk-wrapped in tight, faded denim, he imagined it was spectacular. With a lightweight backpack slung over one shoulder, she looked like she'd stopped off to grab a pizza on her way home from work, like everyone else in line.

Only, she was so incredibly sexy in her aloof indifference, she didn't *look* like any other person in line.

Across from him, Mark said something, but Nick paid no attention. He continued to stare, wishing she'd turn toward him so he could make out the color of her eyes. Finally, as though she'd read his mental order, the brunette shifted, tilted her head in a delicate stretch that emphasized her slender neck, and turned. Sweeping a lazy gaze across the room, she breathed a nearly audible sigh that confirmed she was bored.

Then her eyes met his…and there they stopped.

Hers were brown, as dark as his. As their stares locked, he noted the flash of heated awareness in her stare. She made no effort to look away, watching him watch her. As if she knew he'd been checking her out, she returned the favor, looking him over, from his face down, her stare lingering a little long on his shoulders, and even longer on his chest. Nick shifted in his seat, his worn jeans growing tight across his groin, where heat slid and pulsed with seam-splitting intensity.

Though he was seated and there was no way she could see her effect on him, the stranger began to smile. One corner of her mouth tilted up, revealing a tiny dimple in her cheek. But it wasn't a cute, flirty one…nothing about this woman was cute and flirty, she was aggressive and seductive.

Needing to know her—now—he pushed his beer away and slid to the end of the bench seat without a word.

"Nick?" his brother asked, obviously startled.

"I have to meet her."

"Who?"

Nick didn't answer, he simply rose to his feet, never taking his eyes off the stranger.

Mark turned around. *"Her?"* his brother asked, sounding so surprised Nick wondered if marriage had made him entirely immune to the appeal of a hot, sexy stranger. "You have to *meet* her?"

Already walking away, Nick didn't answer. Instead, he strode across the restaurant, determined to not let her get away. He had to meet the first *real* woman—not a fantasy dressed in rose petals—who'd made his heart start beating hard again since the day he'd gotten home from the war.

IZZIE NATALE HAD A SECRET.

Well, she had *many* secrets. But the secret she was trying to disguise right now was one that would get her thrown out of the windy city for life.

She preferred New York style pizza to Chicago deep dish.

Shocking, but true. In the years she'd been living in New York during her dancing career, she'd fallen in love with everything there, including the food. But she'd be taking her life in her hands if she admitted it. Because, man, they took their pizza *very* seriously here. Her grandfather would turn over in his grave if he found out she'd gone to the dark—thin-crust—

side. Her father, at whose request she'd made this stop at Santori's, would disown her. And her sister, whose husband ran this place, would never speak to her again.

Hmm. That might be a blessing. Considering her sister Gloria never had mastered the art of shutting up when the occasion demanded it, Izzie felt tempted to tell her that not only did she like her crust thin, but she also preferred the Mets over the Cubbies. That would get her stoned in the street.

How am I going to get through this?

It wasn't the first time she'd wondered that in the two months she'd been home, taking care of her family-owned bakery while her father recovered from his stroke. If her friends in Manhattan could see her—covered in flour, wearing an apron, working behind a counter—they'd think she'd been kidnapped.

This could not be Izzie Natale, the former long-legged Rockette who'd had men at her fingertips. Nor could it be the Izzie who'd gone on to land a spot with one of the premiere modern dance companies in New York, short-lived though that spot may have been after her ACL injury had required major surgery seven months ago.

But it was. *She* was. And it was driving her *mad*.

It wasn't that she didn't love her family. But oh, did she wish one of *them* could run the bakery. Because she was not happy being once again under the microscope, living in this big-geographically, but small-town-at-heart area of Little Italy.

Before she could groan about it, however, something caught her eye in the crowded pizzeria. Make that some*one* caught her eye. As she cast another bored look around, half-wishing she'd see someone she'd recognize from her *other* life here in Chicago—the one nobody else knew about—she spotted *him*.

A dark-haired, dark-eyed man was staring at her from

across the place. Even from twenty feet away she felt the heat rolling off him. An answering sultry, hungry fire curled from the tips of her curly dark hair down to the bottoms of her feet.

God, the man was hot. Fiery hot. Global warming hot.

His jet black hair was cut short, spiky. *A military man.*

His dark eyes matched the hair. They were deep set, heavily lashed...bedroom eyes, she'd have to say. His lean face was more rugged than handsome. The strong jaw jutted out the tiniest bit, and his unsmiling mouth was tightly set, as if intentionally trying to disguise the fullness of a pair of amazing male lips.

His shoulders were Mack-truck wide and his chest was football-field broad. And his attitude was all, one-hundred-percent Santori male.

Because Izzie knew it was Nick Santori who'd met her stare from across the room. Nick Santori who'd risen from his seat and was winding his way across the room toward her. Nick Santori who was making the earth shake a little under her feet, just as he always had when she was a teenager.

She told herself to breathe and not let him get under her skin. He sure had once...like at Gloria and Tony's wedding, when she'd been a bridesmaid of fourteen and Nick had been a groomsman. He'd had to escort her down the aisle, and his big, bad, going-into-the-Marines-eighteen-year-old self hadn't liked it. And that day was one she would *never* live down.

Somehow, though, that memory didn't steady the floor. Nor did it cool her off as he came closer. Those dark eyes of his were locked on her face as he effortlessly cleared his way through the crowd with a look here or glance there. Everyone made way for him. The men out of respect. The women... well, the women looked like Izzie imagined she did: dumbstruck. All because of the simmering sensuality of this one sexy man.

The one she'd wanted since the first time she'd felt heat between her legs and understood what it meant.

"Hi," he said when he finally reached her.

"Hey." She felt almost triumphant at having achieved that note of casual aloofness. She even managed to keep slouching against the wall, probably because she needed the support. She might have learned to handle men but she'd never gotten over feeling like Izzie-the-geek around this one.

"Is there something I can do for you?"

Oh, yeah. She could think of several somethings. Starting with her getting some payback for him ignoring her when she was a chubby, lovesick kid. And ending with him naked in her bed.

But getting naked in bed with Nick Santori would involve serious complications. Her sister was married to his brother. The families were old friends. If she so much as looked at the guy with interest the neighborhood would have them married off with her popping out brown-haired Italian babies within a year.

Uh-uh. No thanks. Not for Izzie. Sex with Nick would be delightful. But it came with *way* too many strings.

"I don't think so," she finally answered.

He didn't back off. "I'm sure there's something."

"What, are you a waiter now?" she asked, amused at the thought of him waiting tables. Especially since that chest of his could probably double as one.

Nick had, like all the Santori kids, worked in the restaurant in high school. Just as Izzie had worked in the bakery—often eating her paycheck to sweeten her teenage angst.

But he'd been in the Marines for years. She didn't see him slinging pizzas now that he was back in Chicago. Not after he'd been slinging Uzis or whatever those macho soldier guys carried.

"Maybe. Why don't you tell me what you want and I'll let you know if I can get it for you?"

Thin and cheesy New York style pizza was the first thing that came to mind, but Izzie didn't want to get strung up at the corner of Taylor and Racine. "I already placed my order."

He smiled slightly. "I wasn't just talking about pizza."

God, was that…it *was*. There was a flirtatious twinkle in those blackish-brown eyes of his. He'd been throwing some subtle innuendo at her and it had gone clear over her head.

"Oh," was all she could manage.

Cake flour must have clogged her femme-fatale genes in the past two months. It was the only way someone with her experience with men could have missed his double meaning.

"Want to sit while you wait for your order?" he asked, gesturing toward a few chairs in the waiting area.

"No, thanks." She fell silent. If she opened her mouth again, she might do something stupid like throw out a dumb, "Wow, what I wouldn't have given for you to look at me like that when I was a teenager," line, which she so didn't want to do.

She zipped her lips. She'd be Izzie the uninterested mute. Which was better than Izzie the lovesick mutant.

"How about at a table?"

"At a table…what?"

He smiled again, that sexy, self-confident smile that had probably had woman on five continents dropping their panties within sixty seconds of meeting him. "We can sit at a table while you wait for your order."

God, she was an idiot. "No, I'm fine here, thank you."

She had to give herself a break for being so slow. After all, Nick Santori had been scrambling her brains since she was ten—right around the time her sister Gloria had started dating his brother Tony. And though he'd always had a way with females, he'd never looked twice at *her* that way.

Especially not since Gloria and Tony's wedding. The one

where she'd tripped on her ugly puce gown—which hugged her tubby hips and butt—while they were dancing the obligatory wedding party waltz. She, the kid who'd been in dance lessons since the age of three, had tripped.

Maybe it wasn't so shocking. She'd been worried about what he'd think of her sweaty palms. She'd been *terrified* that her makeup was smearing off her face and revealing that she'd had the mother of all break-outs that morning.

Nervous plus terrified times the pitter-patter of her heart and the achy tingle in her small breasts from where they brushed against the lapels of Nick's tux had left her dizzy. So dizzy she'd stepped off the edge of the slightly raised dance floor and crashed both of them onto a table full of cookies and pastries made especially by her parents for the wedding.

It hadn't been pretty.

Colorful candy-covered almonds had flown in all directions. Her butt had landed on a platter of cream puffs, her elbows in two stacks of pizelles. Her dress had flown up to her waist to reveal the panty girdle she'd worn in an effort to hide her after-school-cookie-binging bulge.

The icing on the five-tiered Italian cream wedding cake— which she'd *somehow* managed to not destroy—had been Nick. He'd gotten tangled up in her dress, and had landed on top of her, sprawled across her chest.

And right between her legs.

It was the first—and last—time she'd figured Nick Santori would be between her legs, which both broke her heart and fueled some intense fantasies throughout her high-school years. Shocked by the unexpectedness and the *pleasure* of it, she'd been slow to part those legs and let him up. Slow enough for the moment to go from embarrassingly long to indecently shocking.

She'd thought her mother was going to kill her afterward.

But that wasn't all. Because Izzie had the luck of someone

who broke mirrors for a living, the incident had also been the money shot of the whole day. The videographer caught the whole thing on film, creating a masterpiece that would taunt her throughout eternity.

She'd been a laughingstock. Everyone in the crowd had whooped and clapped and teased her about it for months afterward. She might as well have worn a banner proclaiming herself, "Lovesick pubescent girl who crushed the cookies and dry-humped the groomsman at the Santori-Natale wedding."

"I haven't seen you in here before," he said, finally breaking the silence that had fallen between them.

"I come here a couple of times a week," she replied.

He shrugged. "I've been gone a long time."

"In the military."

"Right. Things have definitely changed around here in the past twelve years."

"Maybe in some ways," she said. Then she glanced around and saw a minimum of five people she knew—all watching intently as she talked to Nick. Frowning, she muttered, "In some ways it's still the same small town hell it always was."

She surprised a laugh out of him. "I somehow think we have a lot in common."

His laughter softened his tanned face, bringing out tiny lines beside his eyes. It also made him utterly irresistible, as several women sitting nearby undoubtedly noticed.

Nick had been incredibly hot as a teenager. Lean and wiry, dark and intense. As a thirty-year-old-man he was absolutely drool-worthy. Not that he'd changed a lot—he'd just matured. Where he'd been a sexy guy, he was now a tough, heart-stopping male, big and broad, powerful and intimidating.

She didn't suspect he'd changed on the inside, though. Once a Santori male, always a Santori male. The men of that family had always been good-hearted.

Honestly, looking back, if Nick had been a jerk about what had happened at the wedding, she might have gotten over her crush a lot sooner and this moment might be a lot simpler. She could tell him to f-off, remind him he'd once laughed at her and added to her humiliation. Only…he hadn't. Curse the man.

He'd been very sweet, carefully helping her up—once she'd released her thunder-thigh death grip from around his hips. He'd gently wiped powdered sugar and cream off her cheek. He'd helped her pull her dress back down into place without making one crack about her chubby thighs or her panty girdle. He'd pretended she hadn't practically assaulted him. And he'd helped her back up onto the dance floor and continued their dance. Absolutely the only annoying thing he'd done was to start calling her Cookie.

As her mother often said, he'd been raised right. Just like his brothers. He was every bit a gentleman—a protector—and he'd never given her a sideways glance that hadn't been merely friendly. In his eyes, she'd always been Gloria's baby sister—the chubby ballerina who looked like a little stuffed sausage in her pink tutu and tights and he'd treated her with nothing but big-brotherly kindness.

Until now.

Fortunately, though, she wasn't sweet Izzie the cookie-gobbling machine anymore. He hadn't seen her for almost a decade…she no longer blushed and stammered when a hot guy teased her. And she no longer even tried to imagine she could have been a ballerina with her less-than-willowy figure.

Once she'd stopped eating pastries and hit brick-shithouse stature at age eighteen, she'd known her future as a dancer would come from another direction than the ballet.

She'd also learned how to handle men.

Now, *she* was in the driver's seat when it came to seduction. She'd been running the show with men for years. And it was high time to let Nick Santori know it.

"So, when you offered to serve me…what *were* you talking about?" she asked, swiping her tongue across her lips. It was a move she'd perfected in her Rockettes dressing room. Men used to come backstage, trying to pick up the dancers and they all went for the lip-licking. God, males were so predictable. She held her breath, hoping for more from this one.

And she got it.

"I'm talking about me serving you with a line and you tipping me with your number. But since it's crowded and I'm rusty at that stuff, why don't you just give me the number?"

Izzie had to laugh. If he'd come back with a smooth line, the laugh would have been at his expense—because she doubted there was one he hadn't heard. But Nick had been completely honest, which she found incredibly attractive.

She also laughed to hide the nervous thrill she'd gotten when she realized Nick Santori really did want her number. That he really was trying to pick her up.

Her…the girl he'd once complained about having to dance with at a wedding. What were the odds?

"I think I've got *your* number." She'd had it for years.

He didn't give up. "Use it. Please."

He meant it. He wasn't teasing, wasn't trying to make her blush, wasn't treating her the way he treated his kid sister, Lottie, who'd been one of her classmates.

Nick Santori was trying to pick her up. Which shouldn't have been a big deal, but, for some reason, had her heart fluttering around in her chest like a bird trapped in a cage.

"My name's Nick, by the way."

No *duh*. She was about to say that, then she saw the look in his eyes—that serious, intense look. He wasn't kidding. He wasn't pretending they were just meeting.

She sagged back against the wall, not sure whether to laugh or punch him in the face.

Because the rotten son of a bitch had no idea who she was.

2

THE WOMAN HAD FLOUR in her hair. She smelled like almonds. Her apron was smeared with icing and whipped cream. Food coloring stained the tips of two of her fingers.

And she was utterly delicious.

The hints of flavor wafting off her couldn't compete with the innate, warm feminine scent of her body, which assaulted Nick's senses the way no full frontal attack ever had. Though they were in a crowded restaurant, surrounded by customers and members of his own family, hers was the only presence he felt. He'd been drawn to her, captured in an intimate world they'd created the moment their eyes had locked.

"You're name's Nick," she said, as if making sure. Her voice was a little hard, her dark eyes narrowing.

Worried she had an ex with the same name, he replied, "I'll answer to anything you want to call me."

"Anything?"

He nodded, unable to take his attention from that bit of flour in her hair. He wanted to lift his hand and brush it away. Then sink his fingers in that thick, brown hair of hers, tugging it free of its ponytail to fall in a loose curtain around her shoulders. His fingers clenched into fists at his sides with the need to tangle those thick tresses in his hands and tug her face toward his for a brain-zapping kiss.

She had the kind of mouth that begged for kissing. One that

promised pleasure. God, it had been a long time since he'd really kissed a woman the way he *liked* to kiss a woman. Slowly. Deeply. With a thorough exploration of every curve and crevice.

Recently, his sex life had been limited by proximity and his active status. He hadn't had any kind of relationship in years. And the sex he had was usually of the quick, one-night variety, where slow, indulgent kissing wasn't on the agenda.

He could kiss this woman's mouth for *hours*.

Nick didn't understand why he was so drawn to her. All he knew was that he was attracted to her in a way he hadn't been attracted to anyone for a long time. Not just because she was beautiful under the apron and that messy ponytail. But because of the wistful, lonely look she'd worn earlier that said she didn't quite belong here and she knew it. Just like the one he'd had on his face lately.

"You're single?" he asked, wanting that confirmed.

She nodded, the movement setting her ponytail swinging. It caught the reflection of a candle on the closest table, the strands glimmering in a veil of browns and golds that made his heart clang against his lungs.

"What's your name?" he finally asked.

She arched one fine eyebrow. "We haven't settled on what we're going to call *you* yet."

He turned, edging closer to her as a group came into the restaurant. The brunette slid along the wall, farther away from anyone else. Nick followed, irresistibly drawn by her scent and the mystery in her eyes. "I guess you have a Nick in your past?"

"Uh-huh."

"It didn't go well?"

"I'd have to say that's a no."

"Bad breakup?"

"No. We never even dated." One side of her mouth tilted

up in a half-smile. It held no happiness, merely jaded amusement. "He barely even noticed my existence."

"Then he was an idiot."

The other side of her mouth came up; this time her genuine amusement shone clearly. "Oh, undoubtedly."

"He didn't deserve you."

"Absolutely not."

"You're better off without him."

"Nobody knows that better than me." She sounded more amused now, as if her guard was coming down.

"Enough about him," Nick said. "If you don't like my first name, call me by my last one. It's Santori."

He watched for a flare of surprise, a darting of the eyes to the sign in the window, proclaiming the name of the place.

Strangely, she didn't react at all. "I think we've already determined what I should call you. You said it yourself."

Puzzled, Nick just waited.

"Idiot," she said, tapping the tip of her finger on her cheek, as if thinking about it. "Though, honestly, it doesn't quite capture you now. It might have sufficed years ago, but for today, I think we'll have to go with…complete shithead."

Nick's jaw fell open. But the sexy brunette wasn't finished. "By the way, that number you wanted? Here it is, you might want to write it down…1-800-nevergonnahappen."

And without another word, she shoved at his chest, pushing him out of the way, then strode out the door. Leaving Nick standing there, staring after her in complete shock.

"I'd say *that* didn't go well." Mark stood right behind him, watching—as was Nick—as the brunette marched off down the street like she'd just kicked somebody's ass.

Well, she had. Namely his. He just didn't know *why.*

"No kidding."

"I see you haven't lost your touch with women."

"Shut up." Shaking his head in bemusement, he lifted a hand and rubbed his jaw. "I don't know how I blew that so badly."

"But you sure managed to do it."

Hearing his twin chuckle, Nick glared. "At least I'm not wearing a ring. I can still *try* to pick up a hot stranger."

Mark just laughed harder. Which made Nick consider punching him. Only, Mama was standing behind the counter, glancing curiously at them as she waited on the customers. If Nick went after his twin, she'd come around and whack them both in the heads with a soup ladle.

"Hot stranger…oh, man, you are going to hate yourself when you figure out what you just did."

His eyes narrowing, Nick waited for his twin to continue.

"You really didn't recognize her, did you?"

Oh, hell. He should have recognized her? He *knew* her?

"Still not getting it?"

"Tell me how much trouble I'm in," he muttered, praying he hadn't just come on to a cousin he hadn't seen in years. If they were related—and he *couldn't* have her—that would be a crime worthy of a military tribunal. So he prayed even harder that she'd been some girl he'd known in high school.

"Pretty big trouble."

He waited, knowing Mark was enjoying watching him sweat.

"She *is* family, you know."

Damn. All the blood in his body fell to his feet out of embarrassment…and disappointment. "Why didn't you stop me?"

"You shot out of the booth like your ass was on fire."

Rubbing a hand over his eyes and shaking his head, Nick mumbled, "Who is she? Mama's side or Pop's? Please tell me she's not one of Great Uncle Vincenza's thirty granddaughters. Otherwise I just might have to re-up and hide from him and his mafia buddies for the next decade."

Mark's eyes glittered in amusement. The guy was enjoying this. "Not Great Uncle Vincenza. Think closer."

Closer. Christ. "There's no way she's a first cousin...."

"Not a cousin."

Oh, thank heaven. "So who?"

"I'll give you a hint. Did you happen to notice the icing and flour all over her apron?"

Had he ever. He didn't know if he'd ever smelled anything as good as all that messy, sugary stuff combined with the brunette's earthy essence. "Yeah. So?"

"You're not usually this dense."

"You're not usually this close to death."

"Think...the bakery...."

"Natale's? Gloria's folks?" And suddenly it hit him. "No."

"Oh, yes."

No. Impossible. It was out of the question. "Not Gloria's baby sister. *Tell* me that wasn't chubby little Cookie."

"She ain't chubby and I think if you called her Cookie to her face she'd slug you." Mark threw a consoling arm across Nick's shoulders, his chest shaking with laughter. "To answer your question, yes, my brother, that was Isabella Natale."

Nick couldn't speak. He was too stunned, thinking of how she'd changed. It had been at least nine—ten years, perhaps—since he'd seen her. She'd still been in high school and he'd run into her at a Christmas party at Gloria and Tony's when he was home on leave. She'd still blushed and stammered around him. And she'd still been girlishly round—pretty but with such a baby-face he'd never taken her crush on him seriously.

Oh, he knew about the crush. *Everybody* knew about the crush. His brother Tony had threatened to break his legs if he so much as looked at her the wrong way at the wedding.

Huh. He hadn't looked at her the wrong way. He'd just landed on top of her in a pile of cookies. And had been unable to get up because she'd wrapped her limbs around him like she was drowning and he was a lifeguard trying to save her.

He started to smile. "Izzie."

"Izzie. Formerly chubby sister of our sister-in-law, turned sexy-as-hell woman, now back in town working at the bakery."

"Her parents' bakery up the block?"

"That's the one."

"Is she here for good?" he asked, already wondering how things could have turned out this perfectly.

"I don't know. She's been home for a couple of months, since Gloria's father had a stroke. With the new baby, Gloria couldn't help much, and the middle sister's a lawyer."

"So the youngest one came home to take over." Not surprising. The Natales were much like the Santoris—family meant everything.

It almost seemed too good to be true. He'd finally come across someone who not only made his nerves spark and his jeans grow a size too tight, but who also came with a pre-made stamp of approval from the neighborhood. She was gorgeous. She was feisty. Her smile nearly stopped his heart. She'd had a crush on him forever—and was obviously still affected by him, judging by the way she'd taken off in a huff.

And she was *not* a faceless stripper behind a mask.

Enough of that. The Crimson Rose was every other man's fantasy. At this point in his life, Nick wanted *reality.* He was ready for what his brothers and sister had. And he had just stumbled across a *real* woman who he sensed could both drive him absolutely wild with want and be someone he could truly like.

"I think I'm feeling a need for some fresh cannoli," he murmured, smiling as he looked out the window at the sky, streaked orange by the setting sun. Izzie was no longer in sight…she obviously wasn't too desperate for pizza.

Maybe he'd deliver it to her.

"Judging by the way she bolted, you'd better think again."

Nick shrugged. He wasn't worried. After all, Izzie had had a thing for him once upon a time…she had practically chased him down. He just needed to remind her of that.

And to let her know he was ready to let her catch him.

"I SWEAR, BRIDGET, you should have seen his expression. It was as if it was the first time in his life a woman has ever turned him down," Izzie didn't even look at her cousin as she spoke. She was too busy punching into a huge ball of dough, picturing Nick Santori's face while she did it.

Though it had been nearly twenty-four hours since she'd run into him, she hadn't stopped thinking about him. Drat the man for invading her brain again, when she'd managed to forget him over the past several years. Ever since she skipped out of Chicago to follow her dancing dreams, she'd been convincing herself her crush on him had been a silly, girlish thing.

Seeing him had reminded her of the truth: she'd wanted Nick before she'd even understood what it was she wanted. Now that she *knew* what the tingle between her legs and the heaviness in her breasts meant, the want was almost painful.

"Didn't Nana always say the secret to a flaky crust was not to overwork it?" her cousin said, sounding quietly amused.

Izzie shot her cousin—who sat on the other side of the bakery kitchen—a glare. "You want to do this?"

Bridget, who was pretty and soft-looking, slid a strand of long, light-brown hair behind her ear. "You're the baker. I'm the bookkeeper." She sipped from her huge coffee mug. "So why did you walk away? You've wanted him forever."

"Maybe. But I don't want *forever* in general," she reminded her cousin as she floured the countertop and began to work the dough with a rolling pin. "You know I don't want *this* for any longer than I'm forced to have it." She glanced around the kitchen, where she was working alone to finish up the dessert orders for their restaurant clients. Including Santori's.

Not that she'd be the one delivering their order…no way. Her delivery guy would be in to take on that task shortly.

"I know. You'll be gone again once Uncle Gus is well enough to come back to work." Bridget didn't sound too happy about that, which Izzie understood. Her sweet, gentle-natured cousin was an only child, and she'd practically been adopted by Izzie and her own sisters. They'd been very close growing up.

Izzie missed her too. But not enough to stay here. As soon as her father recovered, and her mother no longer had to nurse him at home full time, Izzie would be out of here for good. Whether she'd go back to New York and try to reclaim some kind of dancing career she didn't yet know. But her future did not include a long-term stint as the Flour Girl of Taylor Street.

It also didn't include becoming the lover of any guy who her parents would see as the perfect reason for Izzie to stick around and pop out babies. Even a lover as tempting as Nick.

"So how's your life going?" she asked her cousin, wanting the subject changed. "How's the job?"

Bridget leaned forward, dropping her elbows onto the counter. "I guess I'm not very good. My boss obviously doesn't trust me, there are some files he won't even let me look at."

"Weren't you hired to keep the books at that place?"

Bridget, who'd gone to work three months ago for a local used car dealership right here in the neighborhood, nodded. "They're a mess. But every time I ask him for access to older records, he practically pats me on the head and sends me back to my desk like a good little girl."

Izzie assumed her cousin meant her boss *figuratively* patted her on the head. Because, though Bridget was in no way a fireball like Izzie and her two sisters—she wasn't a pushover, either. It might take her awhile to get her steam up, but Izzie had seen glimpses of temper in her sweet-as-sugar Irish-Italian cousin. That boss of hers obviously hadn't gotten to know the *real* Bridget yet. Because she was about the most quietly stubborn person Izzie had ever met…as anyone who'd ever tried to beat her in a game of Monopoly could attest.

"Why don't you quit?"

Her cousin lifted her mug, leaning her head over it so that her long bangs fell over her pretty amber eyes. She looked as if she had something to hide. And if Izzie wasn't mistaken, that was a blush rising in her cheeks.

A blush. Cripes, Izzie didn't even know if she *remembered* how to blush. The last time her cheeks had been pinkened by anything other than makeup was when she'd burned herself while lying out too long on the deck of a cruise ship a year ago.

Trying to hide a smile, she murmured, "Who is he?"

Her cousin almost dropped the mug. "Huh?"

"Oh, come on, I know there's a guy."

"Um…well…"

"For heaven's sake, you're looking at a woman who used to schedule two dates a night, just come out with it."

Chuckling, her cousin did. "There's this new salesman."

"A used car salesman?" Izzie asked skeptically.

Frowning, Bridget asked, "Do you want to hear this or not?"

Izzie made a "lips-zipped" motion over her mouth.

"His name's Dean," Bridget continued. "Dean Willis. And Marty hired him about a month ago. He's got cute, shaggy blond hair and big blue eyes—well, I assume they're big. They could look bigger because of the thick glasses he wears."

She watched Izzie, as if waiting for a comment. Izzie somehow managed to refrain from making one.

"He's sold more cars than anyone else because he's just so…quiet. Easy to talk to. Unassuming." Sighing a little, Bridget added, "And he has the nicest smile."

Izzie had never heard her cousin go on like this about a man. Must be serious. "So, have you gone out with him?"

Bridget shook her head and sighed again—only, much louder. "He's never even noticed I'm alive."

Snorting, Izzie replied, "I doubt that. You're adorable."

Bridget's bottom lip came out in a tiny pout. "Fluffy teddy bears are adorable. I want to be…something else."

Sexy. It was obviously what Bridget had in mind. Izzie eyed her cousin, considering making her over. Bridget had the basics—she just needed to bring them out a little. But she didn't think Bridget needed much. She was so quietly pretty, so gentle and feminine…any guy would be an idiot to want to change her.

Then again, she'd known a ton of guys, few of whom were Einstein material. "So ask *him* out. *Make* him notice you."

"I couldn't."

"Just for a cup of coffee."

Her cousin snagged her lip between her teeth.

"What?"

"Well, he *did* ask me to go for coffee once, but I was so flustered and nervous, I told him I didn't drink it."

Raising a brow and staring pointedly at the industrial-sized mug in front of her cousin's face, Izzie grunted.

"But it wasn't a date," Bridget added. "At least, I don't think so." Sounding frustrated, she added, "Maybe I should get a collagen injection. I've heard men like big lips."

Ridiculous. Bridget's beauty was the natural kind that needed no false crap like the stuff Izzie had seen other dancers do to themselves. But before she could say that—or threaten to lob a handful of ricotta cheesecake filling at Bridget if she did something so dumb—she heard the bell over the front door.

Glancing at the clock, she bit back a curse. It was nearly five—an hour after closing time. She must have forgotten to lock the door after her part-time lunch workers had left for the day and some customer had wandered in for a snack.

She doubted there was much left to serve. Mornings were their busiest time, with regulars and passers-by coming in for pastries and muffins. During the lunch hour, when Natale's served light sandwiches and salads along with decadent deserts, they were busy, too. Since Izzie had come up with the idea to offer free wireless Internet access to anyone with a laptop, some customers parked themselves at one of the small, café tables and remained there until closing time. They drank a lot of coffee…and ate a lot of sweets. By 4:00 p.m., Natale's display counter was generally wiped out, as this late customer would soon discover.

"Hello?" a voice called.

Grabbing a towel, Izzie wiped her hands on it and tossed it over her shoulder. "Be right back," she told her cousin as she walked down the short hallway to the café. "Sorry, we're closed for the…." The words died on her lips when she saw who stood on the other side of the glass display case, looking so hot she almost shielded her eyes from the glory of him.

"I know." He shrugged slightly. "But the door was unlocked, so I thought I'd take a chance and see if you were here."

Nick stood inside the shadowy café, illuminated by the late afternoon sunlight streaming in through the front window. The light reflected in his dark eyes, lending them a golden glow that seemed to radiate warmth. She felt it from here.

"You found me," she murmured.

"You didn't exactly need to leave a trail of crumbs, Cookie…this place has been here forever."

"*Don't* call me Cookie," she snapped.

He held up his hands, palms out. "Sorry."

Ordering her heart to continue beating normally, Izzie tossed the towel onto the counter, then crossed her arms over her chest to stare at him. "Are you trying to tell me you *knew* I'd be here because you *knew* who I was? Try again."

Nick cleared his throat, averting his gaze. Wincing in a cutely sheepish way, he said, "No, I didn't know you at first."

So, he'd recognized her after she had left?

"Mark told me who you were."

The jerk.

"I'm sorry I didn't recognize you. It's been a long time."

Not long enough to erase *him* from *her* mind, that was for sure. She'd recognize Nick Santori if she bumped into him blindfolded during a blackout. Because his scent was imprinted in her brain. And her body reacted in one instinctive way whenever he was near—a way it didn't react with anyone else, even men with whom she'd been intimate.

He made her shaky and achy and weak and ravenous all at the same time. Always had, for some unknown reason.

"Yeah. A long time," she mumbled, walking over to wash her hands in the small sink behind the counter.

Damn, she hated that he flustered her. She had known more handsome men. She'd been to bed with more handsome men. Maybe none who were as rugged and masculine, or so sensual. But she had dated drop-dead gorgeous actors and millionaires who wanted to notch their bedposts with a professional dancer who could kick her leg straight up above her head. None of them had ever affected her the way this one— who she'd never even kissed—did.

Overexposed

"I have to run, Izzie," a voice said. "I don't want to be…in the way."

Izzie had almost forgotten Bridget was in the kitchen. Seeing the grin on her cousin's face, she blew out a deep, frustrated breath. She'd intended to use Bridget as an excuse— or at the very least as a five-foot-five chastity belt, to keep Izzie from doing something stupid. Like smearing rich cheesecake filling all over Nick's body, then slowly licking it off.

But her cousin was bailing on her, already heading toward the exit. "Nice to see you, Nick," she said.

"How's your family?"

They fell into a brief, easy conversation, like most people who'd grown up in the neighborhood usually did. Except Izzie—who hadn't yet rediscovered that easy camaraderie with all the people she'd grown up with. While the two of them chatted, Izzie tried to regain her cool, forcing herself to look at this guy like she looked at every other guy. As nothing special.

Fat chance. She couldn't do it. He *was* special.

It had to be because he was the first man she'd ever wanted. Never having had him made the intensity of her attraction build. With no culmination—no explosion when she finally had him and got him out of her system—she'd remained on a slow, roiling boil of want for Nick for years.

So take him and get it out of your system.

Oh, the thought was tempting. Very tempting. Part of her desperately wanted to ask him to go with her to the nearest hotel and *do* her until she couldn't even bring her legs together. If she thought he would, and that he'd then forget about it, never expecting a repeat and never—*ever*—breathing a word about it to anyone, she'd seriously consider it.

But he wouldn't. Not in a million years. She knew that just as surely as she knew he'd never have even *kissed* her when she was underage, not even if she'd leapt on him and held him captive. Which, to be fair, she had…at the wedding.

He was a Santori. With everything that went with the name. His upbringing, his family, his own moral code meant he would never have a meaningless sexual encounter with his sister-in-law's younger sister. The daughter of his father's friend. The girl up the block. No way in hell.

He was the kind of guy who would have to *date* a woman he slept with. Dating—neighborhood style—as in hand-holding and miniature golf and pizza at his family's place and cannolis at her family's place. The whole deal. *Gag.*

Not that he'd actually asked her on a date. If he did? Well… that might have thrilled her once—years ago when she had actually thought the bakery and her family and Little Italy were all the world she'd ever need. Now, however, it just made her sad, because as she'd already realized, dating Nick equaled strings. Strings could very well choke her.

"Well, see you tomorrow," Bridget said as she walked out.

Izzie hadn't even noticed Bridget and Nick were finished talking. Cursing her cousin for bailing on her, Izzie cleared her throat, about to tell him she had to get back to work.

He spoke first. "So, do you forgive me?"

"Yeah, sure, no big deal," she replied, forcing a shrug.

A tiny smile tugged at those amazing lips of his and the dark eyes glowed. "No big deal? You seemed pretty mad."

Damn. He'd noticed.

"I wasn't mad. More…amused."

"Sure. That's why my chest is bruised where you shoved me."

Her jaw dropped and she immediately began sputtering denials. Then she saw his wide grin. "You're an ass."

"And a shithead," he replied, his grin fading though the twinkle remained in his eye. "I really mean it, Iz, I'm sorry I didn't recognize you." Stepping around the counter to see her better, he cast a slow, leisurely look at her. From bottom to top. Then down again. "But you have to give me a little bit of a break. You don't look much like you did."

"I'm not addicted to Twinkies anymore," she snapped.

"You weren't chubby."

"I was the Michelin Man in pink tights."

He shook his head. "You were just baby-faced the last time I saw you. A kid. Now you're…not."

"Damn right."

He didn't say anything for a moment, still watching her as he leaned against the counter. The pose tugged his gray T-shirt tight against his shoulders and chest, emphasizing the man's size. Lord, he was broad. But still so trim at the waist and lean at the hips. It was the hips that caught her attention—the way his faded, unbelted jeans hung low on them, the soft fabric hugging the angles and planes of his body.

It really wasn't fair for a man to be so perfect.

"So…about our conversation last night."

When staring at him—overwhelmed by his heat—she could barely remember her own name. Much less any conversation. "Huh?"

"What do you say? Will you give me your number?"

Oh, what she wouldn't have given to hear those words from him ten years ago. Or hell, even two *months* ago—if she'd happened to run into him in Times Square and he'd proposed a sexy one-night-stand for old time's sake. One nobody in Chicago would ever have to know about. She would have leapt on the offer like a gambler on a free lottery ticket.

"I don't think so."

"Come on, you know you can trust me. I'm not some stranger stalking you. We've known each other since we were kids."

Well, he'd known *her* since she was a kid. From the time

she'd met him, Izzie had only ever seen the glorious, hot, sexy *man*. Even if he had been no more than fourteen.

"Just a night out for old time's sake?"

He was so tempting. Because the only old times she recalled were the heated ones of her fantasies. And the incident at the wedding. He'd ended up between her legs during both. "Well…."

He moved again, coming closer, as if realizing she was wavering. Dropping his hand onto the counter near hers, he murmured, "No pressure. We could just go grab a pizza."

She stiffened, any potential wavering done with. The last thing she would consider doing is having a public meal with Nick Santori at his own family's restaurant. Not when her sister would hear about it and tell their parents, who'd then get their hopes up about Izzie remaining safely in the nest, as they'd so desperately wanted her to do when she was eighteen.

Leaving home after high school had been a struggle. She'd been an adult, legally free, but she'd still had to practically run away in order to pursue her dream of dancing professionally. Especially because she was the only one of the Natale daughters who'd inherited their father's gift in the kitchen.

Probably because she loved food so much. As evidenced by every one of her porky-faced school pictures from kindergarten through tenth grade.

Her father had been crushed that she didn't want to work with him. But she had known she had to escape—had to take her shot while she could or risk regretting it the rest of her life.

So she'd gone. She'd hopped a train, determined to stay away until she'd given her dream of being a professional dancer everything she had to give.

Making it at Radio City hadn't eased her parents fears of

her being "out there all alone." It had actually increased them once they'd realized she was unlikely now to *ever* come back.

If they knew just how wild her life had been for the first few years she'd been on her own, they'd have felt justified in their fears. Like any good girl kept on a tight leash, she'd taken great pleasure in breaking every rule in the book once she was free and able to make her own decisions. Especially once she had men surrounding her and money to do whatever she wanted.

It had been wild. It had also been reckless—so in the past couple of years, she'd settled down. Stopped partying, stopped hooking up, stopped blowing every dime. She now had a nice nest egg…which she hoped to use to re-establish her life in New York. She'd been approached about going back to work at Radio City, as a choreographer this time. And she knew she'd probably get the same offer from her other modern dance company.

Or she could teach. She could open her own school…she had the money to at least give it a shot. That was among the things she'd been considering doing when she got back to reality.

Her parents, however, would give anything for her to stay here and never go back to that other life, the one that didn't include them beyond the weekly phone call and twice-yearly visit. Openly dating a local guy—a friend of the family—would raise their hopes unfairly and hurtfully. So she couldn't do it.

Before she could say so, however, he stepped closer. Close enough to stop her heart. "You're a mess," he murmured. He lifted a hand, touching a strand of hair that had fallen across her cheek. Closing his fingers over it, he slowly pulled, wiping away flour or cream or whatever had happened to be there.

The brush of his fingertips against her cheekbone almost made her cry. Almost made her whimper. Almost made her lean forward to press her mouth onto his.

"A sweet, delectable mess," he added, his fingers still

tangled in her hair. He touched her face, rubbing her skin as if he'd never felt anything so smooth, so soft.

Every muscle in her body went warm and pliant, until Izzie wondered how she could still be standing upright. As if sensing her weakness, he moved closer, sliding one foot between her legs, slipping one hand into her tangled hair to cup her head.

"I have to see how sweet you taste," he muttered, sounding as helpless as she felt. "If only once...I have to taste you."

Drawing her forward, he bent closer. Even knowing it was crazy and could go nowhere, Izzie prepared for a kiss she'd wanted for more than a decade. She'd cried over that mouth, had fantasized over those lips for more nights than she could count.

And she wanted it, God how she *wanted* it. Even if it was all she was ever going to get to have of him.

But rather than a simple kiss—the soft brush of his mouth on hers—he shocked her by immediately sampling her lips with his tongue, tasting her, as he'd said he must.

She whimpered, low and helpless.

"Oh, very sweet," he whispered, licking at the seam of her lips again, boldly demanding entrance rather than asking for it with a more typical, closed-mouthed first kiss.

Izzie couldn't deny him *or* herself. With a hungry groan, she opened to him, welcoming his tongue in a deep, sensual exchange that she felt from her head to the tips of her toes.

He'd thought she tasted sweet. She thought he tasted like irresistible sin. He was warm and spicy, his mouth just moist enough to whet her appetite. Just hot enough to send her temperature rocketing higher.

He sunk his other hand in her hair and held her close. Sagging against him, Izzie gave herself over to pleasure, wondering how it was possible for something to be as good as a dozen years of dreaming had promised it would be. It was a kiss more intimate than any she'd had even when making love. Because it was like making love. It was hot and sexy and powerful.

Their tongues found a common rhythm and tangled to it as their bodies melted together. Her nipples ached with need as they pressed against his broad chest. She arched harder against him, easing her legs apart to cup him intimately, whimpering again when she felt his huge erection.

He wanted her. Badly. As much as she wanted him.

The realization was almost enough to shock her into doing something stupid like ending the kiss. This was Nick—the guy she'd always wanted—hot and hard and hungry for *her.*

"Don't say no to me, sweetheart," he whispered as he finally—regretfully—drew his mouth from hers. He moved it to press kisses along her jaw, then down to the throbbing pulse point below her ear. "Say yes."

Yes, say yes! a voice screamed.

Oh, he was so tempting. And she wanted him desperately—wanted him to pull off her clothes, back her up against the counter and make love to her right on top of it. It would be incredible, the culmination of all her dreams and secret fantasies. She could finally put an end to all the years of restless, hopeless wanting.

But it wouldn't be the end. It would be the *start* of something, rather than the end of it. He'd make incredible love to her, make her come with a few more touches of his hands and a few more of those incredible kisses and she'd be alive and happy and completely fulfilled for the first time in her life.

But then he'd want to take her out for a pizza. Or get together with friends. And she'd be caught so deep in a quagmire of family and home that she'd *never* be able to get free of it.

"Say yes, Izzie," he ordered, sucking her earlobe into his

mouth and nibbling it—a tiny bite that she felt clear to the floor. "Give me your number and let's finally get this started."

Get this started. Get *everything* started.

She just couldn't do it. Izzie had always been strong and determined and had taken what she wanted. But she couldn't take *him*. Not now. It was much too late.

Yanking away, she winced as her tangled hair got caught in his fingertips. Her breathing ragged, her body crying out at the injustice, she shook her head, hard. Then she backed away, wrapping her arms around her waist in self protection. "No."

He started to follow, his dark eyes glittering…predatory. "You don't mean it."

She held a hand up. "Yes. I do," she said with a firm shake of her head. "Now, if you'll excuse me, we're closed and I have work to do in the kitchen." Taking a deep breath and striving to keep her voice steady, she added, "I want you to leave."

3

ON HIS FIRST NIGHT working at Leather and Lace, Nick showed up in a bad mood. He'd *been* in a bad mood for two days—since Izzie Natale had shot down his efforts to get closer to her.

The woman was unbelievable. Ten years ago, she might as well have taken out an ad in the Trib declaring her devotion to him. Now she wouldn't throw dog drool on him if he was on fire.

Damn, she was feisty. Had she always been that way? He figured with Gloria for a sister she had been. But considering he'd never seen her as a woman—just as a cute, lovesick kid—he'd never noticed. *Until now.*

Oh, yeah, now he'd noticed. He'd noticed everything about her. And he was not going to give up on her yet. Not when she'd become the first thing he thought of every morning and the star of his dreams every night.

Especially since that incredible kiss they'd shared.

Who would ever have guessed that the cute, pesky girl with the obvious crush on him would prove to be the most sensual, kissable woman he'd ever known? He'd suspected he could kiss her for hours. Now he knew better. He could kiss her for *ever.*

After she'd ordered him out of the bakery the other evening, he'd decided to play dirty, going right to Gloria to ask her for her sister's phone number. His sister-in-law had been glad to oblige. She'd also been more than candid about how Izzie had felt about him in the old days.

Not that Nick had needed her to tell him about it. He'd been well aware—as had everyone else.

"Not anymore," he muttered as he parked his truck—which he'd purchased right after getting home a couple of weeks ago—behind the club. He frowned, wondering how much of a jerk it made him now to be disappointed that a girl who'd had a wild crush on him as a kid didn't give a damn about him anymore. Probably a pretty big one. But he couldn't help it.

Knowing little Izzie had been crazy about him had been a constant during his teenage years. A given. Just another part of his reality. Certainly nothing he'd ever taken advantage of or embarrassed her about. It had just been…kinda cute, thinking there was a girl out there doodling his name in her school notebook. Innocent. Simple.

Man, he hated that that girl wouldn't even look at him now. Especially because he didn't think he'd done anything to deserve her coldness. No, he hadn't recognized her. But he also hadn't recognized the kid who had delivered the newspaper and now ran a newsstand on the corner. Or a couple of guys he'd played basketball with at St. Raphael's.

Mark thought he *did* deserve it. Not because he hadn't recognized her, but because he'd counted on her childhood feelings to give him an edge with Izzie the adult.

Hell, maybe he was right. Maybe he shouldn't have teased her, been so sure of her. He'd known enough women to know how they felt about being taken for granted. He should have taken her out to dinner before kissing her like he needed the air in her lungs to keep on living.

So he needed to start over with Izzie. Start slow, like he would with any other woman he'd just met.

It might not be easy. Because she already affected him more than any woman he'd ever met. He'd dreamed about her this week, thought about her, gone out of his way to walk past the bakery in the hope of bumping into her.

"Tables have definitely turned," he muttered aloud when he walked through the private, employees entrance into the back of the club. "Which is probably just the way she wants it."

Yeah, she could be stringing him along out of revenge. But somehow, Nick didn't think that was the case.

She hadn't been able to hide her feelings behind those incredibly expressive brown eyes. Though she'd sent him away after their kiss, she still wanted him. But something was preventing her from doing anything about it.

He just had to find out what.

"Nick, you're right on time!" The club owner, a beefy, good-natured guy with a Santa Claus-like belly laugh, emerged from his office and extended his hand.

Nick shook it. "Mr. Black."

"Call me Harry."

"Harry, then. Thanks again for the opportunity."

The other man waved a hand in unconcern. "Your big brother, he's one of the few honest contractors I've met in this city. Did beautiful work at a fair price. And if he says you're up to the job, I trust him completely."

Nick had already bought his brother, Joe, a beer in thanks for setting up his interview. He wished he'd made it a pitcher.

"All the paperwork's done, you check out exactly like Joe said you would," Harry said as he gestured Nick toward a seat in his office. "Now, you're clear on what I need from you?"

Nick nodded. "Have there been problems recently?"

Harry tapped his fingers on the desk and nodded. "The Rose has made a stir. Men want to see her and there have been a few *incidents.*"

Nick stiffened reflexively, even though he hadn't met the woman yet. "Incidents?"

"Nothing too serious, thank God. But a couple of grabs, dressing room prowlers. A few disturbing notes." Harry shook his head, looking disgusted. "Can't imagine any man saying stuff that crude to any woman. But she was a sport about it, laughed it off." Staring pointedly, he added, "That's one reason I hired you—she tends to not take it seriously. And I want someone else to."

"I will," Nick replied, confident of his own words.

Harry nodded, obviously convinced. "Other than that, there's not too much trouble on a nightly basis. A guy'd have to be drunk as a skunk or just plain stupid to think he could go after one of the girls at the risk of taking one of the bouncers on. But we don't let anybody get drunk as a skunk in my joint." He chuckled. "And stupid people can't afford it."

That wasn't a surprise. When Nick had come in last weekend, he'd noticed the upscale feel of the club. Far from being seedy or shadowy, like most strip joints, this place was elegantly comfortable, from the earth-toned leather furniture to the framed pieces of classy-looking art on the walls. The prices reflected the ambiance; this was no after-work beer joint.

"I wanted to introduce you to the Rose, but she called and said she's running a little late tonight. I don't imagine there'll be time before her first number."

Nick stiffened, realizing he'd soon be seeing the woman behind the mask. Somehow, during the past few days when he'd been so focused on Izzie, he hadn't let the thought of the sultry stripper drift into his mind. Now, however, knowing he was about to see her again, he couldn't help but remember the way she'd made him feel last weekend.

Hot. Hungry. Needy.

So would any sexy, naked woman after such a long dry spell.

"She's something else."

"I noticed last weekend."

Harry Black shrugged. "Yeah, she's a looker, but there's something special about her even when she's not on stage. Got her head on right—a smart one. But that doesn't mean I'm not worried about her. She could get herself in trouble."

Nick could certainly understand that. Considering how attracted he'd been to her, he could see how a much more desperate man might react to her sultry performance.

"She's not going to like me hiring someone to mainly look out for her," Harry cautioned. "So we'll leave that part between us, okay? As far as she knows, you're just another bouncer."

"Fine." In fact, it was more than fine. He wanted as little interaction with the woman he was supposed to be protecting as possible. Not that he was truly worried about her effect on him—it had been a one time thing, that was all.

He'd been telling himself that for days. He'd also been ignoring the fact that none of the other strippers he'd seen that night had so much as caused his heart rate to increase its regular, lazy rhythm. Only *her.*

Meeting her would take care of that, he was sure of it. She wore a mask, meaning her looks were all from the neck down. She'd have muddy eyes or crooked teeth or a hooked nose. Or a voice like a truck driver. Or she'd snort when she laughed. Something would be wrong. Something would break the spell.

That would be the end of his interest. No doubt about it.

THE CRIMSON ROSE spotted the dark-haired man in black the moment she peeked through the curtains on the stage. And the moment she saw him—immediately recognizing him by his height and the power of his shadowed body—her heart began to beat harder.

He'd come back. For *her*.

This was the first night she'd been back to the club since last Sunday night, when she'd first seen him during her last performance on this stage. Inexplicably, she suspected this was his first night back, too. When she'd asked the other dancers about him, all had denied seeing such a man in the club during the past five nights.

She had drawn him back. Just as he—the very thought that he might be in the crowd again tonight—had worked to draw her here as well.

Not that she needed much of a draw. She loved what she did. She positively came alive while moving under a spotlight. The fact that her clothes were falling off her body as she did so was completely incidental.

She honestly didn't care.

"He came back," she whispered, almost bouncing on her toes, so excited she could hardly stand it.

Not just excited. *Relieved.*

Because though she'd only seen him from a distance, she already felt incredibly attracted to him. He'd be a marvelous distraction from the *other* man who'd been occupying her thoughts lately.

The one she couldn't have.

She began to smile, feeling, for the first time in days, a little upbeat. Working at the club was her one outlet, her only escape from the life she had so wanted to avoid coming back to here in Chicago. She loved these secret, wicked weekends.

And now that she'd realized there was another man—someone else—who could cause an instant, aching sort of want deep inside her, Izzie Natale sensed those weekends simply wouldn't come fast enough.

"You're not the only man in Chicago, Nick Santori," she whispered while the stage crew finished stripping the stage for her signature solo number.

When she'd first seen the ad in the paper for dancers for a Chicago gentleman's club, Izzie had had no illusions about what the job would entail. She wasn't some young dance ingénue who'd turned up for an audition only to be shocked at the very idea of taking off her clothes for a bunch of men.

Izzie had taken off her clothes for plenty of men. Sometimes even groups of them.

It wasn't as if the Rockettes danced in a whole lot of clothes. And during the three months she'd performed with the Modern Dance Company of Manhattan, she'd done two nude artistic performances.

The dancing she did at Leather and Lace wasn't *exactly* artistic. But, then again, she wasn't *exactly* nude, either. After all, she never took off her G-string.

Yes, her audience in Chicago was after sexual titillation rather than cultural stimulation. But, honestly, judging by the way some of the modern dance aficionados had come backstage and tried to pick up the dancers, she figured the motivations were, at heart, exactly the same.

Dancing was dancing. After the dire prognosis she'd received when having her torn ACL repaired several months ago, she didn't care where she was performing, or what she was wearing when she did it.

Honestly, now, having had a taste of it, she realized she couldn't have chosen a better venue. Because here, hidden behind a red velvet mask, she was free to be everything Izzie Natale of the famous Taylor Street Natale's Bakery was not.

Sexual. Uninhibited.

Free.

Before she'd even dragged her mind into readiness, she was introduced and her music had begun. Izzie moved onto the stage, dancing for herself and herself alone, as she always did, letting the petals fall where they may. She remained above everything, even oblivious to the money being tossed onto the stage—the crew would pick it up when she was finished. She also ignored the gasps and avid stares of the crowd.

Except one man's avid stare. His, she wanted to see, though it would prove difficult with him standing in the most shadowy area of the place and her nearly blinded by the spotlight. But when the choreography moved her downstage right—closest to the bar, and *him*—she risked it and looked.

And nearly fell off the stage.

Oh my God, oh my God, oh my God.

She lost the beat of the song and got a little tangled on her own feet. She also had to throw down an extra couple of petals a few measures too soon to try to cover her misstep.

Because in that quick flash when the light had hit him just right, she'd recognized the face, those shoulders, that hair.

It was Nick Santori who stood near the bar. Nick was the same dark, shadowy stranger who'd had her blood pumping through her veins, throbbing between her legs both last week when she'd first seen him here and a few moments ago when she'd glimpsed him again.

The bastard. Was she never going to be free of him? Would no man ever make her feel that crazy/excited/hungry feeling she got whenever he was in the vicinity? And what in the hell was he doing here, anyway?

Worse—what was he going to do about it if he realized she, the woman who'd shot him down in the bakery two days ago, was the Crimson Rose?

Her mind awash with the ramifications of Nick's presence,

Izzie finished her number. As soon as it was over, she darted behind the curtains and stuck her arms into a short, silky robe hanging right backstage. Barely noticing the crew members, who immediately got to work re-setting the stage for the more typical dancers, she hurried down the back stairs toward her private dressing room.

Normally, all the dancers would share one and Izzie was no prima donna who required her own space. But the owner of Leather and Lace had insisted on giving her a private, coat-closet sized room because of how serious Izzie was about protecting her identity. Once he'd realized just how much the "mystery" of the Crimson Rose enhanced the club's reputation—and brought in more customers—he'd upgraded her to one the size of a small bathroom.

Before she could duck into it, she heard his voice. "There you are! Hold up a second, I want you to meet someone."

She was in no condition to meet anyone—especially not another one of Harry's cousins or old fishing buddies. There was always someone ready to play on old friendships or family connection to meet the dancers.

On the positive side, Harry was as protective as a papa bear and the introductions never went further than a quick handshake or a signed autograph. Despite how much some of the men he brought around seemed to want it otherwise.

Pasting on an impersonal smile behind the mask she hadn't yet removed, she turned around.

"This is Nick Santori. I've just hired him to beef up our security."

Izzie sagged against the wall. If it hadn't been there, she might have just fallen sideways onto the tile floor, but thankfully, her shoulder instead landed on some hard wood paneling and it kept her vertical.

More than she could say for her heart. It had gone rolling

down and had landed somewhere in the vicinity of her stomach, which was now churning with anxiety.

"This is…"

"Rose," she quickly interjected, cutting Harry off before he could say her real name. She cleared her throat, seeking the sultry, husky tones she'd always used when greeting fans backstage at Radio City. The one that was quite different from the voice Nick had heard at the bakery just a couple of days before. "Nice to meet you."

He held out his hand. She took it. Time didn't stop or anything, and the floor didn't buckle beneath her feet. But, damn, his touch did feel *fine*.

He had big hands. Strong hands. A soldier's competent hands. They were capable of brute force. Yet equally capable, she knew, of tender care. Like when those hands had helped her pull her ugly bridesmaid dress into place, then gently lifted her back onto the dance platform and back into their waltz so many years ago.

"Nick's brother Joey Santori sent him in. You remember him, don't you? He did all the work upstairs. You met him last month."

Yes, she had…and it had been a closer call than this meeting with Nick, who could see almost nothing of her face because of the mask. She'd barely had time to duck behind a changing screen before coming face to face with Nick's older brother.

Now she had to wonder…had Joe seen her? Recognized her? And was he now playing Mr. Neighborhood Protector by sending his baby brother in to watch out for the girl up the block?

Possible.

God save her from Italian men.

One plus—he hadn't told Tony. Because no way would her overprotective brother-in-law have let Izzie's new job go undiscussed. He'd have come down on her with some big brother lecture about how she simply had to quit now, immediately, if not sooner. Either that or he'd have told Gloria, who would have had a shrieking meltdown over what the neighbors and her sweet, impressionable boys—wild little maniacs, in Izzie's opinion—would think.

"Harry, help! Some CEO's at the door saying he had reservations for ten," a frantic voice called from the top of the stairs. The hostess who worked the front desk came clattering down three stairs and spotted him, relief evident in her face. "You need to get up here."

Muttering under his breath, Harry offered Nick an apologetic shrug. "Sorry. Never fails. Tell you what, why don't you talk to…Rose…get an idea of what her routine and schedule are like and then meet me upstairs in thirty minutes?"

Nick nodded and they both watched Harry walk away. Well, Nick watched Harry. Izzie watched Nick.

She hadn't noticed at first—she'd been too frazzled herself—but Nick appeared tense. The muscles in his neck were rock hard, his jaw jutted out stiffly. Beneath his wickedly tight black T-shirt, his broad shoulders were squared in his military posture and his hands were fisted at his sides.

Interesting.

If she had to guess, she'd say he wasn't particularly happy to meet her. It was as if he actively disliked her…which didn't make much sense.

The only reason he could have for *already* disliking her was that he had somehow recognized her. That he'd looked into her eyes, revealed behind the mask, and seen something familiar. Or heard a note in her voice that he'd heard before. He certainly hadn't seemed very happy with Izzie-the-baker when she'd practically pushed him out of the bakery the other evening and imagined he'd convinced himself she was at best a pain in the ass and at worst a complete tease.

But if he looked at her and saw only a complete stranger…

what could he dislike about her after knowing her for all of two minutes? Nick wasn't the judgmental type. She couldn't see him working here if he had some kind of problem with women stripping.

Besides, his dislike seemed personal, directed only at her. He'd been perfectly fine with Harry.

"So, is tonight your first night?" she asked, keeping her tone low and thick. She sounded sultry—wicked—but that couldn't be helped. She needed to disguise her voice, at least until she knew for sure whether Nick had recognized her. Or if he'd been tipped off by his big brother.

"Yes."

"How do you like the club?"

He shrugged, noncommittal.

"Come now, you're not shocked are you? I imagine you've been in places like this all over the world."

His dark eyes narrowed. "How would you know I've been all over the world?"

Oh, man, that was stupid. She'd just tipped her hand. "I mean…you look like the military type, with the hair and the all-black commando look you have going on. Am I right?"

He nodded once, still not unbending one iota.

Izzie had to force herself not to react to all that simmering, intense male heat. Nick had been adorably sexy when flirting with her and trying to pick her up. And incredibly sensual when seducing her with his kiss.

Now…when he was all dark, intense business, he was absolutely devastating. Dangerous, almost, and though she'd never feared him, she couldn't contain a tiny shiver.

If he decided to kiss her now, it wouldn't be with sweet, sultry persuasion. It would be with raw, overpowering hunger.

She wanted that kind of kiss from him.

"I saw you here last weekend," she said, not even realizing she was going to admit such a thing until the words had left her mouth. That probably wasn't smart. She needed to keep the upper hand here—letting Nick know she'd been aware of him from first glance wasn't a good way to do that.

"I came in to talk to Harry about the job."

"And you watched me dance." She dared him to deny it.

He nodded once. The jaw flexed.

"Did you like it?"

"You're talented."

Oh, if only he knew.

"You're not…uncomfortable around me, are you?" she asked, trying not to laugh. "I mean, having seen so *much* of me?"

He shook his head. The shoulders tensed. "This is a job, Miss…"

"Rose will do."

"As you wish. The point is, I want to keep you…all of you…safe. Meaning we need to implement some new security procedures." He sounded impersonal, but every movement or flex of his body screamed that his tone was a lie. He was definitely reacting to her and Izzie would lay money it had nothing to do with him knowing her real identity.

If he knew who she was, he'd never remain stiff and un-yielding, trying to keep up this professional act. He'd be either seducing her—finishing what he'd started the other day—or else he'd be lecturing her for doing something so out of character for a nice Italian girl from the neighborhood.

Nope. He didn't know who she was. No way in hell. So why he was being so stiff and gruff, she really didn't know.

"Would you like to come in while I change?" she asked, gesturing to the closed door behind her. It had a cheesy little tinfoil star on it—a joke from one of the other dancers, who'd been remarkably welcoming after the first week or two. Considering their clientele had increased significantly since she'd been performing at the club, she figured they were all bene- fiting from the "mystery" of the Crimson Rose.

He hesitated for only a moment. Then nodded. "Sure."

Opening the door, she walked in and ushered him in behind her. "Sorry for the mess."

The space was crowded—one mirror, surrounded by bright lights, covered an entire wall. A long, sturdy vanity, con- nected to the wall, ran the width of the room, reducing the floor space to about a three-foot wide aisle. The vanity was covered with makeup and hair products. Not to mention G-strings and pasties.

He saw those and blanched, quickly looking away. Shifting uncomfortably, he moved back the tiniest bit, but was stopped from going far by the door, which Izzie had closed behind him.

A muscle worked in his cheek and he crossed his massive arms tightly across his chest. His feet spreading a little apart, he looked like a sturdy, unmovable sea captain standing on the deck of a ship. Unapproachable, unweatherable, unflap- pable.

Only, he *wasn't* unreachable. Because she'd seen that look at her sexy, glittery underthings. And his reaction to them.

Which was when Izzie started to get an inkling of what was bothering him. It wasn't a matter of him liking her or dislik- ing her. Of him recognizing her or not recognizing her.

He wanted her. She just *knew* it.

Nick wanted to have sex with a stranger—a stripper—and he didn't like that about himself. He didn't like that weakness. She could practically hear his thoughts now, since she'd been raised exactly the way he had.

It wasn't good. It wasn't nice. It didn't quite fit the whole- some neighborhood-kid image.

It was, however, very honest. And despite how *he* felt about it, Izzie liked that very much. As a matter of fact, she *loved* that he wanted her. Not quite as much as she'd loved that he'd wanted Izzie—the invisible girl—but pretty darn close.

Trying to hide her smile, she walked around behind a changing screen and slipped the silky robe off her shoulders. Tossing it over the top of the screen, she murmured, "You're not...uncomfortable in here with me, are you?"

He didn't reply at first. Glancing at the mirror, she saw his reflection—saw him shake his head. Then he cleared his throat, answering aloud. "I'm fine."

He was turned toward the wall—away from the screen, away from the mirror. Which was probably a good thing, considering the reflection ran all the way to the far wall...even on her side of the changing screen.

If he looked in that mirror, the screen would prove to be completely superfluous. He'd see every bit of her...except her still-masked face.

She took her time getting dressed.

"That's good. If you're going to be working here, I suppose you're going to have to get used to seeing a *lot* of your co-workers." She licked her lips and almost purred as she added, "Much more than you'd see in a normal job."

"I'm not easily shocked," he muttered.

Turn around and we'll see.

But he didn't. Curse the luck.

"Can we talk about your routine, how you drive to work, what time you usually arrive?"

Bending over, she slipped out of the tiny G-string, then straightened and draped it over the top of the screen, answering his questions as she undressed. She never took her eyes off him, waiting for him to turn around, imagining how his eyes would widen and his mouth would drop when he realized he could see every move she made in the mirror.

He remained in the same position; however, the flash of movement must have caught his eye. Because his gaze shifted over—quickly, almost imperceptibly—but he definitely glanced.

She watched his reflection, seeing the way his body grew harder. His black trousers highlighted the clench of his muscular thighs and that tight butt. Though he made no sound at all, he dropped his head forward and slowly shook it, desperation rolling off him though he remained entirely silent.

Triumph surged through her as she realized what was happening. He was dying for her. And desperate to resist her.

Izzie continued to take her sweet time as she pulled on a pair of tiny panties—not much bigger than the G-string she'd just discarded. Then she added a matching lacy bra, cut low, almost to her nipples. Not the type of underclothes one would expect of a baker…they were the types of silky things she wore beneath her clothes to remind herself that she was *not* a sweet Betty Crocker wannabe.

Through it all, Izzie was careful not to dislodge the mask. She was also careful of her clip-in hair extensions. They took her shoulder-length dark brown hair down to the middle of her back, and added reddish highlights that worked well in her act. If he recognized her, the game would be over. And right now, Izzie was enjoying the game too much to let it end.

Particularly because she'd begun to see exactly how it could be played.

With no rules. No restrictions. Complete anonymity.

As the Crimson Rose, she could have him—take him— completely free of the repercussions that would surround her if she dared to do such a thing as Izzie Natale. She could have incredible sex with him, enough to get her deep-rooted need for him out of her system for good, then walk away, without anyone ever knowing the truth.

Including, if she was very lucky, *him*.

The question was—could she pull it off?

Catching sight of movement, Izzie realized Nick had finally turned around. He was reaching for the doorknob of the dressing room, his mouth open as if he was about to tell her he was leaving. Then he glanced toward the mirror and caught sight of her.

Nick's defenses dropped. He looked utterly helpless as he completely devoured her with his eyes. Visible hunger— primal and urgent—rolled off him in nearly tangible waves.

And in that moment, Izzie knew she could, indeed, pull it off. She was finally going to have the man she'd wanted for half her life.

4

HE SHOULD NEVER have come in here. Should never have walked into a small room with a woman who already had his head reeling and his body taut with anticipation. One he was *supposed* to be protecting from guys who'd already threatened her.

Nick had been handling things okay up to now. Even while watching the dancers perform—while watching *her* perform—he'd felt in control of the situation. Yeah, she'd affected him. Any man not affected by the Crimson Rose had to have been castrated or born with no libido. But her effect was purely physical—not mental, not emotional. In his head, he still only saw one woman. Wanted one woman. And that was Izzie Natale.

He'd been feeling cool and confident when Harry had brought him downstairs to meet her. A little of that confidence had disappeared when he'd gotten close enough to her to smell the light, delicate perfume she wore—so at odds with her surroundings and her profession. His coolness had gone right out the window when she'd ushered him into her small dressing room where he'd felt like a bear trapped in a telephone booth.

And now…this…seeing her in the mirror?

Madness.

He'd seen her almost naked on stage and she'd stunned him. Now, close up, she blew his mind. Even wearing something that might pass for clothing on a sun-drenched beach, she was every bit as seductive as she'd been during her naked dance.

She was tall and she was curvy and she was soft and she was breathtaking. Her full breasts were contained by a bra that cupped the bottoms but left the tops nearly bare. Her cleavage spilled over the seam and the dark, pointed tips of her nipples thrust against the white lace, demanding attention.

Every man in the room had seen her breasts upstairs minutes ago, but now, up close, Nick was able to truly appreciate their perfection. How perfectly they'd fit in his hands, how delightful her nipples would taste against his tongue.

Nick drew in a deep breath, letting his attention drift lower. His gaze skimmed over the midriff, the slim waist. It lingered on the generous hips highlighted by the strips of white—the strings of her panties—slung over each one. The elastic top of her panties skated across the pale, vulnerable-looking skin below her hipbones. A tiny tuft of pretty brown curls peeked out from the top of them, the dark shadow behind the white silk was all he could see of the rest.

This was *more* than she revealed in her dance, and every male cell in his body reacted to the glorious sight. His heart rate slowed, the way it did when the world around him became dead serious. He swallowed—his mouth flooding with hunger. And his cock leapt, raging for release against his zipper.

The vanity interfered with the rest of his view, leaving him ripped with curiosity as his mind filled in the blanks of what he was not seeing. Those long legs. She had legs that could wrap around him twice, he knew that much from her dance.

It was all too easy to imagine lifting her onto that strong, flat surface, spreading her legs, then pulling up a chair to sit between them. He'd push her back, then loop her knees over his shoulders. Dipping his head in close for a thorough exploration, he'd sample those pretty curls and the shiny folds that they concealed. He'd pleasure her completely, devour her until his face was wet with the slickness of her arousal. He'd take the edge off his hunger, then focus only on her, giving himself a long time before he'd look up to watch the pleasure on her face as her orgasm rolled through her.

But in the vision, it wasn't the masked face of a stranger he saw. It was *Izzie's* face. This stranger had aroused him. Izzie was the one he wanted to fulfill him.

He needed to get out of here. Now. Because even if Izzie *had* shot him down—if there was absolutely nothing between them—she was still the one he really wanted. The one he'd dream about tonight, whether he got his rocks off right now or not.

He could do this stranger…and it might even be good. But it wouldn't get rid of his hunger. And it sure as hell would complicate things here in his new job.

Logically, he knew all that. The good Santori son who couldn't imagine bringing a woman like this around his traditional family should have been gone long before now.

Something made him stay. Maybe it was the *other* Nick. The one who'd grown predatory on the battlefield and bored in the real world. The one who'd been shot down by the reluctant woman he craved and was face-to-face with a willing one he desired.

They just locked eyes, hers mostly hidden behind that mask she still wore. Her lips slowly curled up into a sensuous smile and her chin came up in pure visual challenge.

Nick couldn't help it. He started to smile, too, a tight, dangerous smile that few would have recognized on the face of one of the affable Santori boys. "I don't think that screen works very well," Nick managed to say, his voice throaty.

"I'd say that depends on what I want it to do."

Knowing better, he asked, "If not giving you privacy to change, what is it you want it to do?"

The smile widened, a glitter of pleasure appearing in those shaded eyes. "Perhaps just heighten the anticipation. It's amazing how much more arousing it is to see some…but not all."

"You show almost all on stage."

"Almost," she conceded. "But if you noticed, it's mostly flash and petals, and only a tiny glimpse at the end."

His jaw clenched. "I noticed."

"Did it make you want more? Did a glimpse make you hunger for a look…which in turn made you ravenous for a touch?"

Which would make him insane for a taste.

He didn't answer, he didn't need to. She saw the answer in his face. As if tired of the game, she stepped out from behind the screen, still wearing only three things: the minuscule panties, the skimpy bra and the red velvet mask which was bigger than either of the other two.

"Why don't you take that off?" he asked, needing to see her face. He needed to find something about her that turned him off so he could get upstairs where his boss was waiting. So he could put her out of his head and get his libido back under control.

Quirking a questioning brow, she pointed to her bra, which startled a small laugh out of him. Because hell, yes, he'd like to see her without the bra—up close—but he knew he couldn't let that happen. Not if he wanted to keep his job. Not if he wanted to have the kind of life his brothers had.

Not if he wanted to work things out with Izzie.

"No. I mean that." He nodded toward the mask.

"I don't think so."

"You really take this anonymity seriously?"

"More than you know."

She moved closer and Nick honestly didn't know which pleased him more—feeling her warmth as she approached, or seeing her both in the flesh and reflected in the mirror. The woman's panties were not only tiny, they were thong-style and he could see the succulent curves of her ass in the mirror. His hands clenched with the need to fill them with those curves.

She reached for his left hand and lifted it. "No ring."

He shook his head.

"So there's no one…special?"

He hesitated a second before answering. A week ago the answer would have been an unequivocal no. Right now he wasn't so sure. He hedged. "That one's in the air right now."

Her bottom lip edged out in a tiny pout, glistening and wet against the red velvet cupping her mouth.

He wanted to bite it. Suck it into his mouth and lick the plumpness of it, then pull her down on his lap and explore all those curves and soft angles of her body.

"I'm unattached, too," she murmured, licking her lips as if she'd read his thoughts. "And frankly, in my line of work, I don't have much use for dating and get-to-know-you chats."

He suspected he knew where she was going. With some other woman—just about any other woman—he'd watch for signals, wonder if she was trying to pick him up. With this one, he knew she'd be very frank about what she wanted.

Her hand came up, she trailed the tips of her fingers across his shoulder, her nails scraping the cotton of his shirt. He felt the touch *everywhere.* Her scent overwhelmed him. Her heat screamed to him in pure sexual invitation.

She made it even more clear. "I want to have sex with you."

His heart skipped a beat. His pants shrunk across his groin and if the woman looked down, she'd know he could quite easily accommodate her. Several times, if she'd let him.

Before he could say a word, she quickly continued, "Despite what you might think since we just met, I'm not making this suggestion lightly. As Harry could confirm…I'm not in the habit of letting men in my dressing room. You are, in fact, the first one I've been alone with since I started working here."

Interesting. She sounded as if she was worried he'd question her morals or think she was trashy. He'd known trashy women. But in his experience, they were women with low self-confidence and lower self-esteem who grasped at sex with anyone in an effort to feed their egos and fill their empty hearts.

He could already tell Rose wasn't like that. She was *incredibly* self-confident. She could lift a finger and have any man upstairs ready to give her anything she wanted…and she knew it. She didn't need physical devotion to feed her self-esteem. In fact, he suspected it was her unshakeable self-esteem that enabled her to take off her clothes in front of a room full of men and yet remain so completely out of reach of all of them.

She could strip for them, entice them, seduce them…but never lower herself to a level that said she'd *ever* give them what they wanted.

But now, that's exactly what she was doing. Offering herself…to him. "I'm flattered," he said, his tone husky.

She reached for him, scraping the tips of her fingers along the waistband of his pants, tugging a little at his shirt.

"But it's not going to happen."

Her hand stilled. "You said you weren't attached."

"That's not the only issue."

"You're attracted to me."

He couldn't deny something so obvious. "We work together."

Shrugging in unconcern, she stepped closer, sliding one bare foot between his so that her leg scraped against his thigh. "Working together is what makes it so very…convenient."

She tilted her head, glancing toward the sturdy-looking vanity, and Nick knew she was picturing a very similar scenario to the one that had filled his mind earlier.

It would be shockingly easy to lift her onto that surface, step between her legs and drive into her body. Or to turn her around, lay her over it and come into her from behind. Their eyes would meet in the mirror…but he wouldn't see the passion in their depths. He could barely make out their color behind the fabric of her mask. And he knew one thing for sure—he would never make love to the woman as long as she wore the thing.

"I'm sorry, Rose. You're very attractive and sexy, but you're just not who I'm looking for right now," he said. "I've done the one night-stand-thing and I've had enough of it."

"Who said anything about one night?" Her words were flippant. Her husky tone was not.

The idea of having more than one night appealed to him. But it didn't change the basics: she was not the kind of woman he needed to get involved with right now. Not even on a purely sexual basis. "I'm sure there are a hundred guys upstairs who'd take you up on this in a heartbeat."

"I don't want any of them," she murmured. "I want you."

"You don't even know me."

"I don't have to know you to want to have sex with you."

"I'm not wired that way."

She made a sound of disbelief. "You've never had raw, wild, uninhibited sex with someone just for the sake of feeling good?"

"Just to get off, yeah," he muttered, making no effort to be delicate. "But only because time and expediency demanded it. I don't operate that way anymore."

"I could make it so good for you." She lifted his hand again, this time putting it on her bare hip.

Nick couldn't help squeezing it. "I don't doubt it."

"*Let* me," she ordered. "Let's see how good it can be."

His jaw stiff, he pulled his hand away. "I *know* how good it could be. I don't doubt we could screw ourselves senseless and make each other come a dozen times in an hour."

Her eyes closed behind the mask. He could see her pulse fluttering in her neck. Still talking in that throaty, sultry whisper, she asked, "And what would be so bad about that?"

Nothing would be so bad about that. In fact, it would be incredible. But he'd feel like shit afterward. He knew it as sure as he knew his brother Mark was never going to let him forget he'd been born twelve minutes before Nick had.

Some things were inarguable.

Like the fact that he couldn't have sex with this woman tonight and still look Izzie—the woman he sensed could be right for him for all the *right* reasons—in the eye tomorrow. So glancing at his watch, he found some nugget of resolve and said, "Harry's waiting for me upstairs. I'll see you later."

Without giving her a chance to try to stop him, he turned around and walked out of her dressing room. Judging by the way something went flying in that tiny room once the door was closed behind him, he knew he'd left a very angry woman in his wake.

"So HOW YOU DOIN', little brother?" Nick heard a woman's voice ask as he sat in a booth at Santori's the next day. It was early Sunday afternoon and the church crowd hadn't yet shown up for their traditional Sunday big mid-day meal, so he'd taken advantage of the lull to grab some lunch. Glancing up, he saw his sister-in-law, Gloria, Izzie's older sister.

They didn't look much alike. Gloria was pretty—especially for a thirty-something mother of three—but she didn't have Izzie's flamboyant looks. Her face was sweet, not dramatic. Her mouth soft, not sensual. She didn't have Izzie's amazing figure. Nor had she inherited her sister's desire to escape from here.

Gloria personified the world in which he'd grown up. She'd worked in her parents' business, gone to high school right here in the neighborhood. Married an Italian boy up the block. Gone to work in *his* family's business. And proceeded to produce lots of little Italian babies who looked just like her husband.

Though they were both hard-headed and volatile, and had been known to shout the street down when they got going, Tony and Gloria were absolutely crazy about each other. They had the kind of marriage anyone would want to have. The kind he would be lucky to have…once he figured out if he really wanted it.

Not knowing what he wanted was proving to be a real pain in the ass. Made more painful by the very sexy distraction called the Crimson Rose. He'd been able to avoid her for the rest of last night while working at the club, but every time their eyes met, she reminded him that she knew he was attracted to her.

"Nick?" Gloria prompted. "Everything okay?"

"I'm good, where are the boys?" he asked, looking past her for his two older nephews, or the carriage holding the baby one.

"I came in through the back…Tony Jr. and Mikey are in the kitchen with their father." She raised her voice, never shifting her eyes toward the swinging door leading into the kitchen. "Who had *better* not be giving them candy outta Pop's candy jar if he wants to *live* another day."

From the back room came the sound of Tony's deep

laughter. Nick would lay money the boys were already high on Pop's secret stash of gummy bears. "What about the baby?"

Gloria frowned, glancing toward the door of the restaurant. "He should be here any second. It's hard enough bringing the boys to mass without Tony there to help me. No way could I handle three of them. So he stayed with Auntie Izzie." Smiling in relief, Gloria nodded. "Here they are now."

Something about seeing Izzie pushing a baby carriage into the restaurant made Nick's stomach twist. Not because she looked like an absolute natural doing it…but because she looked miserable. Uncomfortable as hell.

He had to laugh. The woman was *so* unlike anyone else around here. Maybe that was why he couldn't get her off his mind.

"Hey, Iz, how'd you do with my little prince?"

"He puked in my hair. Twice."

Gloria swooped in and lifted the three-month-old out of the stroller, cuddling him close. "Aww, what'd you do to him?"

"I told him if he puked on me again I'd take him to the zoo and drop him in the bear cage," Izzie muttered. "What do you think I did to him?"

Gloria patted the baby on his back. "It's okay, Auntie Izzie's just grumpy because she doesn't have a sweet man to cuddle up with…much less four like Mommy's got."

Nick almost choked on his water at that one. If Gloria had been facing her sister, she would have seen the death ray that had come from Izzie's eyes. Apparently she heard him… because suddenly that death ray was sent in his direction.

Nick held up his hands, palms out, in a universal peace gesture. "I'm with you. Don't drop me in a bear cage."

Her glare faded and she half-smiled. "Don't tempt me."

"Careful, Nick," Gloria cautioned, still focused on the

baby, "our Izzie's not quite the sweet young thing you remember. You don't want to tangle with her."

Oh, yeah, he did want to tangle with her. Tangle his hands in her hair and his tongue in her mouth and his arms around her body and his legs between her thighs. Mostly he wanted to tangle in her life…and tangle her in his. At least enough so she'd give him a chance to win back some of that interest she'd once felt toward him.

Before Izzie could say anything, the door opened and more family members poured in. His parents and his brother Joe— with wife and baby in tow—led the way. Folks from the neighborhood followed. Next came lots of cousins and aunts and uncles, all of whom came to the restaurant every Sunday for a big family meal.

Izzie's whole body went tense. He could see it from five feet away. She didn't want to be part of this—didn't *feel* a part of this. And Nick, more than anyone else in the room, understood. So without saying a word, he got up, took her hand, and tugged her toward his table.

She resisted. "What…"

"Come on, it'll be okay," he whispered as he pulled her down to sit beside him. "I'll tell you who I recognize, you tell me who you recognize and we'll get through this together."

She stared at him, her eyes wide, her mouth trembling. Looking for a moment like a trapped deer, she seemed on the verge of fleeing. She appeared unable to deal with something as innocuous—yet painful—as a neighborhood gathering.

"It's okay," he repeated. "You can do it."

It took a few more seconds, but that panicked look slowly began to fade from her eyes. As family friends and neighbors greeted her, he felt her begin to relax beside him. She even chatted a little, smiling at people she hadn't seen in years.

Everything went fine. Right up until the minute some old

lady from the block clapped her hands together, then pinched Izzie's cheek. "Oh, you're a beautiful couple!" she exclaimed. "At *last* you've got your man, Isabella Natale. All those years and you've finally landed him!"

Everyone fell silent, immediately turning in their direction. Especially Gloria. And Nick's parents.

"Shit," Izzie mumbled under her breath. Her face turned as red as a glass of the chianti Pop loved so much.

Nick put a hand on her leg under the table. But she pushed it off. And with a quick goodbye to her sister and the family—and a glare at Nick—she strode across the restaurant and stalked out the front door, not looking back. Not even once.

OVER THE NEXT couple of days, Izzie gradually began to lose her mind. Began? Heck, she'd been losing her mind since the night she'd toppled onto a table full of cookies and Nick Santori had landed on top of her. The man had been consuming her for *years*. This week, however, he was on track to win the gold medal in the Let's Drive Izzie Crazy games.

After her failed seduction attempt at Leather and Lace, he'd avoided her as much as he could when on the job. They hadn't been alone at all the rest of Saturday night, or when they'd both worked again Sunday. Just as well. She was still ticked about what had happened at the restaurant that afternoon.

He did take his job seriously, making sure she went nowhere alone. But *he* hadn't been alone with her for one minute. It was as if he feared "Rose" would make another move on him the first chance she got, and was making sure she didn't get the chance.

Grr…men. So untrusting.

But if Nick was frustrating her with his aloofness at the club by night, he was absolutely killing her by day. He'd come by several times in the past few days, popping into the bakery for a muffin and a coffee. Every time he was all cute and sweet and sexy. So different from the dark, brooding guy at the club that she'd have thought they were two different people.

She honestly didn't know which man appealed to her more. Probably whichever one she happened to be with at the time. Funny…he knew her as two different women. And while his name was Nick either way, she knew him as two different men, too.

Both of them were messing with her head. She'd been making all kinds of stupid mistakes at the bakery today—like using peppermint extract instead of almond in a batch of cookies.

Giving up in the kitchen since she had several hours before the restaurant orders had to be delivered, she decided to do some paperwork before closing. It was well after lunch, she was working alone but could hear the bell if anyone came in.

But even that didn't go well. She'd added up a column on a deposit slip four times and still hadn't gotten it right. She was tempted to call Bridget to ask her cousin to straighten out her books. But judging by the conversation they'd had earlier in the day, Bridget had finally worked up the nerve to ask her shaggy-haired used car salesman out. And Izzie didn't want to do anything to distract her.

Izzie just wished *she* had a distraction. Because she couldn't get Nick out of her head. He'd invaded her life. No, *both* her lives. When he stared at her across the club and devoured her with his eyes at night while physically spurning her, she felt ready to howl in fury.

Showing up here by day—the handsome guy next door who wanted to lick the cream out of her cannoli—and her having to refuse him? It was pure hell.

She wanted Nick the bodyguard at night. Not Nick the sexy guy up the block by day.

She wanted sex. Not romance.

Wanted temporary. Not ever after.

Wanted to *do* him. Not date him.

It was simply a matter of wills to determine which of them got what they wanted first. God, she hoped it was her.

"Izzie?"

Startled, Izzie yelped and spun toward the front of the shop, seeing a customer at the counter. So much for thinking she'd hear the bell—she'd been deafened by her own thoughts.

Recognizing the woman, a weary smile curled her lips. Lilith was a regular, who could supposedly read the future. A bit out there, but a good customer, and a nice one. "I'm sorry." She wiped her hands on her apron. "My head was in the clouds."

"If the clouds all smell like this bakery, that's not a bad place to be."

Maybe for the customers. But after practically living in this place for two months, Izzie was *over* the nauseatingly sweet smells that invaded her nostrils from morning till night. "Believe me, it's not so great going home from work with hair scented like anisette and clothes that reek of ginger."

"On the positive side, they say the scent of licorice is great for dieters because it controls your appetite."

Didn't seem to her that the sexy, short-haired brunette had anything to worry about in that regard. Frankly, neither did Izzie. She'd long since lost her taste for sweets…no more cookie-induced panty girdles for her. "Twizzlers can keep it. I try to ignore the smells unless someone burns something."

"Oh, come on, no one at Natale's ever burns anything."

Quickly washing her hands, Izzie had barely dried them before Lilith pointed with impatience at the lone cannoli remaining in the front display case.

When Lilith told her she'd be eating in, rather than taking the cannoli to go, Izzie asked, "Got a reading?"

While she didn't entirely believe in that stuff, Izzie knew a lot of regulars swore by Lilith's spiritual readings. Though she'd never considered it before, Izzie half-wondered if the other woman could help her figure out the quagmire that was her life. Especially the Nick part of that quagmire.

"Nah, I'm taking a break from the medium world right now."

"Just my luck. For the first time in my life I think I'd actually *pay* to have someone tell me who the heck I'm going to be next week."

Izzie the baker? Izzie the stripper? Izzie the New Yorker? Izzie the Chicagoan? *Izzie the horny?*

That was the one she really wanted an answer to. Was she ever going to get laid again, and oh, please, please, please, would it actually be Nick Santori who did the laying?

She didn't ask Lilith any of those things, though the medium promised she'd try to help her as soon as she was "back in business"—whatever that meant. But that might be too late. She might already have done something stupid—like having sex with Nick the bouncer as the Crimson Rose. Which would be fabulous but would make him hate her if he found out the truth.

Or something *more* stupid, like going out on a date with Nick, the guy up the block, which would have her parents planning their wedding. Then she'd hate *herself.*

Ordering a cappuccino to go with her treat, the mysterious brunette made herself at home at a front table, firing up a laptop. After making the frothy cappuccino, Izzie carried it over. "Doing some surfing?"

"I'm going to try. The most I've ever used the Web for is updating my Web site and answering e-mail."

"Don't forget shopping. Or maybe you're going to start haunting chat rooms?"

"No, I'm doing research."

Leaving the woman to it, Izzie went back to work. Concentrating on cleaning out the display cabinet, she was surprised to hear the bell jangle as another late-day customer came in. This one she didn't recognize—and she definitely would have, if she'd seen her before. The leggy brunette was dressed entirely in sleek, black leather and she looked like a predatory cat. The sexy little motorcycle parked outside the door suggested the woman was a risk-taker and a rule-breaker.

Izzie liked her on sight.

"Hey, Izzie," Lilith called, "what do you know about computers?"

Offering the new customer a quick smile, she answered, "Well, I don't know how to find any naked pictures of Heath Ledger, and I haven't figured out how to send a death ray to spammers, but I do the Web site for the bakery." It was a basic one, but Izzie was pretty proud of it.

"I hear ya. So you know how to enlarge pictures? Other than ones of naked movie stars?"

Izzie grinned. "Yeah, give me a sec." She looked at the newcomer. "What can I get you?"

"Espresso and a cannoli."

"Sorry, Lilith took the last."

Settling for just the espresso, the woman paid her and waited for her drink. After making it, Izzie went over to Lilith to see what help she could offer.

It wasn't much. It turned out the medium needed to enlarge a grainy newspaper picture in order to see a ring on some guy's finger. And Izzie just didn't have the know-how to do it.

The newcomer in black leather, however, did. Joining them, she asked a few questions, then bent over Lilith's computer and went to work. Watching her type, her fingers flying on the keys, Izzie figured she was experienced at this. But when the woman acknowledged that she was hacking into the newspaper Web site to try to find the original photo, she suspected there was a lot more than simple ballsiness to the woman.

She was mysterious. Maybe even a little dangerous.

They *both* seemed that way, really. Lilith with her supposed psychic abilities. This woman with her risky, who-gives-a-damn attitude. So unlike little Izzie of the bakery.

Maybe, however, not too unlike the Crimson Rose. She wondered what these two would think if they knew she wasn't quite the sweet, simple bakery worker she appeared to be.

"Who is this guy, anyway?" the stranger asked. "Don't tell me you're trying to figure out if that ring is a wedding band and he's the asshole you've been dating for the last three months."

"Ew."

"So he's not your lover."

"Say that again and I'll dump the dregs on you. He's a jerk I'm investigating."

"A jerk?" The stranger snorted. "What makes him different from every other man on this planet?"

"Good question," Izzie muttered, though her heart wasn't really in it. Nick had always been one incredibly good guy. The fact that he wouldn't have sex with her as a stripper didn't mean he was a jerk.

Even though he was.

She wandered away from the other two, cleaning off the empty tables in preparation for closing. As she worked, she kept up with the other women's conversation, trying to stay out of it, but unable to when she heard who Lilith was currently dating. Hearing that the sexy medium had hooked up with Mac Mancuso, a nice boy-next-door type turned Chicago cop, she had to put her two cents in. Mainly because their situations—whether Lilith would believe it or not—were very similar.

"Mac's not a jerk. He grew up just a few blocks from here. Our families know each other. I'd think any woman would love to catch a good, honest cop like him."

The stranger in black immediately stopped typing. "You're sleeping with a cop." Somehow, Izzie suspected the woman was allergic to anyone official—especially the police.

"I'm sleeping with him, not married to him," Lilith insisted. "Trust me when I say that my definition of right and wrong varies from his by huge degrees."

Huh. Sounding more and more like Izzie's situation. She almost wished she and Lilith were alone so they could talk.

"Keep working and your next ten espressos are on me," Lilith told the other woman.

"I won't be around that long, but thanks for the offer."

"Add her to my tab," Lilith told Izzie. "Any time she stops in, coffee's on me." Glancing at the stranger, she asked, "What's your name?"

"Seline."

Amused since Lilith's tab currently took up two pages in her accounts book, Izzie asked, "Does that mean you're actually going to pay it someday?"

Lilith shrugged in unconcern, watching as Seline kept working. When she finally struck pay dirt and got Lilith the information she wanted, they both seemed triumphant.

Izzie only wished her problems with Nick could be solved with an Internet search. Unfortunately, if she searched for the stuff she wanted to do with Nick Santori on the Internet, she'd probably get inundated with spam from sites like bigpenises.com from now till eternity.

Finishing up her cappuccino and shutting down her

computer, Lilith thanked Seline for helping her out, then turned to Izzie. "Thanks for the sugar boost and the wi-fi."

"Anytime." Unable to help it, Izzie called out, "Lilith, don't be so quick to write off a great guy like Mac. Maybe you and he can find a way to make it work, even if you think there's no way it ever could."

And maybe she was a sucker who should still be reading fairy tales. But hey, it didn't hurt to dream, did it? Even if she was dreaming on behalf of someone else.

Once Lilith was gone, the other woman, Seline, approached the counter. Even her walk was feline—sultry—and Izzie wondered if she'd ever danced before.

"Here," Seline said. She put a one-hundred-dollar bill on the counter. "For her tab. I sense that she needs the money more than I do. And I don't have to be psychic to figure that out."

Stunned, Izzie murmured, "Thanks." She opened her mouth to say more—to offer the money back—but the mysterious woman in black had already turned toward the door, her coffee in hand. She walked out into the bright sunshine without another word, got onto her sleek motorcycle and roared away down the street.

BRIDGET DONAHUE had always known she would never be wildly sexy and self-confident like her cousin Izzie. But there were times when she allowed herself to think that, maybe, since they were related, Bridget had a tiny bit of Izzie-power trapped deep inside her. So ever since she was a kid, she'd played a game. WWID, aka *What Would Izzie Do?* And then she'd try to do that.

Asking Dean Willis to go out with her one day at lunchtime had definitely been a WWID moment. And Bridget still couldn't believe she'd gone through with it. But if she hadn't, she wouldn't now be sitting at a coffee shop, looking across the table at his handsome face. Make that staring at his face.

Staring. Izzie wouldn't stare. Bridget ducked her head down, focused on her cup of Earl Grey tea. Not the double shot espresso she probably needed—because of her "I don't drink coffee" fib—but okay…mainly because of the company.

"You ready for a refill?" Dean asked.

Bridget shook her head. "I'm fine, thanks."

They weren't at her uncle's bakery, but at a big chain place not far from her apartment. Bridget had chosen the spot, which seemed safe, neutral and impersonal. Not the kind of place that said she thought they were on a date. Not the kind of place where a date would be absolutely out of the question.

God, she sucked at this. Izzie would have met him at a hotel bar.

Small steps, she reminded herself. Asking a man out was a first for her. It wasn't that she'd never dated—or that she was completely inexperienced. But if Izzie was on the top rung when it came to dealing with men, Bridget was still pulling the ladder out of the cellar.

They sat in an alcove by the front window. Bridget had her chair pushed back from the table, to accommodate the length of his legs beneath it. He looked crowded—bunched up in the small chair and the small corner—but he hadn't complained.

"You must be tired of hearing me rattle on about my land-lord problems," she said as the conversation lagged. "I haven't seemed to shut up."

He shook his head. "You're easy to talk to."

"You haven't been doing much talking…just listening."

"You're easy to listen to," he replied with a small smile.

Nice answer. And it was mutual, because he was also very easy—easy to like. But she still didn't feel like she knew anything about him. "So how do you like working for Marty? You've sold more cars in the month you've been there than any other salesman has sold in the past three."

He shrugged. "It's not hard when you have good products to sell." Lowering his gaze, he reached for his cup. "I guess you'd know that since you've worked for Marty longer than I have."

Sighing, Bridget shook her head. "Not much longer."

"Really?"

"I started just a couple of months before you did so I don't know much of anything, either."

He frowned. "But you keep the books, surely you know how things are going. I bet the place is raking in the bucks, huh?"

Grunting in annoyance, she admitted, "I have no idea. I see just enough to keep the books balanced and not much else."

Dean stopped stirring his tea and lifted his eyes to hers. Leaning forward over the table, he asked, "You don't know *anything* about what's going on at Honest Marty's Used Cars?"

"I know Marty's a bit of a con artist," she said tartly. "Honesty is just one of his…embellishments."

She suspected her boss also embellished some other things—like stuff he told the IRS. But she didn't have proof and was not about to say such a thing to anyone else.

He persisted. "But you must make the deposits, pay the invoices, keep an eye on the accounts receivable."

"I take what he gives me and do what I can." Shrugging, she added, "Honestly, I don't know much of anything about the business, it's all I can do to keep the checkbook balanced."

He held her stare, his blue eyes looking searchingly into her face, as if he was trying to find the answer to some question. She couldn't imagine what. She had no idea why he was so interested in the financial dealings of their employer.

Then she thought of something. It *could* be a matter of job security. Dean was personable and a good salesman, but he didn't exactly dress like someone who had a lot of money.

The sports coats he wore to work usually didn't fit well across his broad shoulders, and his pants were sometimes a little shabby.

Dean hadn't said a lot about what he'd done before coming to Honest Marty's. For all she knew, he'd been put out of work by poor management at his last job. That would certainly be enough to make anybody ask questions, especially somebody who lived paycheck to paycheck, as she suspected he did.

Not wanting to embarrass him, she carefully tried to set his mind at ease. "Look, I don't know specifics, but I know the dealership's doing well. I see the number of cars coming onto the lot and the number leaving it. You don't have to worry."

He frowned, as if not understanding what she meant. Some impulse made Bridget reach across the table and put her hand on his. She almost pulled her hand back right away, surprised to feel a warm tingle where skin met skin. But, swallowing for courage, she left it there. *Like Izzie would.*

If this was a date, he'd interpret her touch as a signal that she wanted more. If it was *not* a date, he'd interpret it as concerned friendship. Bridget considered it a little of both. "Your job is secure."

He was staring at their hands, still touching. "My job?"

He sounded—distracted. As if he was as affected by their touch as she was, which gave her a little thrill. "Marty would be a fool to let you go. You're the best salesman he's got."

He said nothing at first, he just slowly twined his fingers in hers, rubbing at the fleshy pad of her palm with the tip of his thumb. Her pulse raced and she wondered if he could feel it throbbing right there below her skin.

She somehow managed to concentrate on getting a positive message across, ignoring the tingling in her fingers and the flip-flopping of her heart. "It's okay, I know what it's like to worry about making ends meet, but please don't worry about the company. I'm sure you're not going to lose your job."

He looked up at her, his jaw dropping. "Lose my...."

"I thought that's why you were curious."

Dean's mouth snapped and he mumbled, "It's okay." He pulled the hand she'd been touching away and dropped it onto his lap. "Well, they probably want this table for other customers. I guess we should go."

Oh, God, she felt like a fool. She'd ruined this, he probably thought she had been pitying him or something. "Dean, I really didn't mean anything..."

"Hey, don't worry about it. I just wasn't sure what you meant at first. It's good to know the company's doing so well," he said, still sounding distracted. "Thanks again for meeting me. I'm glad we got the chance to get to know each other better, since we'll be working together."

Bridget managed to suck her trembling lip into her mouth, recognizing a brush-off when she heard one. Either he'd never intended this as a get-to-know-you date at all, or he *had* and she'd blown it. But whatever the case, it was finished now. He was not interested in seeing her again.

WWID...Izzie wouldn't cry. So she blinked. Hard.

"Bye, Bridget," he said as he escorted her outside.

She somehow managed to sound perfectly normal when she said goodbye too. But deep inside, she felt anything but normal.

In fact, Bridget felt a little bit broken.

5

OVER THE NEXT WEEK, Nick went out of his way to change Izzie's mind about going out with him. He stopped by the bakery, phoned in orders for stuff he didn't really want and made sure he was the one to sign for any deliveries at the restaurant, just in case she happened to be the delivery person.

She never was.

But he wasn't giving up. While at first she'd been a sexy stranger who'd caught his eye, she'd now become something of a challenge to him. He wanted to work his way around her protective wall and see if the smiling, funny girl was still there behind that to-die-for woman exterior.

Maybe it was just as well that Izzie consumed his thoughts by day. Because it made it easier to resist temptation by night. It definitely had on Saturday and Sunday night.

He'd worked at Leather and Lace for a second weekend. This time, knowing what he was in for, he'd been careful to avoid being alone with Rose, the club's sultry star performer, and hadn't even exchanged a word with her. Even still, it had been impossible to keep his eyes off her.

Especially when she danced.

Especially when she watched *him* while she danced.

If she'd made another move on him, he honestly didn't know that he'd have been able to refuse. So ensuring he was never alone with her was probably a good thing.

Hell, he honestly wasn't sure why he was resisting. As long as he kept the woman safe, he didn't see Harry Black being the kind of man who'd have a problem with it. After all, he was married to one of his own former star performers.

And letting off a little sexual steam didn't have to have anything to do with Nick's normal, daytime life. In fact, nobody in his family ever needed to know about it. There was no law that said an unattached man couldn't have sex with a willing woman, just because he was interested in another woman.

One who wasn't interested in him.

Damn. That's why he hadn't done it. Because it was driving him crazy that Izzie wasn't interested in him.

Frankly, he'd never worked so hard to get a woman's attention in his life. The fact that Izzie was the woman in question made the whole situation that much more challenging.

She'd been crazy about him once. He'd get her to see him that way again if it was the last thing he did. Even if it meant doing stupid, sappy shit like showing up at her bakery with a handful of flowers.

Like he was right now.

God, how the guys in his unit would laugh to see him, standing on a street corner on a hot August day, holding a brightly colored bouquet he'd bought off a guy on the corner.

"What are you doing?" she mouthed through the glass late Thursday afternoon when he knocked on the locked front door.

"I'm bringing you flowers," he yelled back. "Open up."

"Don't bring me flowers."

Shrugging, he flashed her a grin. "Too late."

"I mean it."

"Like I said, too late. Come on, let me in. They're thirsty."

She glared at him. Seeing pedestrians stopping to watch the show, she went a step further and bared her teeth.

Man the woman was *hot* when she was hot.

"Go away!"

Tsking, he shook his head. Then he looked at the closest woman who'd paused mid-step to see what was going on. "Can you believe she doesn't want my flowers?"

A teenager and her girlfriend, who'd also stopped nearby, piped in together, "We'll take them!"

The older woman, an iron-gray haired grandmother, frowned. "What did you do?"

Good question. He wasn't *entirely* sure. "I didn't recognize her after not having seen her for ten years."

The grandmother's eyebrow shot up. Pushing Nick out of the way, she marched up to the glass, stuck her index finger out and pointed at Izzie. "Take the flowers you foolish girl." Rolling her eyes and huffing about youth being wasted on the young, she stalked down the street.

Izzie, still practically growling, unlocked the door, yanked it open and grabbed his arm. "Get in here and stop making a fool of yourself."

"I wasn't making a fool of myself," he pointed out. "You were making a fool of me."

"You don't require much help."

Shaking his head and smiling, he murmured, "What happened to the sweet, friendly, eager-to-please Izzie?"

"She grew up."

She yanked the bouquet out of his hand, stalking behind the counter and grabbing a glass to put it in. Watching her, he noticed the surreptitious sniff she gave the blooms, and the way she squared her shoulders, as if annoyed at her own weakness.

Nick didn't follow her, tempted as he was. Instead, he leaned across the glass counter, dropping his elbows onto it. "The flowers are a peace offering."

"Are we at war?"

"It's felt that way to me ever since I was stupid enough to not recognize you that night at Santori's."

Ignoring him, she finished filling the glass with water, turned off the tap and plopped the flowers in.

"I still can't believe you're punishing me over that."

"Don't flatter yourself. I'm not punishing you over anything. I'm just not interested in you, Nick."

"Yeah, I got it." Only he didn't. He was in no way ready to concede that. Something had caused Izzie to put a wall up between them…and he was going to find out what it was. "But there's no reason we can't go back to being friends, is there? We were once."

"No. We weren't. You were the stud of the known universe and I was the puppy dog with the big, humiliating crush. You can't seriously think I'd go back to that."

"I tell ya, Izzie," he said, hearing the frustration in his voice, "I don't know for sure *what* I want from you. I just know I can't stand that you won't even look at me."

She finally did just that. Looked at him, met his direct stare. In those dark brown eyes he saw stormy confusion. It was matched by the quiver of her lush lips and the wild beating of the pulse in her throat.

"You liked me once," he said softly. "And we did pretty well helping each other out at the neighborhood-prying-session disguised as lunch last Sunday. Can we at least try being friends?"

She opened her mouth to reply. Closed it. Then, sighing as she pushed the vase of flowers to the center of the counter, slowly nodded. "I *guess.*"

It was a start. Maybe not the start he wanted to make with her…but at least the start of something.

"Do you want some coffee?" She didn't sound particularly enthusiastic about the invitation.

He glanced at the industrial coffeemaker, scrubbed clean

for the night, and shook his head, not wanting to put her to the trouble.

"I have a small coffeemaker in the back."

"Sounds good."

Nick followed her down a short hallway between the café and the kitchen, trying to remember that it wasn't very polite to stare long and hard at the ass of someone who was just a friend. It didn't work. Because though she wore loose-fitting khakis and an oversized apron, the woman had a figure to die for. Every step pulled the fabric a little tighter across her curves, and the natural sway in her hips made him dizzy.

Friends. That's it. And *not* friends with benefits.

"How do you like being back in Chicago?" he asked as he sat at a tall stool beside a butcher block work counter.

Izzie ground fresh beans. At last—a woman who knew how to make coffee. One more thing to like about her, aside from the cute way her ponytail wagged when she moved and the way she smelled of sugar and butter and everything nice. "About as much as I like getting a root canal."

"That bad? You don't like being back in the family business?"

She glanced around the kitchen, immaculately clean and stocked with every baking supply ever invented. "My prison smells like anisette."

"Mine smells like marinara," he muttered, meaning it.

She nodded, not asking him to elaborate. She obviously knew exactly what he meant. "Not easy to come home, is it?"

He shook his head. "Not easy at all. My parents still haven't forgiven me for moving into an apartment, not back into my old room. It still has my high-school posters on the walls."

She snickered. "Mine, too. Though I don't suppose yours were of ballerinas and Ricky Martin."

"Uh…definitely not." A grin tickling his lips, he admitted, "Demi Moore and *Lethal Weapon 3*."

Izzie laughed softly. There was a twinkle in those dark brown eyes of hers and a flash of a dimple he remembered in one cheek. At last.

"Are you…"

"What?" he asked.

"I'm sorry," she said, "it's none of my business."

"What's none of your business?"

"I guess I was just wondering if you felt…a little…out of place with your family."

"I feel like I belong with the Santoris about as much as that kid in the Jungle Book belonged with the dancing bear."

She nodded, as if in complete agreement. "But if I recall correctly, I think he *wanted* to belong with the dancing bear and couldn't understand why he didn't quite fit in."

Nick said nothing. She'd made his point for him.

Izzie seemed to realize it. "Yeah. Me too."

"Something else we have in common," he said.

"Don't get too excited about it," she muttered, "I'm still not giving you my phone number."

"You must know I already have it."

She rolled her eyes but didn't frown. "Gloria. Dead sister walking." The coffee had finished brewing, so she poured two big cups. "Cream or sugar?"

"Neither." Taking the cup from her, he inhaled the steam. "My mother makes lousy coffee. So does your sister, who seems to have decided even the *smell* of caffeine can make our hooligan nephews bounce off the walls."

"Decaf's for quitters," she muttered.

Startled, Nick barked a laugh. This was no sweet little Izzie, the girl he remembered.

"I lived on coffee in Manhattan," she admitted. "It was the only way I could maintain my schedule."

He sniffed appreciatively, allowing the rich aroma to fill

his head. When combined with all the other scents permeating this room, it was making him weak with physical hunger.

Or *she* was. He honestly wasn't sure which.

"I think I would have killed for something this good even when it was one-hundred-twenty degrees in the desert."

Izzie sat on one of the other stools across from him, her cup on the counter between them. Watching him intently, with a bit of trepidation, she forecast her curiosity before the words left her mouth. "How did you make it through every day?"

What a good question—and one nobody had asked him yet. Oh, he'd been asked about the action and the things he'd seen. Asked if he'd shot anyone, killed anyone, saved anyone. Asked what he'd done to relieve the boredom, to accomplish his mission.

But nobody had asked him what it was that had held him together every single day. Not until now.

"I'm sorry, that's probably none of my business."

"It's okay. If you want to know the truth, it was *this* that held me together." He gestured around the room.

She frowned skeptically.

"I don't mean the bakery. I mean this lifestyle. Home, family, all the safe, secure stuff I grew up with that I thought would be exactly the same when I got back. Only, it wasn't."

Staring at him, Izzie revealed her thoughts in her expressive brown eyes. She understood what he meant—got it, exactly. Nick didn't look away, liking the connection even though they were separated by several feet of sweet-smelling air. Mentally, though, they were touching. Bonding. Sharing the unique brand of estrangement they had each been feeling from the world they'd grown up in.

She finally shook her head. "Well, obviously you have some things to figure out, man-cub."

He grinned, remembering what he'd said about the Jungle Book. "Yeah, well, so do you, right? You didn't get what you bargained for when you came home, did you?"

She shook her head.

"What'd you do in New York, anyway?" he asked, never having gotten the whole story. He knew she'd had a good job but had given it up to come home and help her family.

"I was…in the arts," she murmured, lifting her cup to her mouth. She blew across the surface of the coffee, sending steam curling up into the air. It colored her cheeks, already flushed a delicate pink from the heat of the yeasty kitchen. "On the stage."

An actress. The idea stunned him for a second, though it made sense. Izzie had looks and personality and a lot of self-confidence. He suspected she was amazing on stage.

"But I got hurt last winter and haven't worked since."

He lowered his cup, waiting.

A tiny frown line appeared between her eyes as she explained. "I tore my ACL in my left knee and had to have surgery. It required a lot of rehab."

"And you're on your feet working in a kitchen all day?" he asked, appalled at the idea of how much pain she had to have experienced. He knew guys who'd had those injuries during his high-school sports days. They were not fun.

"I'm better." She pointed down to the stool on which she sat. "And I work sitting down a lot."

Nick wanted to know more. Lots of things. Like what kind of life she'd led in New York and whether anyone had shared it. And what her neck tasted like. And what she planned to do once her father was well enough to come back to the bakery. And what she'd eaten today that had left her lips so ruby red. And why she was resisting something happening between them.

And when she was going to be in his bed.

But the phone interrupted before he could ask, much less get any answers. Excusing herself to answer it, she revealed her frustration with the caller with every word exchanged. Nick heard enough to understand what was going on—her part-time delivery person was calling in sick.

"I can't believe this," she muttered after she hung up the phone. "All these orders and he bails on me." Almost growling, she added, "Are the Cubs playing today? It sounded like the little bastard was at the ball park."

Fierce. He liked it.

"Don't sweat it, Iz. I'll help you out."

Blinking, she replied, "Huh?"

"I'll help you make the deliveries." Hopping off the bench, he walked over to a tall cart, laden with cardboard boxes labeled with the names of several local restaurants. "After all," he said, offering her a boyish smile over his shoulder, "what are friends for?"

FRIENDS WERE FOR going to the movies with. Sharing bad date stories with. Getting through boring reunions with. Crying over breakups with. Dieting with. Drinking with. Clubbing with.

Friends were *not* for having sex with. Or lusting over. Or inspiring lust simply by the way they handled a few heavy boxes and filled out their soft, broken-in jeans.

Nick Santori was no friend of hers. Because oh, God, she had already broken every "friend" rule in the book and she'd only agreed to his terms a few hours ago.

When they'd talked in the kitchen, he'd been friendly and warm. That boyish smile he'd flashed her when he'd offered to help her with the deliveries had made him seem so charming and endearing. Completely the *opposite* of the brooding, simmering hunk of male heat she'd watched through covetous eyes at the club last weekend. It was like he was two people in one body.

And she wanted both of them desperately.

She couldn't believe she'd thought she could handle being merely his friend. Now, having been closed up in a delivery van with him for the past couple of hours, she was definitely having second thoughts.

He was being so damned *wonderful*. Not just offering to help her, he had refused to let her lift a single box. They'd gone to a dozen shops and restaurants, delivering cakes, pies and pastries to some places for their dinner customers tonight, and muffins and coffee cake to others for their breakfast crowds tomorrow. He'd charmed her customers, and *her*. He'd even driven, since Izzie hated dealing with the traffic. She'd sat in the passenger seat of the bakery van, reading off the list of stops, trying not to notice how big he was and how small the van felt with him in it.

She also tried not to notice how wonderful he smelled. How the sound of his low laughter rolled over her, more warm and sultry than a summer breeze. How his short hair curled a little behind his ear. How strong his lightly stubbled jaw was and how thick his body was beneath his tight T-shirt. How he warmed her from two feet away.

And how very, very much she wanted him.

Especially after the cannoli. It was the damn cannoli that put the nail in her coffin…and the wetness in her panties.

They had an extra box. Izzie had been so wiped out from working so many hours, both at the bakery Tuesday through Saturday, and at the club Saturday and Sunday nights, that she'd miscounted. She'd boxed up an extra two dozen of the decadent ricotta-and-cream filled treats. Once they'd finished all the deliveries, thanks mostly to Nick's strong back—oh, heavens, that strong back—she'd noticed the extra box and realized her mistake.

So, when they'd gotten back to the bakery and parked in the small private lot behind it, she'd offered him one. He'd immediately taken her up on it, not even getting out of the van before digging in. And seeing him eat it with such visceral, sensual appreciation, was making her a quivering, shaking mess.

"God, these are amazing. No wonder they sell out every day at Santori's," he said as he licked at the creamy center of the tube-shaped pastry.

Izzie shifted in the seat. Licking. It was not a good thing to watch a man do if you wanted to have sex with him but couldn't.

He nibbled some of the flaky crust.

Nibbling. Also bad. She added it to her mental list of no-nos to watch.

Then he bit in and closed his eyes in rapturous delight. Oh, Lord. Biting—anything that put that look of intense pleasure on his face—was absolutely out of the question.

Thankfully, he finished the thing so quickly—devouring it in three bites—that she didn't have time to do something foolish, like, say, offering him her tongue to lick and her breast to nibble and her inner thigh to bite.

"You are going to let me have another one, aren't you?" he asked. Not waiting for an answer, he got out of the driver's seat and bent over to step into the back of the van. Metal racks were attached to each side of it, with an aisle down the middle. Opening the lone box remaining on one shelf, he held it toward her. "Come on, have one."

She hadn't voluntarily eaten a cannoli since tenth grade, the day after she'd split her pants while trying to do a sit-up in gym class. They'd torn with a resounding flatulent sound and she'd almost dropped out of school then and there. "Uh-uh."

He smiled, his eyes glittering in the near darkness. Dusk had fallen while they were out making the rounds, and it was now after eight o'clock. The book shop next door was also closed, their private parking spots empty, and the small lot was entirely quiet and deserted. Very private.

She really should hop out of the vehicle and go inside. Being out here, in the near-dark, alone with Nick, was not a very good idea. Of course, being inside the closed shop, in the light, alone with Nick, probably wouldn't be much safer.

"One little taste. How can you tell how good you are at doing it if you never give it a try?"

Nearly choking, she repeated, "How good I am at *doing* it?"

"You know. Making them."

Yeah. Sure. That's what she'd thought he meant.

A small smile continued to play on those incredible lips of his as he watched her, as if he knew what she'd been thinking. And had intentionally put those thoughts into her head.

Get out. Now.

But she didn't reach for the door handle. Instead, like a kid lured by the ice cream man, she ducked into the back of the van with him. There wasn't room to stand, but Nick had already sat down on the carpeted floor. One leg was sprawled out in front of him, the other bent and upraised. He was carefully picking his way through the open box of pastries, as if searching for just the right one to satisfy his craving.

Izzie sat down across from him, cross-legged, wondering whether the temperature in the van had just gone up forty degrees or if it was her imagination. Considering it was a breezy summer evening and the front windows were open, she somehow doubted the air had gotten hotter…only *she* had. In fact, being this close to Nick was setting her on fire.

"You going to let me tempt you with one?" he asked, still looking down at the box, not at her.

They did look good. *So* good. "I really shouldn't."

"Just a taste," he whispered. Not waiting for her to answer, he lifted one out, then put the box back on the shelf. He scooted forward…close, so close she felt his heat wash over her and his warm, masculine scent fill her lungs. He lifted one of his legs over her crossed ones, until her right knee brushed his hot, jean-covered butt.

She didn't move. Not one inch.

"Won't you have one little lick?" he murmured, lifting the cannoli to her lips.

Staring at it in his hands—the flesh-colored cookie, the pale creamy cheese oozing from the end—she suddenly realized just how phallic the thing looked. Her mouth flooded with hunger—she wanted to lick, to taste, to devour.

Not the pastry. *Him.*

Almost whimpering, she lowered her mouth to it, scraping her tongue along the flaky crust, brushing his finger as she did. He shifted a little in response, as if no longer comfortable sitting the way he had been. The way they were sitting, she quickly realized why.

He was rock hard, his erection thick and long against her leg. She almost drew her legs together, the pressure in her sex demanding relief.

Izzie could hardly think or breathe. Unable to resist, she moved her leg a little, rubbing it against him, and got a low groan in response.

"Taste, Izzie."

She tasted. Imagining it was him she was sampling, she nibbled at the filling, brushing her lips against it.

She didn't need to invite Nick to share it. He was already there, kissing the corner of her mouth, his tongue flicking out to clean some of the sweetness off her lips. "Good," he whispered.

Oh, *very* good.

She licked again, dipping her tongue inside the cookie shell for a deeper taste. Nick tasted deeper, too. He covered her lips with his, stealing some of the cream right out of her mouth, their tongues tangling over it for a long, delicious moment.

"Get your own," she whispered with a soft laugh when he pulled away to offer her another lick.

"I'd rather have yours," he murmured, moving his mouth to her cheek, then lower. He nibbled her jaw, scraping his lips along it until he could nuzzle the sensitive spot just below her ear. "Actually, I'd rather have *you*."

His words washed over her, echoing in her head. With his warm breaths on her neck, his mouth on her skin, his hard body radiating heat just inches from her own, she couldn't remember a single reason why she shouldn't have him.

"I noticed." She shifted back far enough to uncross her legs. Without thinking or considering, she draped them over his thighs, scooting close—so close—that that thick ridge in his jeans pressed against the damp seam of hers.

He arched forward reflexively, grinding against her, and Izzie gasped. Moisture flooded her and her sex swelled almost painfully against her clothes. Her clit felt as if it had doubled in size and she bucked into him, needing to come so badly she could almost taste it.

"More?" he asked.

She arched harder. She definitely wanted more.

He lifted the cannoli. She shook her head, then let it fall back. She wanted to *be* the dessert now. Right or wrong, stupid or not, she wanted Nick Santori too much to resist him again.

When they stepped out of the van, the real world would return. He'd still be the great neighborhood guy she couldn't publicly date. But for now—oh, for now—she wanted him desperately, with a longing that had built in her for more than a decade. "Have me, Nick," she whispered, saying yes to the question he hadn't quite asked.

He made a low sound that might have been unrestrained—want or might have been triumph. Honestly, Izzie didn't care. Especially when he nibbled her earlobe, then worked his way down her neck. "Mmm, you taste like sugar and almonds." He kissed his way down to her collarbone, lightly biting her nape, and she shivered.

Never taking his mouth off her, he reached up and pulled her ponytail holder off. Her thick hair fell around his hand and he twined it through his fingers. Cupping her head and supporting her, he pushed her back a little so he could have better access to her neck.

When she felt the cool wetness touch the hollow of her throat, she gasped. The ricotta filling felt good against her heated skin. When Nick licked it off, it felt amazing.

Dropping back to support herself on her elbows, she watched through heavy-lidded eyes as Nick began slipping open the buttons of her sleeveless blouse. After every button was freed and another bit of skin revealed, he dabbed filling on her. Soon there was a trail of dots from her throat, down her chest, in the middle of her cleavage, and all the way down to her belly.

He wasn't tasting them. Not yet. She twisted and arched up, desperate for him to, but he ignored her silent plea.

Once he tugged the top free of her jeans, it gaped open. Shrugging, she let it fall off her shoulders, then watched him devour her with his eyes. His breaths grew audibly choppy as he saw the way her breasts overflowed her skimpy bra. Bent back as she was, she could barely keep the thing in place, and one nipple was actually peeping freely above the lace.

"Beautiful," he muttered hoarsely. He lifted the pastry and dabbed some of the filling on her nipple.

This time he didn't move on. He stopped for a taste.

"Oh, God," she groaned as Nick bent over and covered her nipple with his mouth, licking and sucking at the cheesy filling. He lapped up every bit, pushing her bra all the way down so he'd have complete access to her breast.

"You are glorious," he said as he lifted a hand to cup her. His fingers were dark and strong against her pale skin, and she literally overflowed his hand. "You hide a lot behind that apron you usually wear."

She hid a lot more behind the mask she sometimes wore. The thought flashed through her head, but she thrust it aside. This was not the time to be thinking about her alter-ego…or what Nick might do if he ever found out they were one and the same.

Now was for savoring. Indulging.

Reaching for the clasp of her bra, he unfastened it and pulled it off, catching her other breast as it spilled free. Scooping out a large fingerful of filling, complete with tiny chocolate chips, he smeared it all over the taut tip, then devoured it as completely as he had the other side.

Her legs clenched, heat shooting from her wet nipples down her body, straight between her legs. She jerked up, dying to be freed of her jeans. "I need…"

"I know," he whispered. He dropped his mouth to hers for a deep kiss that shut her up and zapped her brain. He tasted sweet and hot and decadent.

Izzie worked at Nick's shirt as they kissed, pulling away so she could tug it up and off him. Then she sagged back, staring in disbelief at the perfection that was his body.

In his clothes, he was an incredibly well-built man.

Out of them he almost defied description.

He was rock hard, not an ounce of excess on him, with a massive chest and thickly muscled shoulders. His huge arms rippled as he moved, highlighting a sizeable tattoo—a Marine Corps logo. Just the perfect amount of dark, curly hair emphasized the breadth of him before narrowing down to his waist and hips, where he was incredibly lean.

"I'm not finished my dessert yet," he muttered when she reached for his waistband.

He tossed the tiny bit of cannoli away and grabbed another one out of the box. Taking her hand, he pushed her arm over her head until she had to lie flat on the floor. Then he worked his way down her body, kissing, nibbling and licking off all those spots of cream he'd deposited on her earlier.

"It tastes sweeter now," he said when he dipped his tongue into her belly button and swirled it there. "It just needed one more ingredient to make it absolutely addictive."

Her. It needed her.

And she needed *him*.

His hands. His mouth—oh, heavens, his mouth. His amazing body. And that big, hard erection she could feel pressing against her leg as he slid farther down her body.

He didn't even move his mouth off her as he undid her pants and pushed them down her hips. Izzie lifted up to help him…and unintentionally offered herself to him *much* more intimately.

He was *on* her immediately.

"Nick!" She gasped and panted when he covered the front of her tiny panties with his mouth, breathing through the fabric, sending warm tendrils of pleasure right where she needed them most. "Please."

"I bet this will taste even sweeter," he whispered as he tugged the satin away.

Izzie barely breathed as he pushed her clothes down and off, until she lay naked beneath him. And she absolutely flew out of her skin when he took the new tube-shaped pastry and smeared one creamy end of it through her curls and across her sex.

"Oh," she groaned.

He pushed at her inner thighs and Izzie parted her legs, giving him the access he'd silently demanded. When he took a first, slow lick at the filling, thick and heavy in her curls, she came up off the floor.

"Oh, definitely sweeter," he said. He moved farther down, sliding his tongue over every inch of her, eating every drop of sticky cream as if it was the best thing he'd ever tasted.

Izzie was a quivering mess, shaking, panting, bucking. Desperate for more, she didn't know whether to beg or remain still for fear he'd get distracted from what he was doing.

He didn't get distracted. And before she knew what he was up to, she felt the flaky shell of the cookie scraping across her clit. She cried out again, feeling the climax build inside her. When he licked at her again, working her clit with his tongue and his lips—lathing, then sucking—she finally got what she'd been waiting for. Pleasure erupted through her, rocking her hips, sending a pulse of heat through her.

Nick didn't even pause, beyond muttering a soft "Yes," in acknowledgement of her orgasm. He just kept going, sliding the cannoli further...following it with his tongue. Until finally he began working the delicacy between her drenched lips.

"You're not...you can't..." she gasped.

But he did and he was. He slid the tip of it into her wet crevice—sending a cacophony of sensations rushing through her. The roughness of the delicate shell, the smoothness of the filling, she'd never felt anything like it. It was wicked—erotic. A little outrageous.

And she loved it. "Nick..."

"I'm not quite finished with dessert. Though I'm just about full," he murmured.

She only wished she were.

She didn't get too impatient, however, because she was too anxious to see what this supposedly "nice neighborhood guy" would dare next.

He wanted to keep playing, obviously. He slowly sunk the treat deeper, as far as he could, then gently tugged it out. He did it again, leaving Izzie to wonder how long it would take before the shell broke and the oozy cream filled her.

Finally, when she thought she'd die of the wild wantonness of it, he started working it out with his teeth, rather than his fingers. He nibbled off little pieces as it came out of her, whispering sweet words about how good it tasted…how good *she* tasted. How juicy and creamy she was.

His words were almost as arousing as his touch.

"Gotta make sure I got every drop," he whispered once the last of the cookie was gone. And he did, plunging his tongue into her and stroking—in and out—until she lost her mind and came again.

She threw her head back, closing her eyes, giving herself over to the rocking of her body, which seemed to go on forever. When it had finally eased up, and she opened her eyes again, it was to find Nick over her.

She lifted her legs, realizing his were bare. His lean hips brushed her inner thighs, and his thick cock lay heavy on her pelvis.

Whimpering, she looked down. "Let me see you."

"Feel me," he whispered, burying his face in her neck. He slid up and down, his cock separating the slick lips of her sex, hitting her clit at the perfect angle.

"See *and* feel," she insisted, sliding her arm between their bodies to reach for him.

She caught his erection in her hand, shocked at how big and hot it was. He'd already sheathed himself with a condom, but she could feel his pounding pulse through the rubber.

"You're bigger than that cookie," she said, nibbling on her lip as she acknowledged just how much Nick Santori had been hiding beneath his clothes.

He groaned and dipped closer, sliding in her a little at a time. "You're sweeter than that cookie." He pushed a bit more, easing into her with incredible restraint. "And you are definitely creamy enough to handle me."

She didn't doubt it. He'd aroused her half out of her mind and right now, she wanted him plunging to the hilt inside her. Grabbing his hips, she dug her nails into his butt and arched up for him. "Take me, Nick. Fill me up."

He seemed to forget about restraint because he did exactly what she asked, plunging hard and deep until Izzie howled at how good it felt.

He stretched her, embedded himself in her, then drew out and plunged again. "Oh, my God," she groaned. "This is amazing."

Better than amazing. It was absolute perfection. Worth every one of the years she'd waited for it.

Thrusting up, Izzie took what he gave and demanded even more. When she became too frenzied, he slowed the pace, showing so much control she wanted to sob in frustration. But he wouldn't relent, taunting her with slow, deep strokes and teasing half-ones. He kissed her so often and so deeply she wasn't sure she'd remember how to breathe when she wasn't sharing the breath from his lungs.

Finally, though, she heard the tiny groans he couldn't contain. His hips thrust harder, more frantically, and she wrung as much as she could out of every stroke.

"I can't…oh, Izzie…"

"Do it," she ordered, feeling another climax building in her from the friction of their locked bodies. "I'll come with you."

That seemed to satisfy him—that he had her permission—and he finally lost his head and gave her the deep, pounding thrusts they both needed. Again. And again. Until he threw his head back and shouted as he reached his climax.

She found hers a second later and wrapped her legs tightly around him to ride it out.

As if knowing the floor was hard against her back, Nick scooped her in his arms and lay down, dragging her on top of him. They were both panting, gasping for air, and he kissed her temple, smoothing her hair away from her sweaty face.

"Izzie? I have to tell you something." His words were rushed. Choppy.

"Yes?"

Closing his eyes, he dropped his head back onto the floor. "I'm going to call you Cookie until the day I die."

6

FUNNY. Nick had once thought that having absolutely mind-blowing sex with a woman would make her friendlier. At least more approachable.

No. Uh-uh. Not Izzie Natale. Because within *minutes* of their incredible lovemaking in the back of the delivery van, she was back to freezing him out, trying to act like nothing had changed between them.

After sex like that, he'd kind of expected to be invited in for a cup of coffee…if not dessert. Oh, man, he was *never* going to look at a cannoli the same way again.

But she hadn't invited him in. Hadn't answered him when he'd asked if she wanted to go get a bite to eat somewhere. And over the next couple of days, hadn't returned his calls. Hadn't even met his eye in the past couple of days.

The woman was killing him, she really was.

When he'd finally confronted her on the sidewalk in front of the bakery Friday afternoon, she'd erupted. "It was a one time thing, Nick. It was fabulous, I loved it, but it's not going to happen again. Because if it does, then you're going to be *more* of a pain about wanting me to go get a pizza with you, or go visit the folks, and then the whole neighborhood will be congratulating poor little Izzie for finally landing her man."

She'd stalked inside without saying another word. He hadn't needed to. He got the message, loud and clear. She'd loved the sex, she just didn't want all the stuff that went with having a sexual relationship. Or any relationship whatsoever.

He thought about proposing that they just set up a weekly sex-buddy meeting in the parked van behind her shop, suspecting he could have her on those terms if he wanted her.

He didn't want her on those terms.

"Hell, admit it, you want her on any terms," he muttered aloud as he walked out the back door of Santori's that night. He hadn't even realized anyone else was there until he saw his brother, Joe, who'd just parked his pickup in one of the empty spots in the alley. Fortunately, Joe hadn't heard Nick talking to himself and so wasn't dialing for the rubber-walled wagon.

"Hey, where you off to?" Joe asked as he hopped out and pocketed his keys. "I was going to take you up on that pitcher you owe me."

"I'm not very good company right now," he admitted.

Joe, who was the best-natured of all of the Santori kids, threw his arm around Nick's shoulders. "Then what better time to share a beer with your brother?"

He had a point.

"Okay. But not here," he said, looking back at the closed door to the kitchen. "I really need someplace quiet."

Joe's smile faded and he immediately appeared concerned. "Everything okay? Is there a problem?"

"No problem. Just a case of family overdose."

"I hear ya. Come on, let's go across the street."

Following Joe into a neighborhood bar on the corner, Nick ordered a couple of beers and paid the tab. If Mark had been sitting across from him, Nick knew he'd be getting one-liners aimed at making him say what was on his mind. Lucas would be doing his prosecutor inquisition. Tony would throw his oldest-brother weight around and try to browbeat him into talking. Lottie would jabber so much Nick would say anything to get her to shut up.

Joe just watched. Listened. Waited.

"Thanks again for pointing me toward the job," Nick finally said, filling the silence. The bar was pretty empty—it was too early for the weekend regulars, who'd be drifting in for a long night of drinking and darts before too long.

"How's that going?"

"Pretty well. I've only worked the past two weekends but the money's good."

"You still haven't told the rest of the family?"

Nick shook his head. "Just Mark."

Joe nodded. "Probably just as well. I know Pop and Tony are talking nonstop about you coming in on the business."

Yeah, they had been to him, too. Nick couldn't prevent a quick frown. Because managing a pizzeria was not the way he saw himself spending the next six months, much less the rest of his life.

"It's okay, Nick. Nobody can force you to do anything you don't want to do."

"Guilt goes a long way," he muttered.

"Don't I know it. But guilt didn't stop you from enlisting. It didn't stop me from picking up a hammer and learning construction. Didn't stop Mark from strapping on a gun or Lottie from…well, from doing whatever it is Lottie does."

"Like marrying a man who killed someone?" Nick asked dryly, still not having gotten used to the idea that his new brother-in-law, Simon, had killed a woman, even if in self-defense.

"Let's not go there," Joe said with a sigh. "She's happy, and he's crazy about her."

True. Lottie and Simon's recent marriage had contributed to the 95 percent marital success rate in the Santori family.

"The point is, you can live your life the way you want to live it, and nobody will try to stop you." As if realizing he'd left Nick with one major argument, he added, "Except for Mama's crying. Which we're all used to and you can get past. You just need to figure out what you want to do, and go after it."

Good idea. And lately, Nick *had* been figuring out what he wanted to do, especially since he'd been working at the club. "An old buddy of mine from the service is putting something together with a couple of the other guys. They're talking about opening up a protection business."

"Professional bodyguard?" Joe asked, looking surprised.

"I have the military background for it and I like what I'm doing at the club."

Joe smiled. "Especially when the people you're guarding are very easy on the eyes."

"Like you'd *ever* look at another woman."

The twinkle in his brother's eyes confirmed that. "Hey, I'm not *you*. You're the single one. Have you met anybody, uh… interesting?"

Nick felt heat rise up his neck. Because that was a loaded question. He had definitely felt interest in the Crimson Rose. But now that he'd had Izzie—tasted her, consumed her, made love to her—he knew he didn't want any other woman. But he couldn't very well explain that to Joe…without hinting about what had happened with Izzie. She'd never forgive him if that little tidbit became common knowledge. "I guess."

"Their star performer?" Joe sipped his beer. "I hear she's one-of-a-kind."

Clearing his throat, Nick sprawled back in the booth. "She is that."

"Have there been any more problems with her?" Joe sounded only casually interested, but Nick's guard immediately went up.

"Problems?"

"Threats, freaks trying to grab her?"

Nick sat up straight. "No. What are you talking about?"

"Didn't Harry even tell you why he hired you?"

He had, but only in the most general terms. Nick didn't realize Rose had actually been threatened. "What do you know?"

"Just what the guys were whispering about when we were working at the club. That there had been a few incidents that had disturbed Harry and scared the dancers. Especially the featured one."

Harry Black had said almost nothing about any specific threats. Rose had said even less. Why would they hire him and then tie his hands by not giving him all the information he needed to do his job? He just didn't understand it. "Maybe whoever was causing the problems got caught and the threat has been eliminated," he murmured, speculating out loud. "Because I haven't gotten any kind of specific heads up."

Joe kept his eyes on his beer, for some reason not looking Nick in the eye. Which made him wonder about his brother's interest in the stripper.

He immediately discounted any suspicion that Joe was interested in the woman for himself. He was married to the sexiest kindergarten teacher ever born, and he adored her and their baby daughter. Besides, of all the Santoris—who'd been raised to equate cheating with a mortal sin—Joe was the very last one who'd ever stray.

"Well, if I were you, I'd stick close to the featured attraction at Leather and Lace. I think she might be more of a target than she or Harry would like to admit." Shaking his head, Joe added, "There are some really sick guys out there who like stalking vulnerable women."

Suddenly feeling on edge, Nick nodded, anxious to get to the club and question Harry Black. He didn't particularly want to confront Rose—not alone, anyway—but one thing was sure. He had been hired to do a job: protect her. It was about time he stop letting his physical response to the woman interfere with doing that job.

And it was well past time for him to stop letting his feelings for Izzie Natale consume so much of his attention that he didn't even *realize* a stalker might be threatening someone he'd been hired to protect.

That had to end. Starting right now.

So it looked like Izzie was finally going to get what she wanted. Him…out of her life.

"HEY, SOMEBODY SENT you flowers."

Izzie hesitated, her hand on the doorknob of her dressing room. One of the other dancers, a young blonde with a sweet smile and a killer body, approached her. "They were waiting on the stoop at the back entrance when I got here. Had your name on the envelope. I put them in your dressing room."

Izzie's first reaction was a tiny little thrill as the image of Nick's handsome face filled her mind. But it quickly dissipated. Nick had no idea she worked with him every Saturday and Sunday night.

Damn good thing. Because if he found out now, after she'd had such incredible sex with him, he was going be mad. More than mad—irate. Especially because of how insistent she'd been that it was a one-shot deal.

Boy did she wish it didn't have to be a one-shot deal. She still got shaky and shivery and weak and wet thinking of that amazing interlude in the van. It had been the most intensely sensual experience of her life.

But not to be repeated. Never.

Not as Izzie. Not even as the Crimson Rose. Because now that he'd had her naked in his arms, it was all too possible that he'd recognize her as Rose. Dancing and interacting with him at work was going to be difficult enough. If she let him get close—the way she'd invited him to that night in her dressing room—there was no way she'd be able to keep her secret.

So tell him the truth.

The idea had merit and Izzie knew it. Part of her truly wanted to—it wasn't easy maintaining a double life with no one to talk to about it. He'd listen—she knew he would. And she even suspected he wouldn't judge her about what she was doing. Given the things he'd said about feeling so hemmed in by his own family and their expectations, she thought he might even understand. A little.

But telling him—bringing him in to her alternate life—would mean involving him deeper in her real one. Each secret shared would be another rope tied to her body, holding her down, dragging her back into the world she'd fought so hard to escape.

If he knew she was Rose, there would be no reason they couldn't get more involved, at least at work. That, however—a secret, sordid affair conducted in dressing rooms and closets at Leather and Lace—wouldn't be enough for him. She knew it down to her very soul. He'd insinuate himself in her daily life, start tangling her in the ropes of a relationship, make her fall for him even harder…so he would be even harder to leave.

No. She could not tell him.

"Rose? Didja hear me?"

Realizing the other dancer was waiting expectantly for her reaction to the flowers, Izzie nodded. "Yes, thanks Leah."

"Not a problem. It was pick 'em up or trip over 'em," she said with a cheery smile. Without the stage makeup and the sequins, the young woman looked so fresh-faced and wholesome an average set of parents would have asked her to babysit.

She'd been the first of the dancers to befriend Izzie when she'd first taken the job at Leather and Lace. The others had been slower to warm up, especially Harry's wife, Delilah, who'd been the featured dancer up until a couple of years ago when she married her boss. Now she served as a sort of warden to the others…and hadn't liked that Izzie wasn't inter-ested in her rules and regulations. She *especially* hadn't liked that she couldn't get her husband to order Izzie to listen to her…and that the Crimson Rose had become hugely popular.

The rest of them had all come around, though, especially since they had all started bringing home more money every weekend that she performed.

"How did you get into this, Leah?" she asked.

The girl shrugged. "Typical story. My parents divorced, father split out west somewhere. Mom remarried an asshole who tried to touch me after she'd passed out on their wedding night."

Izzie instinctively reached out and put her hand on the other woman's shoulder. "I'm sorry."

"Hey, I survived. Stabbed him in the wrist with a fork and took off. Never looked back."

"Do you…" she didn't know how to proceed without seeming judgmental. It just seemed so sad to think of this young woman making this, dancing at Leather and Lace, her only career goal. For Izzie, it was a part-time thrill to stay in shape and save her sanity. Some of the women here, however, saw no other future for themselves.

"What?"

"Do you think you'll do something else when you get tired of this?"

Leah nodded, her blond curls bouncing around her pretty, heart-shaped face. "I got my GED last year and I'm taking college classes. I'm planning to be a nurse."

"Good for you."

Hearing footsteps upstairs, Izzie glanced at her watch. It was only six—a couple of hours before her first number. Usually Nick showed up later than this. But hearing the deep, male voice from upstairs, she immediately stiffened.

"That's our sex-on-a-stick bodyguard I hear up there."

"Damn," Izzie muttered, immediately whirling around. "Stall him if he comes down the stairs, okay?"

"You still playing the 'nobody can see me' game with him?"

Izzie nodded. "I *don't* want him to see me. Please help me."

The woman offered her a big smile. "You got it...in exchange for one of those flowers your secret admirer sent you."

"I'll do you one better," Izzie said as she pushed open her dressing room door. She grabbed the vase and thrust the bouquet at the young woman. "You can have all of them. Just don't let him near my door."

Either Leah was true to her word, or else Nick hadn't yet ventured downstairs. Whatever the case Izzie had privacy for the next twenty minutes. Long enough to get her hair extensions clipped in place and put her mask on. Only after she'd yanked it into position did she realize she'd forgotten her false eyelashes.

"Damn Harry for not giving me a lock," she muttered, glancing at the closed door. If she took the mask off to put her lashes on, she risked Nick walking in on her. No, he hadn't exactly gone out of his way to be alone with her as the Crimson Rose, but she couldn't count on her luck lasting forever.

Frowning at her reflection, she did a quick evaluation, wondering if she really needed the lashes. Her eyes had disappeared. She looked like the Marquis de Sade.

"Need the lashes," she muttered.

She'd been putting false lashes on her eyelids for years, she could probably do it...well, not blindfolded, but *masked*.

"Sure," she whispered as she bent toward the mirror. Grabbing one lash, she dabbed special glue on it, then carefully reached into the eyehole of her mask and applied it.

"One down," she said as she blinked rapidly, pretty proud of herself.

The second one was a little trickier, mainly because it was hard to see out of the first heavily lashed eye. But she managed it. And a moment later, when she heard voices in the hall, she was very glad she hadn't taken the chance and removed the mask.

"Hey, Nick, how's it shakin' baby?" a woman's voice said. Loudly.

Bless you, Leah.

"I need to talk to Rose." He cleared his throat. "I mean, I need to talk to all of you, *and* Rose."

Huh. Still too chicken to see her alone.

She quickly squelched the thought. That man had the most incredible, powerful body she'd ever seen in her life. He was afraid of nothing.

Besides, refusing to see her alone was exactly what she needed him to do. Even if it wasn't what she *wanted* him to do.

Tightening the sash on her robe, she reached for the doorknob and opened the door. Nick's immediately looked over, stiffening when he saw her there.

He *so* didn't want to be attracted to her, his expression said it all. Knowing he didn't want anyone else made Izzie, the baker he'd made such incredible love to a few days ago, amazingly happy.

"I need to talk to you, and all the other girls, in the greenroom for a few minutes," he said. Without waiting to see if she was coming, he spun around and walked toward it.

Shrugging, Leah followed. So did Izzie. Once they were

inside, Izzie realized all the other dancers—nine or ten of them—were already present, including Delilah with her two-foot-tall pile of red hair on top of her head and three inches of makeup on her face.

In varying states of undress, all the other dancers practically licked their lips when Nick walked into the room. She couldn't blame them. In his tough/bodyguard mode, he looked incredibly hot. Gone was any trace of the sweetheart who'd helped her deliver baked goods. Or the sensual lover who'd given her more orgasms in one lovemaking session than she'd had in entire previous relationships.

In their place was a frowning—scowling almost—man, dressed all in black, looking not only menacing but dangerous. And absolutely delicious.

"I asked you all in here to discuss your security."

"Let's discuss your ass," one of the dancers cracked.

"I'd rather talk about his shoulders."

"I vote for his co…"

"Ladies," another voice said as Harry entered the room. Rolling his eyes, he gave Nick an apologetic look. "Please go ahead, Nick."

Nick got right back on track, hitting them all over the head with the need for tighter security around the place. Though he was talking to everyone, he looked at Izzie so often, she knew she was the one on his mind.

There wasn't any reason to single her out. Well, not *much* reason. Yes, she'd had a few persistent customers. One guy had lunged at her on the stage a few weeks back. Another had burst into her dressing room. And there'd been a few parking-lot lurkers who'd been chased away by one of the bouncers, Bernie, who'd been watching out for her since her first night. Long before Nick had come on the scene.

In this job, she'd expect nothing else. But Nick was relentless in his lecturing. He kept on about how they all needed to look out for one another, report anything suspicious. Yadda yadda. Izzie zoned out somewhere between "drive a different route home from work every night" and "have a buddy when you go to the restroom."

That one did spark an "I'll be your bathroom buddy, Nick," from one of the girls, a glare from Delilah and another long-suffering sigh from Harry.

Finally, though, the meeting broke up and the other dancers raced to finish getting ready. Izzie quickly ducked out of the room, hoping Nick wouldn't see her. She'd gotten about ten steps from her dressing room when she realized he'd followed.

"Rose, wait a minute."

She froze, but didn't turn around.

"I'm particularly concerned about you. The 'who's behind the mask' element puts you at higher risk. Some whackjob might decide to try to find out for himself."

She glanced over her shoulder. "Thanks for the warning." *Now go away.*

Before she could look away again, she saw a dark frown pull at Nick's handsome face. "What in the hell?" he muttered, staring at her face.

Fearing he'd recognized her, she quickly lifted her hands to ensure her mask was still in place. It felt okay—but Nick was still staring at her, blinking in confusion.

"What?" she snapped. Remembering at the last minute that she needed to lower her voice to the sultry whisper he'd grown familiar with, she rephrased. "Is something wrong?"

He reached for her. Izzie immediately lurched back, almost tripping over her own feet. If she hadn't backed herself up against the wall, she would have.

"Careful," he muttered, still frowning. "It wouldn't look

good on my résumé if somebody I'm supposed to be guarding trips and breaks her neck."

Right. He needed to guard her.

Not look at her. Not watch her. Not batter at her defenses with every flex of that body, every whiff of his spicy scent that filled her head whenever he was near.

God, this was hard. So much harder than it had been last weekend, when she hadn't *had* him. When she didn't know what he was capable of.

"You have something on your…it's…."

Shrugging uncomfortably, he reached for her again. This time, she stayed still. At least until he yanked at her eyelashes hard enough to jerk her eyelid off her face. "Ouch!" she yelped, slapping his hand away.

His hand was still stuck to the lashes so when she smacked him, she only ended up hurting herself more. As his hand flew away, he took the lashes with him, ripping them off her lid.

"I thought it was a bug," he said with an uncomfortable grimace.

She yanked her false eyelashes out of his fingers. "A *bug?* You thought I had a bug on my face?"

"It's not like you'd be able to tell if you did with that stupid mask on. Why do you wear it when you're not on stage, anyway?"

Oh, boy. A question she definitely couldn't answer.

"You don't have to keep up this mysterious woman act for the staff, do you? So why not take it off and take a deep breath?" Swiping a frustrated hand through his short, spiky hair, he added, "Or at least put your damn false eyelashes on more securely?"

She almost growled in annoyance. *He* was the reason she'd had to put the lashes on through the eyehole in the mask. "I want a lock on my dressing room door," she whispered harshly.

He glanced at the knob. "You don't have one?"

"No." Thinking quickly, she added, "And that's one reason I keep the mask on all the time. I have no place to go for complete privacy. A reporter who did an article on the club a few weeks ago came creeping around down here one day, trying to get a picture of the real me."

Nick moved in close, towering over her, burning her with his heat. Putting his hands on the wall on either side of her, he trapped her in. "Who is he?"

Izzie nibbled her lip, trying with every ounce of her strength not to throw her arms around his shoulders and her legs around his waist. Or to shove him away so he'd stop looking searchingly at her, seeing her eyes…how could he not recognize her eyes? How could he be this close and not know the smell of her body?

It was good that he didn't, she knew that. But it was also starting to tick her off.

"Just some reporter," she murmured.

"Have you had any problems with him since?"

"No, he hasn't been around since the story came out. Would you relax?"

"You tell me if you see him." Then, staring hard at her, he slowly pulled back, releasing her from the prison of his arms. An odd look appeared on his face, as if he'd suddenly realized just how close they'd been and wasn't happy at himself for it. Clearing his throat, he added, "I'm sorry I hurt your eye."

"It's all right." Slipping away from him, she headed again to her door, relieved to have escaped his scrutiny. Good thing he'd let her go, because the longer he stayed so close to her, the more angry she was going to get that he didn't know her.

Especially because a mask would never prevent *her* from knowing *him*.

Huh. Men. So painfully unobservant.

"I hope you're taking me seriously," he said, that gruff, no-nonsense tone returning to his voice, his apology obviously done.

"I am, I am." She practically bit the words out from between her clenched teeth, ready to smack him if he didn't shut up and let her go get herself back under control. And fix her eyelashes.

"No more running out to your car alone to get something you forgot."

"Yes, your majesty."

"No more coming back upstairs and mingling close to closing time."

She seldom did that, anyway. Whirling around, she offered him a sharp salute, and snapped, "Got it, chief." Then, determined not to listen to another word, spun on her heel and strode into her dressing room, slamming the door shut behind her.

It was only after she'd shut him out that Izzie realized how *stupid* she'd just been. Nick had annoyed her so much—both because of his overbearing protective bodyguard schtick and his inability to see what was right in front of his face—that she'd completely forgotten her role in this. The role she played as the Crimson Rose.

Because during those last three words, when anger had overtaken common sense, she'd forgotten to speak in her sexy, husky voice.

She'd been pure, 100 percent Izzie.

7

Leather and Lace employed a few burly bouncers to watch the doors and to stand in the back of the crowd during the show. Their presence was mainly to inspire intimidation to keep the audience on its best behavior. And they did their job well, especially the tallest one, Bernie, whose beefy build concealed a guy with a deep belly laugh and a good sense of humor.

Nick, however, wasn't technically one of them. His job involved more than rousting out rowdy drinkers or breaking up any fights. He was there to make sure nobody touched the dancers. Especially Rose. And the bouncers were his backup.

He typically moved around during the performances—sometimes in the audience, sometimes backstage, sometimes downstairs. He kept a low profile, his eyes always scanning the crowd, looking for the first sign of trouble.

Tonight, he was standing close to the dance floor, in a shadowy corner just left of the stage. He couldn't say why. It wasn't as if he expected anyone in the front row to leap up and try to grab Rose or one of the others. Yes, it'd happened. But usually not until at least the second set, late in the night, when the patrons had consumed more than a few fifteen dollar shots of top-shelf whiskey. And when they'd forgotten how big the bouncers were or how stupid they were going to feel having to call their wives to get bailed out of jail.

Tonight, Nick was close to the stage because he wanted to watch *her*.

Something had happened earlier, something that was still driving him crazy. Oh, she drove him crazy in any number of ways, already—mainly because of that blatant sexuality oozing off the woman. But this didn't have anything to do with her attractiveness, or Nick's reaction to it.

It was something else. Something he couldn't define. Ever since he and Rose had exchanged words outside her dressing room, a voice had been whispering in his head that there was something he wasn't seeing. Some truth he had overlooked.

He had replayed their entire conversation, thinking about every word, wondering what had seemed so *off* with it. Aside from her being such a smart-ass about the self-protection tips he'd asked her to follow, they hadn't been confrontational. Hadn't been unpleasant in any way, other than when he'd accidentally almost ripped her eyelid off.

So why are you so tense?

Good question. He was wound as tight as a ball of rubber bands, his jaw flexing, his hands clenching. His heart wasn't maintaining its usual pace, it was rushed, as if adrenaline had flooded his body.

When they introduced her, something *did* flood his body. Heated awareness. Maybe adrenaline, too.

She didn't spot him when she started, and from here Nick had a perfect view of every move she made. She was using the pole tonight, taking advantage of it to showcase her strength and flexibility. Not to mention inviting every man in the audience to imagine being the one she was writhing against, the one cupped between her incredibly long legs.

He tensed, then thrust away the flash of jealousy. It was none of his business what Rose did—in her professional life or in her personal one.

She'd begun removing her petals now, they fluttered onto the stage, one even wafting so close it was only about a foot away from Nick's corner position. Something made him step closer, to reach for it. Whether to give it back to her, or to save it as a souvenir, he couldn't say. Fingering it lightly, he stuck it in his pocket and kept watching.

When this close, he had a very good view of the Crimson Rose…a view of a trim waist made for his hands. Of supple legs he could almost feel wrapped around his hips. Of slender fingers that had tangled easily in his hair. A delicate throat for nibbling. Lush round breasts for cupping. And when she removed the petals covering those breasts, his mouth flooded at the image of sucking on those dark, pebbled nipples.

Every bit of her was familiar…to his eyes, and to the rest of his body. He knew what it would be like to taste her, to touch her, to hear her soft little moans of pleasure.

To hear her….

Her voice. That *voice*. That body.

"Oh, my God," he whispered, certain he'd lost his mind but unable to chase the thought away. Because as he watched the performer disappear behind the curtain after her dance, he saw a face behind that mask. A face he saw in his dreams every night.

Izzie's face.

"It can't be," he mumbled, staggering back into the shadow. He hit the wall in the corner and slid down it, bending over so his hands landed on his knees. Sucking in a few deep breaths, he kept his head down, thinking over everything he knew about Izzie Natale. And about the Crimson Rose.

She'd taken dance lessons throughout her childhood, he remembered that. She'd gone to New York to become a performer. On the stage. She hadn't exactly said she'd been an actress.

My God, had she been a stripper at some high end Manhattan club? And when she'd been forced to return to Chicago after her father's stroke, had she taken up the same profession here—wearing a mask so she wouldn't possibly be recognized?

Their bodies were so alike—how could he not have seen it before? Then again, he had never seen Izzie naked before, until two nights ago, so he couldn't possibly have known that her legs were as long and supple as a dancer's. That her hips were full enough to make a man hard just at the thought of getting his hands on them. That her breasts were big, high and inviting.

She'd hidden a lot behind the apron. So much that he hadn't registered that Izzie and Rose were the same height, had the same builds. Or that their hair was close in color—the length of Rose's obviously caused by some kind of hairpiece or wig.

Now it registered. But it still seemed impossible. Absolutely unbelievable that cute little Izzie, Gloria's baby sister...the girl who'd crushed the cookies for God's sake...was the woman driving men all over Chicago insane with lust.

Including him. *Especially* him.

At that moment, he knew it was true. He'd been reacting to Rose and to Izzie the very same way from the moment he'd seen each of them. With pure, undiluted want based on absolutely nothing but instinct and chemistry.

They were the same. His body had known that immediately. His brain had finally caught up.

Somehow, he managed to stay on the sidelines and finish doing his job throughout the long night until the club closed at 2:00 a.m. He stayed upstairs, sending one of the other guys down every so often to do a sweep outside the dressing rooms. He didn't trust himself to go down there and confront her yet.

If he did, it might get loud. And neither one of them might be ready to go back to work after they had the blowout fight Nick suspected they were going to have.

It was definitely going to be a blowout, and probably not for the reasons Izzie would suspect. Yeah, it bothered him that his sister-in-law's kid sister was working as a stripper. But he was no prude, nor was he judgmental. He'd seen her act…she was not only good, she was damn good.

As someone who was—and might again be—Izzie's lover, he was not happy. Couldn't deny that. But again, not so much because of other men looking at her, but more because she was working in a very risky field. Putting herself in danger.

The real reason he was fuming was because she'd lied to him. She'd been deceitful, letting him chase after Izzie by day while Rose pursued *him* by night. The woman had nearly sent him out of his mind—for what? Some twisted game? A power trip?

He didn't know. He just knew he wanted answers. And when the club finally shut down and everyone began to drift away, he walked downstairs, determined to get them.

Nick knew she hadn't left yet, he'd been watching her car in the parking lot, which was emptying as everyone departed for the night. She usually left much earlier—since her last number took place around midnight. And it didn't take her long to get ready since she didn't bother taking her mask off before getting into her car and roaring away. Obviously for his benefit.

But she was still here. So he could only assume one thing: she was waiting in her dressing room, either hiding in the hopes that he'd leave first. Or preparing herself for his arrival.

Because she had to know he'd figured her out. All she'd have had to do was look out at him in the audience during her second set and see the steam pouring out of his head. And the fire burning out of his eyeballs.

Reaching her closed door, he remembering she'd said it had no lock. He gave her a one-knock warning, then entered without waiting for an invitation. It wasn't like she had anything to hide…he'd seen her body, both as Izzie and as Rose.

"What do you think you're doing?" she asked, staring at him from across the room, where she'd been slipping a jacket on. She was dressed casually, in a loose, comfortable-looking pair of baggy pants and a tank top. If she hadn't been wearing the mask, she'd have looked just like the girl next door.

Like Izzie.

God, what a blind idiot he was not to have seen it before. The eyes were the same—though "Rose's" were shadowed by the mask. Those lips couldn't be denied. The shape of her jaw, the length of her neck. Everything about the Crimson Rose was Izzie under a sexy microscope. Everything about Izzie was the Crimson Rose in nice girl trappings.

"What do you want, Nick?"

"You're here late," he murmured, stepping inside and shutting the door behind him.

"Um, yes, I guess so," she replied.

"You don't usually stay until closing time."

She tilted her head back, her chin up, displaying outright bravado. She was going to try to bluff her way through this, since she couldn't be certain she'd been busted. "One of the other dancers got sick and had to leave. I wasn't sure if Harry would need me to cover for her."

He hadn't. Nick knew that much. If he'd had to watch "Rose" in a third performance on the stage, he would have lost it. He didn't know that he'd have been able to keep himself from going up there and confronting her right in front of the audience.

She fell silent, just watching him. Waiting. Nick said nothing, not giving himself away yet. He wanted to see what she'd do. How far Izzie would go to maintain her secret.

God, it killed him that she didn't trust him. He had no illusions about why she'd put that mask on her face in the beginning. Her parents would be upset if they found out. He could even see why she'd kept quiet the first couple of times he'd worked here—before she knew she could trust him.

But now he was her lover. She'd trusted him with her body. She *should* have trusted him with her secret.

"Well," she said, "I guess it's time to go."

"So soon?" he murmured, leaning back against the closed door, blocking her escape. He crossed his arms and stared. "But this is the first time we've been alone in quite a while."

She licked her lips nervously. Nick almost felt that moist tongue on his own mouth and had to force himself to stay cool.

"It's late."

"I know. It's also nearly deserted. You and I might be the very last ones here," he said. Watching her closely, he saw the way she gulped as that truth dawned on her. They were practically alone in this big building. No one would hear if she decided to shout for help.

As if Nick would ever *hurt* her. He'd sooner cut off his own arm. That didn't mean, however, that he didn't intend to torment her just as much as he possibly could.

She was nervous, quivering, her whole body in miniscule motion. And he knew why. He *could* just put her out of her misery and confront her on her deception, but something made him string her along a little more. Maybe it was the way she'd been stringing him along. Maybe it was just because he liked seeing the wild flutter of her pulse in her neck. Plus hearing the choppy, audible breaths she couldn't contain.

He liked having her at a disadvantage for once. He also knew how to put her at more of one.

"So, Rose," he said, finally straightening and stepping closer, "about our very first conversation?"

She slid back, trying to increase the space between them

again, but couldn't go far before hitting the folding screen. Nick pressed closer, relentless in his silent, stalking approach. "I've been giving it a lot of thought."

"You have?" she whispered. "I haven't been, not at all."

What a liar. "Really? Because I think by the way you watch me, you've been thinking about it a lot." Lifting an arm, he put it on the top of the screen, blocking her with his body. They were close enough for him to feel the brush of her pants.

"I need to go."

"I need you to stay." Tracing the soft line of her neck with the tip of one finger, he added, "I've changed my mind about your invitation."

Her mouth opened. "You don't mean…"

He tipped her mouth closed, sliding his thumb across her bottom lip. That juicy, full lip he had tasted the other night and wanted to lightly bite now. "You're very attractive, Rose."

"But…"

"I can't take my eyes off you."

Though she sighed at his touch, her soft body also stiffened. Her fists curled. She obviously didn't know whether to melt or erupt. It was all he could do not to laugh.

"You were so dead-set against it," she said in that hot whisper. "Why now?"

"Men can change their minds, too. You're all I've been thinking about for weeks."

The fists rose to her hips. The sultriness disappeared. She looked indignant, verging on angry. "Oh, yeah?"

"Most definitely." He dropped a hand onto her shoulder, feeling the flexing of her muscles. He kneaded it softly, easing away the angry tension, knowing he was only going to build it back up again. "I want to touch you, everywhere."

She shook under his hand.

"Want to taste you." Knowing how to make the top of her

head blow off, both with lust and with fury, he leaned close. Moving his mouth to the side of her neck, he placed an open-mouthed kiss at her nape, licking lightly at her skin, flavored the tiniest bit with salt from her energetic dancing. "Aww, Rose, do you know what I want to do to you?"

She just whimpered, not saying a word.

"I'd like to smear something luscious and sticky all over you, then lick it from every sweet crevice of your body."

That did it. Izzie/Rose shook off her half-hungry, half-worried daze and reacted with gut fury. She lifted one of those fists and whammed it toward his face. If Nick hadn't been prepared for it, he might have been caught in the jaw. As it was, he deflected the blow by grabbing her hand in mid-air.

He didn't let go, holding her tightly as she struggled to pull away. "Damn you, Nick Santori," she spat out, completely forgetting her sultry whisper.

"What's the matter, sweetheart," he snapped back, "you afraid to get a little oral?" Sliding an arm around her shoulders, still gripping her first, he added, "Or do you just like to *give* it rather than *get* it?"

"Put *anything* in my mouth and I'll bite it off."

"Oooh, rough. I like it." Tracing the opening in the velvety fabric with his finger, he added, "I couldn't *fit* anything in your mouth with that thing on your face. Especially not my cock, *as you well know.*" He pressed hard against her, pushing her back against the wall, grinding into her. Because while her actions and her continued deceptions drove him crazy with anger, her nearness was driving him crazy with lust.

He was rock hard for her, raging with need.

She whimpered and stopped wriggling for a second, her hips bucking toward his in response—once, then again. She lifted one leg slightly, tilting her pelvis so his bulge hit her in the spot she most needed it to. "Oh, God," she mumbled, "I get the point, you've got a lot to offer."

She'd whispered that, calming herself down, and Nick almost groaned at her determination.

She *still* hadn't quite let herself believe it had already gone too far, that her masquerade was over. Izzie had lost her temper at the thought that he'd play the same sexy, wicked games with another woman that he'd played with her the other night in the van. And she'd reacted with honest—if momentary—fury.

Now, having realized it, she was almost desperate to convince herself she could salvage the situation. She was hoping he *hadn't* been talking to Izzie, who knew firsthand what he had to give her since she'd taken him into her body the other night. And that he was instead talking to Rose, who was right now feeling the size of his cock as it pressed against her.

Bending to the side, he grasped her bent leg, gripping her thigh to tug her up for a better fit. She groaned as their bodies came together more intimately. He could feel the heat of her—her moisture—through her thin pants and his own. She was wet and aroused, flushed and ready.

Yet still too damn stubborn to whip off the mask and take him on open, honest terms.

"So you ready to play those kinds of games?" he muttered as he rocked against her, inhaling her little cries of pleasure.

"I don't like to be manhandled," she muttered through hoarse breaths. The excited pulse in her throat and the desperate tone in her voice made a lie of that statement. She liked it. A lot.

He bit lightly on her bottom lip. "Yes, you do."

She started to shake her head, but he kissed her, thrusting his tongue against hers, loving the silky feel of her mouth almost as much as he hated the scrape of the mask against his cheek. That mask was what finally brought him back to his senses. He didn't want the masked woman, he wanted the real one. The one who trusted him and exhibited honesty. And guts.

He'd had enough. Enough of the lying, enough of the deception. Even enough of tormenting her.

So he dropped her leg. "I think we're done."

She sagged back against the wall. Even with the mask he could see the way her eyes widened with shock. And hurt. *"What?"*

It wasn't easy to stay back, keep his hands off her, ignore the heat in small room and the overwhelming smell of sexual want filling his head. But he did it. "I changed my mind."

Turning his back to her, he took one step toward the door. Then he heard her whisper, "You son of a bitch, you *do* know."

He put his hand on the knob. Glancing over his shoulder to meet her stare, he frowned and sighed. "Yeah, Izzie. I do."

Then he walked out.

For the first time in the nearly three months that she'd worked at Leather and Lace, Izzie called in sick Sunday night. She told herself she was a coward ten times over. But that didn't change the way she felt.

She couldn't face him. Not after what had happened in her dressing room Saturday night.

His anger had been undeniable. His revenge understandable.

But it was his *hurt*—that glimpse of sadness on his face as he'd looked at her over his shoulder before walking out the door—that had been the real punch in the gut.

He'd been pursuing her relentlessly for weeks and had finally caught her that night in the van. He'd been nothing but honest about what he was going through—with his family, his life, his attraction to her.

And she'd been lying to him from the first moment. Lying about her secret job, lying about her feelings for him. Lying about what she really wanted.

Hell, she'd even been lying to *herself* about those last two. She'd been denying her feelings for him though they had existed for as long as she could remember. And she'd pretended she wasn't dying for him physically when the thought consumed her every waking moment.

Even her parents had zoned right in on her mood when she'd gone to visit them Sunday. She'd tried so hard to paste on a smile, especially around her father, who was just now starting to seem like his old self. But her mother had immediately noticed something was wrong and had questioned her about it.

She'd covered…promising everything was fine.

One more lie to add to her list. She was becoming quite adept at it. And frankly, she hated herself for that.

"You deserve to feel this way," she told herself as she sat in the closed bakery a few evenings later. It was her quiet time again, when the café staff had left for the day but the evening kitchen and delivery help hadn't arrived. She was sipping a big, fattening cappuccino laden not only with whipped cream but a swirl of caramel. Feeling like absolute scum.

"Iz?" a voice called. A female one.

Turning on her stool, she saw her cousin, Bridget, enter through the employees' entrance in the back.

"Hey," Izzie mumbled.

"I've been calling."

"I don't usually answer the phone after hours."

Bridget frowned. "I mean your cell phone."

"Turned off." Izzie blew on the steaming coffee drink. "There's more if you want to make yourself one."

Bridget looked longingly at the mug and fresh whipped cream and got to work. She remained quiet as she did it, but Izzie saw the worried sidelong glances her cousin cast her way.

When Bridget had finished—topping her hot drink with a sprinkle of cinnamon—she took a seat on the opposite side of the counter. "You look like hell. You haven't been sleeping."

"Thanks. And you're right. I haven't been."

Bridget sighed. "Me, neither."

Finally looking seriously at her cousin, she saw the dark circles under her pretty eyes and the droop of her normally smiling mouth. It was an unusual combination. Bridget was not the cheerful, constantly giddy sort, but she was always quietly happy. And her face reflected that.

Not today, though. "What's wrong?"

"I hate men."

"I hear ya," Izzie mumbled, though her heart wasn't in it. She didn't hate Nick, not at all. She just hated that look of disappointment on his face. Hated how it made her feel.

Low. Rotten.

Yes, she'd had a reason to keep her identity hidden from most of the world. But once she'd let Nick lay her down in the back of that van and do things to her that would cause a real good little Catholic girl to faint of shock, all masks should have been torn away.

"I don't understand them."

Sensing her cousin was talking about one man in particular, Izzie set aside her own emotional misery. "What's going on?"

"It's that guy at work I mentioned a few weeks ago. Dean."

"The new salesman?"

Bridget nodded. "I finally met him for coffee one day, kind of figuring it was our first date. But obviously I totally misread him. He made it clear he was just interested in getting to know a coworker. And he hasn't asked me out again."

Izzie frowned, disliking the look of unhappiness on Bridget's face. "Have you made it clear you're interested?"

"I went out with him, didn't I?"

"Yes, but did you make it *clear* that you were looking at him as more than just a coworker?"

"How was I supposed to do that?"

"I don't know—flirting, smiling, brushing up against him. All the typical weapons of the female romantic arsenal."

"I…don't suppose I did. We talked mostly about business…at least when I wasn't griping about my landlord."

"So, he might not even know you're interested in him *that* way. Which means, you need to let him know, then figure out if he gave you the brush or retreated out of self-preservation."

Bridget blinked. "Self-preservation?"

"Some men won't make a move on a woman unless they're sure she's interested. It takes a lot of self-confidence."

Self-confidence like Nick's. It had taken a boatload of it for him to keep pursuing her when she'd kept turning her down.

"Is that what *you* would do? Make it more obvious?"

"Yeah. I would."

Her cousin mumbled something, then cleared her throat. "You know, I'd think you're right. But there's something about Dean that makes me think he's not quite as nice and shy as he seems."

Izzie instantly stiffened. "Has he done anything to you?"

"*Done?* Oh, goodness, no. He's barely looked at me since the day we went out. But there have been one or two times when I've caught him staring at me—with this, oh, God, it sounds so stupid, but I'd swear he looks almost *hungrily* at me when he thinks I'm not looking."

"Hungry's good. If it's coming from someone you *want* to want you." Not just a room full of horny men turned on by a naked dancer. Her audience sometimes annoyed the hell out of her. Sometimes it seemed like dancing naked alone would be better than dancing naked in front of a crowd. Of course, she wouldn't get *paid* for that. A definite drawback.

"Not if he constantly hides it. And there's more, he sometimes just comes across so much harder—tougher—than this nice, quiet, soft-spoken salesman. It's almost like he's trying really hard to be on his best behavior."

Izzie didn't like the sound of that. Guys who tried that hard to be on their *best* behavior had to be pretty *bad* during their not-quite-best behavior. She said as much to her cousin, but Bridget waved away her concerns.

Though they talked a little while longer, Izzie couldn't keep her mind on anything. Her cousin noticed her distraction and tried to get her to talk about it, but she wasn't ready to.

It wasn't that she didn't trust Bridget to keep her secret. Or that she feared her cousin would be shocked by it. But the truth was, it didn't seem right for Bridget to be the one she talked to about this. Not when Nick was the first one who'd realized what she was doing on Saturday and Sunday nights.

She wanted to talk to him.

She wanted him. Period.

She just didn't know if it was too late to get him. Judging by the way he'd slammed out of her dressing room Saturday night, she greatly feared it was.

It took every ounce of willpower Nick possessed to avoid going into Natale's Bakery that week. Something inside him insisted that he go up there and confront Izzie now that he felt at least moderately calm. Unlike the way he'd felt Saturday night at the club.

Something else demanded that he stay away, let her figure

out what the hell it was she wanted from him and clue him in when she was ready. Maybe he'd accommodate her. Maybe he wouldn't. It depended entirely upon what she wanted: him in her life, him out of her life? A secret affair, or a public one? A lover…a friend?

There were a lot of different possibilities. He honestly wasn't sure which he was most hoping for. The only thing he knew he wanted was for Izzie to come clean with him about everything. Then they could figure out the rest.

He assumed it would take a while. Considering she'd called in sick from work Sunday night, he had the feeling she was going to avoid the confrontation for as long as possible. But, unless she quit working at the club, she wasn't going to be able to avoid him forever.

Quit working at the club. He couldn't deny that his first reaction had been to want her to.

He didn't want other men looking at Izzie. He didn't want other men fantasizing about her. And he most certainly didn't want anyone getting fixated on her…fixated enough to stalk her, threaten her or hurt her.

Once he'd calmed down, though, he realized he understood exactly why she'd gone to work at Leather and Lace. It was probably for the same reasons *he'd* gone to work there.

She was every bit as out of her element in this old-new environment as he was. Fitting in about as well as he did.

Fitting in…hell, what he was doing right now was proof he didn't fit in. It was Thursday night and he was holding a brown paper bag clutched to his side. Walking to his building, his eyes scanned side to side in the hope that he didn't bump into his parents or another elderly relative who'd rat him out.

Chinese carry-out was probably grounds for his mother to call for an exorcism. Especially since he'd refused yet another doggy bag full of calzones and Pop's lasagna tonight. If he bit another piece of pasta, he was going to explode like the giant marshmallow man in *Ghost Busters*.

"Tough," he muttered, his mouth watering for the Kung Pao Chicken he could smell from the bag. Not to mention the eggrolls, fried rice...he'd bought enough to feed an army.

Nick knew a little something about clandestine missions. Enough to know that when you were on one, you accomplished as much as you could the first time, in the hopes that you could delay going back. And a big bag of food meant leftovers. Enough to last a week or so, meaning no more dangerous, secret excursions to Mr. Wu's for a while.

Unless, of course, he had unexpected company for dinner. Female company. Like the female standing right outside his apartment door, her hand lifted to knock.

"Izzie?" he mumbled as soon as he stepped off the elevator, wondering not only how she'd gotten into the building, but also how she'd found out where he lived.

She whirled around, her eyes wide and bright. She hadn't knocked yet, which meant she hadn't quite prepared herself to face him. He'd caught her off guard.

Nick tried not to wonder what this meant, tried to remain casual. Tried not to notice how curvy and inviting her body looked in her tight tank top and sexy short skirt.

It would be like not noticing an earthquake shaking your house down around you. She was just too beautiful to ignore.

As they continued to stare, he finally murmured, "Hi."

"Hi."

They said nothing else for a moment. Long enough for him to notice the smudges of shadow beneath her pretty brown eyes and the paleness in her cheeks. She was practically biting a hole in her bottom lip as she tried to figure out what to say.

He couldn't help taking pity on her...at least taking pity on that gorgeous lip before she bit a hole right through it.

Shifting his bag to his other hip, he walked to the door and lifted his keys to the lock. "You hungry?"

She glanced at the bag. "No pizza?"

"Nope. I've got egg foo young, lo mein, couple of different chicken dishes, you name it."

"Oh, God, feed me," she exclaimed, following him into the apartment with a smile on her face.

Once inside, she tossed her purse onto his couch, a large one that dominated the small living area of the very small apartment. He didn't mind—compared to sharing a barracks with twenty other guys, this was pure luxury. He'd picked the place because it was clean and high, with a great view of the college a few blocks away. And he'd barely started furnishing it, figuring he'd get the most important things first.

Big, comfortable reclining leather couch. Big TV for watching football. He could live for a while on that…plus the huge, comfortable bed dominating his bedroom.

A flow of warmth washed through him at the thought of that bed. He'd imagined Izzie in it many times. He'd *dreamed* of her in it many times.

Now, here she was. So close he could smell her perfume and hear her breaths. Like a fantasy come to life.

"Minimalist, huh?" she asked as she stared pointedly at the couch and the big screen TV.

"I'm working on it."

He couldn't believe how normal they sounded. Like two old friends getting together for dinner. Considering the last two times they'd been alone they'd been either fighting or practically ripping each other's clothes off, he figured that was a pretty good trick.

"I, uh, wanted to…"

"Save it," he muttered, not wanting to start their discussion yet. "I'm hungry. Let's eat first."

Relief washed over her pretty face as she followed him into the kitchen. When she lifted something up onto the counter, he realized she hadn't come empty handed.

"Peace offering." She pointed toward a six-pack of beer.

"Are we at war?" he asked, repeating a question she'd once asked him.

"We've been doing a lot of battling."

Yes, they had. And he, for one, was tired of it.

Getting some bowls, plates and silverware, he spread all the food out on his small kitchen table, and they each loaded up, smorgasbord style. "Where…"

"Do you mind the floor?" he asked.

Shrugging, she followed him into the living room, watching as he sat down in front of the sofa, stretching his legs out in front of him, with his plate on his lap. It wasn't quite as easy for her, since she wore a skirt.

Nick forced himself to focus on his food, not on her long, sexy legs so close to his on the floor. Picking up the TV remote, he flicked the power button, then channeled up to a station playing soft music. It was background noise, filling the silence that grew thicker as they ate…as they drew closer to the conversation they both knew they were about to have.

When they'd finished, he took their plates into the kitchen. She followed, working on putting away the food. Within a few moments, there was nothing left to do—no dinner to eat, no dishes to clean—nothing to do but face each other.

"I don't want to do this," he said, surprising them both.

"Do what?"

"Fight with you. Do battle. Whatever you want to call it."

She shook her head. "I don't want to either. But I need to tell you…I need to get this out."

Crossing his arms, he leaned back against the kitchen counter and waited. "Okay."

She closed her eyes, then spoke in a rush. "I'm sorry I was dishonest with you about being the Crimson Rose. At first, I didn't trust you—didn't trust *anyone*. I'm sure you know that my parents wouldn't be happy about what I'm doing, and I don't want to do anything to add to my father's health problems."

"I understand that." He did. It made perfect sense for her to go incognito at her risqué job. "But once you and I…"

"I know." She raked a hand through her brown hair, which was loose around her shoulders tonight, rather than up in its usual ponytail. "I should have told you immediately. Instead I panicked and pushed you away."

"Yeah. I gotta say, I felt pretty damn humiliated when I figured it out. I should have known you."

"I *am* a performer. I know about portraying someone else."

"About that…when did you start in this line of work?"

"Stripping's not my line of work. Dancing is. I was with the Rockettes until a year ago."

"You were one of those kick-line chicks?"

She glared at him. "It's harder than it looks."

"Right. Tough life dancing with giant nutcrackers and Santa Claus." He quickly put his hand up. "I'm joking. You must have been damn good to make it."

"I was," she said, with complete confidence. "But I got bored with it and went with a modern dance company in Manhattan. Then came the injury. Then came Dad's stroke. Now I'm here."

Her life in a nutshell.

"And now what?" he asked, knowing that was the question he really wanted answered. Where was she going from here? Where did she see him fitting into that?

"I don't know. Right now I'm biding time, trying to figure out what I want." Her jaw tightening, she continued. "But it's not the bakery, and it's not the neighborhood. It's not Gloria's life—a repeat of my mother's. And it's not my sister Mia's life as a hard-ass lawyer with tons of drive and no happiness."

"I understand," he murmured.

Nodding, she said, "I'm sure you do. If anyone would, it's you." The tension easing from her shoulders, Izzie walked across the small kitchen, covering the distance between them in a few short steps. Putting her hand on his chest, she looked up at him, her eyes bright. "Which is why I have to repeat this: I am sorry, Nick. Please say you'll forgive me."

He hesitated, then offered her a short nod. Appearing relieved, she began to pull her hand away, but he covered it with his, not letting her go. "Where do *we* go from here?"

She hesitated, so he pressed her. "We can't be just friends."

"We can't be a couple."

Their eyes locked, they both said the same four words at exactly the same moment. "We can be lovers."

Nick chuckled as Izzie smiled. Tightening her fingers in his shirt, she scraped the tips of them along the base of his neck. "Where I'd *like* to go right now is into your bedroom to see if it's furnished any better than your living room is."

Lifting her hand to his mouth, he pressed a warm kiss on the inside of her palm. "Oh, it is, angel. You bet it is."

8

MAKING LOVE TO NICK in the back of the van had been erotic and spontaneous and incredibly hot. It had also been a week ago and in that week, Izzie had begun to wonder whether it had really been as amazing as she remembered.

As soon as Nick led her into his bedroom, turned her to face the mirrored door of his closet, and slowly began to kiss her neck, she knew it had been. He was so slow—so patient—so deliberate. The man had incredible control and he had used it to drive her absolutely wild.

Izzie had flipped the light switch on as soon as they entered the room, determined to see all, savor all, enjoy every minute of this experience. When Nick studied her in the mirror, consuming her with his eyes, she was very glad she had. She liked watching him watch her. Liked having his eyes on her. And she wanted to watch everything he did to her.

"You've been driving me absolutely insane since I saw you that night in the restaurant," he whispered, his lips hovering just above the sensitive skin below her ear.

"You've been driving me insane since you landed on top of me on the cookie table."

He turned her to face him. "Izzie, I'm sorry I didn't…"

"I was a kid. You needed to wait until I caught up a little," she said with a smile.

He glanced down at her, his stare lingering on the scooped

neck of her shirt and the clingy fabric hugging her breasts. "You caught up a lot."

She reached up and unfastened the top button of his shirt, then moved to the next. "Oh, more than you know," she whispered, feeling incredibly free. A sensual woman capable of knocking him back on his heels the way he'd knocked her back last week.

Their first time together had been about him overwhelming her senses. Tonight it was Izzie's turn.

She was not going to lie back and *take* the pleasure he wanted to give her, she intended to *give* with every lustful molecule in her body. He'd offered her an experience she would remember until the day she died. Now she planned to do the same.

Using the one thing she did best.

She quickly scanned the room, thinking ahead. "Where'd that come from?" she asked, pointing to an old-fashioned, straight backed chair in the corner. It, a simple, immaculately clean dresser and an enormous four-poster bed were the only things in the room. The chair didn't look at all new like the rest.

"My parents insisted on giving me stuff…I had to take *something* and there's no room for it in the living room."

"It won't fit with that TV that's more suited for the Jolly Green Giant's living room," she said with a low laugh. Licking her lips, she pointed to the chair. "Go sit down."

One of his eyebrows rose, but he obeyed, watching with interest to see what she was up to. Izzie glanced around the room, looking for a radio, a boombox, something.

No luck. Nick's bedroom was nearly empty, with just the furniture and a smaller TV on the dresser. There wasn't a piece of clothing on the floor, or a speck of dust anywhere. It was nearly Spartan…military, she assumed. And it lacked the warmth she knew Nick possessed.

She hoped that someday he allowed that warmth to spill free and become part of his home as well as a part of his life.

"You got me where you wanted me," he drawled from the chair. He put his hands behind his head, his fingers laced, and leaned back against the wall. His sleeves were rolled up to his elbows and his forearms bulged and flexed. His big, strong legs were sprawled out in front of him and for a second, Izzie was tempted to climb right onto his lap.

She could unzip his jeans, tug them out of the way, release that big erection she could see from here. It would be delicious to slip her panties off, lift her skirt, then slide down onto him to ride him to her heart's content.

Not yet. First she needed to delight his senses the way he'd delighted hers last week. He'd focused on her sense of touch and smell—she could still inhale and remember that sweet, cheesy filling he'd smeared all over her. And her body tingled at the memory of his lips and tongue removing that filling.

They'd played games with food. She intended to whet his taste buds with something else.

The sight of her body.

Suddenly remembering what he'd done with the TV in the other room, she grabbed the remote control and turned on the bedroom one. Punching in a few numbers—familiar, since she liked listening to the same station at her own apartment— she landed on a channel that played sultry Latina music.

Because luck was a woman, the song was a slower one with a sultry back-beat and a sensuous rhythm. Easy to dance to.

"What are you…"

"Watch me," she whispered. *Watch me and I'll make you burn.*

She began to move, closing her eyes and letting the music roll through her. Since childhood Izzie had had an affinity for music—all types of music. It had always made her want to move. To sway or to spin, to leap or to bend. She just had a dancing gene that demanded release whenever the right beat hit her ears and rolled on down through her body.

This one was perfect for seduction.

Keeping focused on her own instincts—giving herself pleasure by the simple act of moving—she knew Nick would gain pleasure, too. At first she simply danced. Her eyes still closed, she threw her head back and tangled her hand in her hair. Rocking her hips, she gyrated against an imaginary partner, sliding down and up against an invisible thigh, quivering under the touch of a hand that wasn't there.

She heard Nick groan softly. Licking her lips, she slid her hand down her own body. Her hips still rocking, she touched her stomach, then slid her hand lower, resting her fingertips on her pelvis. Her other hand she moved across her chest, scraping her nipples, already rock hard in anticipation and excitement.

"Izzie…"

"Shh."

She didn't look at him, didn't let him distract her. Instead, she tugged her top free of her waistband. Flicking at the snap and pushing down the zipper of her skirt, she rocked until the thing fell to the floor. She kicked it out of the way, never losing the beat, her body in constant, sensual motion.

Her top came next. She dragged it up—slowly, so slowly— letting the fabric fall back an inch for every two she raised it. She could hear Nick's ragged breathing over the music. Could hear her own heart pounding in her chest, too. Every move she made was an invitation and a promise.

She pulled the top off, sensual even when untangling her hair from the material. Clad in nothing but a skimpy bra and thong panties, and her high heeled sandals, she bent over and swung her head, letting her hair fly free.

"You're killing me here," he whispered.

"So take care of yourself. Get ready for me," she replied, coming closer—but not too close. "Do what you *want* to do when you watch me dance."

"I want to *have* you when I watch you dance."

Tsking, she shook her head in disbelief, still swaying like a woman being sexually aroused by the touch of the musical notes on her body. "Pretend you don't know you're going to have me, Nick. Let me see what you'd do then."

She turned around, her back to him, returning her attention to her dance. Bending at the waist, she put her hands on her thighs and did a booty rock that she knew would drive him out of his ever-loving mind.

His low groan told her it had worked. But Izzie ignored it, Grabbing the end post of Nick's bed, she used it, hooking one leg around it and bending back. The wood was hard against her swollen sex, but she needed it—got off on it—rubbing up and down in a way she never rode the pole at the club.

"Izzie," he whispered hoarsely.

She glanced over and almost smiled in triumph. He'd finished unbuttoning his shirt and it hung from his shoulders.

Even better, his jeans were open, his briefs pushed down. And his hand encircled his huge erection.

"Yes. Imagine it's *me* touching you," she told him.

He never took his eyes off her, beginning to stroke, up and down, his movements timed to match her strokes against the bedpost. But when she let go of it, he didn't stop.

"The bra," he ordered.

"Just as the customer desires," she whispered, taunting him with every bit of her sexuality.

She unfastened the bra, dragging out the moment before it fell away to reveal her breasts. This usually marked the end of one of her numbers, but tonight, Izzie was just getting started. She touched herself, showing him the way she wanted to be touched. Crossing her arms—her hips still rocking—she cupped each breast. Capturing her nipples between her fingers, she tweaked and rolled. The pleasure she gave herself—and the way Nick reacted to it—sent pure liquid want rushing to her sex, already dripping with readiness.

Hearing Nick clear his throat, she glanced over and saw he held a twenty dollar bill in his hand. He was enjoying this game. Getting into the fantasy.

"You have something for me, mister?" she asked, almost purring the words as she danced closer, wearing nothing but her skimpy panties and shoes.

"Uh-huh. But you have to work for it."

She moved again, closer, stepping over one of his legs to straddle it. She lowered herself closer to his thigh, rocking a few inches above it. Her breasts swayed close to his face. "What'd you have in mind?"

He leaned up, his mouth moving toward her breast.

"Uh-uh, no touching," she said, easing back a little. "I can touch you…you can't touch me."

"Those the rules?"

"Uh-huh."

"Not sure how long I'll be able to obey them."

"You'll just have to keep your hands busy *elsewhere* until I say you can break them."

He flexed his hand again, lazily working the erection that still jutted out of his unfastened pants. "That means the rules *will* eventually be broken?"

She bent down again, low, brushing her silky panties over his strong thigh. "If you're very, very good." Her mouth watering, she inched closer, so her leg could brush against all that male heat. He instinctively arched toward her, branding her with that ridge of flesh that had given her such intense pleasure last week.

She wanted it. Badly. In every way it was possible for a woman to take it.

"You want a lap dance, mister?" she asked in her heavy, Crimson Rose whisper.

His eyes narrowed. "I didn't know you gave them."

"I don't. But you're an extra *special* customer."

Izzie had never done this particular type of dance, but she figured she could fake it. Frankly, she didn't think Nick would care if she didn't get it exactly right.

So she went with her instincts. With both hands on the back of the chair, she swayed over him, brushing her breasts against his cheeks, shivering at the delicious roughness of his skin. She danced above him, writhing just above one leg, then the other, then straddling both. He watched with glittering eyes, groaning with need as she taunted him—coming close, so close—then pulling away.

"Gonna have to break that rule soon, lady," he growled.

"We'll see."

Driving them both closer to the brink of insanity, she dipped lower than she'd ever gone, until the silky wet fabric between her thighs met his arousal and set them both completely on fire. He grabbed her hips, helping her rock up and down on him until they both moaned with the pleasure of it.

"You're touching," she said.

He thrust up harder, the hot tip of his erection easing into her, bringing her silky panties along. "I'm going to be touching you a lot more in a minute."

Oh, she liked playing these wicked, sexy games with Nick. It was unlike anything she'd ever done with anyone before, and Izzie sensed she could be happy playing bedroom games with him and *only* him for a very long time.

"But you still haven't paid me." She licked the side of his neck, biting lightly on his nape. Feeling the scrape of the bill against her skin, she pulled away just enough to watch him slip it into her panties. "Big tipper."

"You're worth every penny."

"I think maybe you should get a little bonus for being such a good customer."

She needed a little bonus herself. Needed to do something she'd been aching to do since she'd first seen him take off his pants in the back of the van.

Sliding back, she lowered herself to the floor, then moved between his thighs. She reached for his hand, covering it with hers, mimicking his slow, easy movements up and down his erection. Eventually she pushed his hand away, pleasuring him with her fingers and her palm. Encircling him as best she could, she slid down to the base of his shaft, then eased back up. She trailed her fingers across the thick, bulbous head to moisten them with his body's juices, then repeated the motion.

But it wasn't *quite* enough. Izzie inched forward, wetting her lips with her tongue.

"Iz…"

"Let me," she murmured.

She didn't wait for permission. Kneeling between his spread thighs, she drew closer, flicking out her tongue for a quick taste of the sac pulled up tight beneath his erection.

He jerked up, thrusting harder into her hand, which still encircled him. Izzie didn't stop. Parting her fingers to make way for her mouth, she licked her way from the base of his shaft all the way up to its tip. "You taste so good, Nick," she whispered before flicking her tongue out to catch more of that fluid dripping out of him.

"So do you." Still sprawled out before her, he tangled his hands in her hair. "But I'm hungry. I want some, too."

Mmm…mutual oral pleasure. She'd love to savor that experience with Nick. But for right now, she wanted to concentrate on him. So, ignoring his comment, she moved over the thick, pulsing head of his cock and took it into her mouth. As she sucked, he hissed. The deeper she went—taking as much as she could—the louder his groans.

Shifting around for better access, Izzie began to slowly make love to him with her mouth, getting off on hearing *him* get off. She slid up and down, taking more with every stroke, wanting to swallow him all the way down, though he was, of course, much too big for that. But she gave it her all, focused on his sounds of pleasure, the smell of sex rolling off his body, the feel of his hands delicately stroking her hair and the back of her head.

"Ride me, Izzie," he whispered, not demanding but pleading. "Come up here and take me."

Take him. Izzie had never had a man beg her using those words, though she, herself, had spoken them. She found herself liking the sensuous power of it. He didn't just want her, he *needed* her. Was desperate for her.

With one last little suck, she pulled her mouth away and looked up at him. He was staring down at her, his dark brown eyes gleaming with want. Reaching for her shoulders, he began to tug her up and repeated his plea. "Take me, Izzie."

Offering him a half-smile, she rose to her knees. She was nearly naked, but Nick was still half-wearing his clothes. So she reached for his waistband and pulled his pants and briefs down. He lifted up to help her, kicking his shoes off and his clothes with them. His shirt fell off his shoulders with a simple shrug, and now the tables were turned—she was the only one wearing a stitch of clothes.

It was, of course, a tiny stitch. And as she rose to her feet, Nick didn't take his eyes off it. Reaching for her hips, he tugged her closer until he caught the elastic seam of her panties with his teeth. Nudging them down, he tasted her with two quick, heart-stopping flicks of his tongue. Her clit swelled against his lips. "Please," she whispered, not knowing what she needed more—for him to lick her into an orgasm, or to tear her panties off and plunge down onto him.

"Since you asked so nicely," he murmured, returning his mouth to her most sensitive spot. Taking her hips in his hands, he pushed the panties down and nuzzled in deep in her curls.

Feeling a climax rocket through her, Izzie threw her head back and groaned. She was still groaning when Nick tugged her down over him. He glanced at his jeans. "My pocket…"

"We're safe," she assured him since she was on the pill. "As long as you're comfortable with that."

"Oh, I am so comfortable with that," he muttered hoarsely. "I cannot wait to feel you wrapped around me, skin to skin."

Straddling him, her toes on the floor, Izzie rubbed against him, loving the tangle of his chest hair on her rock-hard nipples. Nick dipped his head down to suck one of them, hard and demanding. "Ride me," he ordered, his mouth still at her breast.

She eased onto him, taking the hot tip into her wet channel a little at a time. He was right—skin to skin was incredible. She could feel every beat of his pulse through his velvety smooth erection.

"Can't…take much…" he said through choppy breaths.

As if he'd reached his breaking point, he squeezed her hips and thrust up, impaling her hard and deep. "Oh, Nick," she groaned, shocked at the full intensity of it.

It took her a second to catch her breath, he filled her so deeply. But when she did, she had to move. Had to slide up and then ease back down. She rode with slow strokes, her arms on his shoulders, looking down into his face as he stared up into hers.

Nick lifted one hand and cupped her cheek, drawing her toward him. Covering her lips with his, he kissed her deeply, sliding his tongue in and out of her mouth in strokes matched by the ones deep inside her core.

The kiss went on and on, slowing or growing frenzied in mirror reactions to the movements of their bodies. Izzie rode him, took him as he'd demanded, using muscles she didn't even remember she had to stretch out their pleasure.

Their position was perfect for pleasing her both inside and out. And within moments, the friction on her clit provided her with another mind-blowing orgasm.

Finally, though, her legs began to weaken. She wasn't sure how much more she could take. As if he knew, Nick wrapped his arms around her, cupping her backside, and rose from the chair.

The strength of the man defied description.

Still buried deep within her, he continued kissing her as he walked the few steps to the bed. He dropped her on her back, coming down with her, and took over control.

"Yes, Nick," she gasped, her legs around his lean hips.

He didn't reply. He was gone now, mentally just *gone,* at the mercy of his wildly plunging body. Izzie held on for the ride, whispering frantic words of pleasure, telling him how much he pleased her.

Until she, too, was incapable of words. Together they lost themselves to the power of it until Nick shouted and came deep inside her, sending Izzie spiraling over the edge again, too.

BRIDGET HAD BEEN thinking about her cousin's words nearly all night Thursday. So much so that she barely slept and climbed out of bed long before her alarm went off Friday morning.

If there was one thing Izzie knew, it was men. And if she thought Bridget hadn't been sending out strong enough signals to Dean, she was probably right.

Izzie would make her interest more obvious.

So that's what Bridget would do.

That morning, she dressed for work a bit more carefully than usual. Her regular workday attire was typically a pair of pastel capris or a pair of slacks and a blouse. Today, she shimmied into a yellow skirt that cupped her butt like she'd sat in a tub of butter. Pulling a tight white tank top on with it, she glanced in the mirror and was surprised at what she saw.

She didn't look much like Bridget, the nice, smiling book-keeper. In fact, she looked sexy. She had curves...nice ones. Her breasts were high and shapely, highlighted by the scooped neck of the tank top. And while she didn't have es-pecially long legs, they looked pretty good in the skirt.

Feeling almost armored for battle, she donned a light-weight sweater—which she intended to remove as soon as she saw her quarry—and headed to work. She wanted to get there early so she could get used to walking around the office in the minuscule skirt and high-heeled sandals without tripping and making a fool of herself.

Usually, she was the first one at the dealership, anyway. The lot didn't open to customers until ten o'clock, with most of the sales staff showing up around nine...a half hour or so after her regular starting time. By the time she got to the lot, it was only seven-thirty, an hour early even for her.

The inside was dark, as expected, and as she entered, she reached for the switch to turn on the bank of overhead lights. But before she did it, something caught her eye...a sliver of light coming from beneath the door to the business office. Where *she* usually worked.

She supposed she could have forgotten to turn the light

off last night when she left. But she was still cautious as she approached. This was a pretty safe area, but occasional robberies certainly weren't unheard of. She wasn't about to open the door and surprise some junkie looking for a petty cash box.

When she got to within a few feet of the nearly closed door, she heard a voice from inside. She tensed for the briefest second, then recognized the voice and relaxed.

It was Dean. He'd obviously shown up early for work. Though she didn't hear whoever he was talking to, she figured someone else must have come in early, too.

Too bad. Had he been alone, she might have been able to put her "send stronger signals" plan into action. If, of course, she had the nerve, which was questionable.

Reaching for the knob, she paused when she heard Dean speak again, answering a question she hadn't heard asked. That was when she realized the conversation was one-sided. He was talking on the phone to someone.

Not wanting to eavesdrop, she stepped away, catching only the snippet of a comment Dean made. Something about a deal going down. Sounded like their star salesman had landed another buyer—one who liked to close deals very early in the morning.

When she heard his voice stop, she figured she'd see if he was done, and knocked once on the door. Feeling a little foolish—since she was, in essence, knocking on her own office door—she pushed the door open and stepped inside.

"Good morning, early-bird," she said.

He jerked his head up, so surprised he dropped his cell phone right onto the floor near her feet.

"Sorry, didn't mean to startle you," she said. Normally, she'd wait quietly and let him pick up the phone himself. But Izzie's words kept ringing in her ears. So instead, she carefully bent at the knees, reaching down to pick it up for him.

She kept one hand on her skirt, to hold it in place, but Bridget couldn't deny that it slid up several inches, high on her thighs, despite that.

Still appearing shocked, Dean didn't say a word. His narrowed eyes were locked on her thighs. His jaw was visibly clenched and he breathed over parted lips.

He looked…hungry. Just as she'd seen him look at her once or twice in the past. More than that, he seemed dangerous. Not nice Dean looking at a pair of woman's legs, but wickedly sexy Dean looking at a pair of woman's legs and imagining them wrapped around his waist.

She could do that. She could definitely do that. Whether it was what Izzie would do or not.

It is.

"Here you go," she said, handing him the cell phone.

He took it from her, their fingers brushing lightly. Standing, he stuffed the phone in his pocket. His lean face looked weary, as if he hadn't slept well.

"So, was it worth your early trip in?" she asked, knowing she sounded coy. She couldn't help channeling Izzie a little bit. "Everything…satisfactory?"

His pale blue eyes narrowed. "What do you mean?"

"I mean, did you get whatever deal you're working on taken care of this morning?"

He nodded slowly. "The deal. Yeah. It's all good."

"Good. You might set another sales record this month."

With a casual manner she had never suspected she could pull off, she tossed her purse onto her desk, which was laden with files, legal paperwork and financial stuff. Holding onto her courage, she slipped her sweater off her shoulders. She had to move close to Dean—very close—to reach the coat rack on the wall. Her arm brushed against his as she lifted the sweater onto one of the hooks.

"Bridget…"

Smiling, she turned and glanced up at him. "Yes?"

He wasn't looking at her face, his attention was focused lower. On the scooped neck of her tight, spandex tank top. The heat in his stare warmed her all over and she felt her body reacting to it. A lazy river of want flowed through her veins. She clenched her thighs in response to it. But there was no way to disguise the way her breasts grew heavier, her nipples hardening to twin points that poked against her shirt.

He noticed. Most definitely.

Swallowing hard, he growled, "Why are you dressed like that?"

"Like what?"

"Like you're trolling for men at a club rather than working with a bunch of used car salesmen and wrench jockeys at an auto shop?" he asked, his tone harsh.

Bridget instinctively stepped back. A little hurt. A little confused. "I just…." *Channel Izzie. WWID?* Taking a deep breath, she tilted her head back and jutted her chin out. "What business is it of yours what I wear to work?"

He reached for her, grabbing her arm as if he couldn't help himself. "Put your sweater back on."

"*Make* me."

His whole body tense with frustration, he lifted his other hand and grabbed her other arm. Bridget wasn't sure what he was going to do—shake her or haul her into his arms and kiss her.

She was most definitely hoping for option two.

She should have been intimidated, maybe even scared given his size. But she already knew he wouldn't do anything to hurt her. He was attracted to her, she was sure of it now, and he just didn't know what to do about that attraction since they were coworkers.

"Either take your hands off me or do something with them," she snapped, still thinking the way her cousin would.

"Damn it, Bridget."

But before he could do either one, they heard the sound of voices coming from right outside the door. They weren't, it appeared, the only two who'd arrived to work early.

Dean instantly released her and stepped away. He shook his head, as if to clear it, and eyed her warily. Finally he said, "I really think you should put your sweater on."

Bridget hid a smile, liking the tiny thrill of power she felt at having this big, handsome man react so strongly to *her*. Crossing her arms in front of her chest—which pressed her breasts even higher and harder against her top—she shook her head. "I don't think so, Dean. If you don't like the way I'm dressed…I suggest you don't look at me."

Knowing her bravado wasn't going to last for much longer, she sashayed past him, out onto the showroom floor to greet the other salesmen who'd arrived. Leaving Dean watching her with eyes that blazed like the sun.

IZZIE HAD SPENT the night in Nick's arms, but she'd slipped away early—around dawn. Knowing the bakery would open soon, he didn't protest.

He wanted to, of course, but he kept his mouth shut.

Izzie's whole reason for being here in Chicago was her devotion to her family's business. He wouldn't even think of interfering with that. Because he *liked* her working at the bakery. Right here close by.

As for her other job, at the club? Well, that, Nick had to admit, might be a tougher proposition. He hadn't yet been tested, but he didn't imagine it would be easy watching the woman he was absolutely crazy about take her clothes off for a roomful of other men. Especially since he'd almost certainly be picturing what had happened last night, when she'd taken her clothes off only for him.

It had been the most unbelievable night of his life. And he had to wonder how she'd had the strength to get up and walk this morning considering he'd spent so much of the night between her legs.

Izzie wasn't the only one who had to go to work. Nick had promised Tony he'd help him handle the delivery of a new wall oven at Santori's. So after showering, he got dressed and walked the few blocks up to Taylor. He passed right by Natale's on the way, but, mindful of Izzie's feelings, he didn't pop in. It felt strange as hell to walk on by and not say hello to the woman he'd made love to in so many wild, different ways the night before.

But she wanted their relationship to remain entirely between them. Meaning he couldn't single her out, couldn't grab her hand in public, couldn't ask her to do so much as walk across the street with him.

"This is gonna suck," he muttered aloud as he reached the restaurant. He had no idea how long he'd be able to maintain this secret, nighttime-only relationship with Izzie.

He only hoped she'd change her mind. That she'd realize she didn't have to give up *herself* to become part of a relationship with him.

A relationship. Yeah. He wanted one. He was falling for her in a big way, just as he'd suspected he could when he'd seen her looking so bored and aloof on the other side of Santori's all those weeks ago.

It was pretty ironic, really. He was starting to think he really could have found the perfect woman. He was already falling in love with her. And a union between them would absolutely delight everyone in both their families.

But Izzie didn't want one.

"Women," he muttered as he pushed into the restaurant.

His brother Tony, who'd been standing right inside the door, greeted him with a clap on the back. "Can't live with 'em...but they're sure as hell better than living alone."

As usual, his larger-than-life older brother coaxed a smile out of him.

Fridays were usually busy at Santori's, so the day flew by quickly. And, as usual, the rest of his family started drifting in after their workdays had ended. By eight o'clock, all of his brothers were here with their wives and kids, as was his sister, along with her new husband. Those two were cuddling like the newlyweds they were. Though he'd been skeptical, given what he knew about Simon Lebeaux's shady past, even Nick had to admit the two of them were obviously crazy about each other.

Besides, if Lebeaux could put up with his mouthy little sister, he had to be one hell of a strong man.

"Come on, take a load off," Mark said to Nick as he emerged from the kitchen, where he'd been helping his father.

"Yeah, I guess my slave-driver boss will let me knock off now," he replied, glancing over his shoulder at Tony, who stood in the swinging doorway.

"Not boss...partner," his brother reminded him with a grin.

Uh, no. Not in Nick's opinion. But he still hadn't wanted to have that conversation.

His siblings and their families took up several tables in the restaurant—tables that would probably have been appreciated by the paying customers lining up near the front counter. But Mama would never dream of shooing them out to free up the space. She clucked around, ordering them all to eat, cooing over the grandbabies and beaming when Noelle, Mark's wife, offered to let her feel the baby kicking in her stomach.

In Nick's opinion, that was Twilight Zone stuff. But *all* the women got into it, and Mark looked like he thought it was the coolest thing since Optimus Prime and the Transformers. Nick, however, was freaked by the very idea. The only thing he wanted to feel moving around inside a woman was his own cock. A baby? Forget it.

Unless the woman was Izzie.

The thought was crazy—bothersome, even. But it wouldn't leave his head.

"Hey, look who's here," Gloria called, waving toward the front door. "My baby sister! How you doin', Iz?"

Nick immediately swung around, seeing Izzie at the counter.

"Ah, Isabella, you haven't been to see me too much. What's wrong with you, eh?" Mama said as she bustled over. She cupped Izzie's face in her hands, pressing a kiss on her forehead, then grabbed her arm and dragged her over.

Smacking Lucas on the shoulder, she said, "Move over and make room for Gloria's little sister."

"Yes, ma'am," his older brother said with a grin. Luke was the next oldest above Nick and Mark and, as a prosecutor, was used to ordering other people around. But, like all of them, he couldn't refuse a command from their bossy mother.

"How's everything, Iz?" he asked as he stood and moved his chair out of the way. "You remember Rachel, right?"

Izzie nodded, smiling at Luke's pretty blond wife, the only fair-haired one of the bunch. A die-hard southerner, she'd somehow made herself fit in so well that Nick couldn't imagine what the family would be like without her.

Fortunately, the room Mama had forced Luke to make was between his chair and Nick's. Rosa Santori stole an unused chair from a nearby table and slid it in place, nearly pushing Izzie down onto it. Which had Nick ready to kiss his mother's hand, even though Izzie looked less than happy.

"I was just picking something up for dinner on the way home from work," she said, sounding almost dazed at how quickly she'd been shanghaied into a family dinner.

He understood the feeling. His mother was a powerhouse.

"Such a silly girl," Mama said. "You will eat here, with the family. You're one of us!" Trying to squeeze past her to get back to the kitchen, Mama said, "Scooch over a bit, eh?" and she pushed on Izzie's chair until it was so close to Nick's their thighs touched under the table.

Nick would lay money that his mother had done it on purpose. When he saw the smirk on her face as she left to check on dinner, he knew it was true.

Everyone wanted them to hook up. *If only they knew....*

"Hey *Isabella*," he whispered from the side of his mouth. She kicked him under the table.

"So, how do you like being back in Chi-town, Izzie?" his brother Joe asked. "Guess it's pretty tame and unexciting after your life in New York. You must really need a creative outlet."

There was a surprising twinkle in Joe's eye. As he and Izzie exchanged a long stare, Nick began to have a suspicion that Joe knew a little more than he'd let on about Izzie's night-time life. Remembering the way Joe had steered him toward the job, and had been so adamant about Nick taking care of the "featured dancer" at Leather and Lace, he had to wonder if Joe had seen Izzie there during the renovations.

"It's okay," Izzie replied. Smiling, she added, "I'm just busy trying to avoid resuming my cannoli addiction. They're my absolute weakness."

Everyone at the table laughed. Except Nick. Because there'd been a sultry purr in her voice and he believed she'd been speaking only to him.

When he felt her hand—concealed by the red-and-white checked tablecloth—drop onto his leg, he was sure of it.

There was something really hot about having a woman you were supposed to just be casually friends with feel you up under a dinner table. Especially when that table was filled with curious family members who would love to see any sign of interest between the only two singles there.

Izzie was careful. So they definitely didn't see her hand creep up his leg to trace the outline of his dick. That, he assumed, would be taken as a definite sign of interest.

He was going to make the woman pay for her sensual torment. Right now, however, he was enjoying it too much to try slipping his hand down to beat her at her own game.

The conversation soon resumed, Izzie falling into it as if she'd never been away. She traded barbs with his brothers, reminisced with his sister Lottie about their school days.

She fit. She just fit. Like a normal neighborhood girl.

But no normal neighborhood girl he knew would be working Nick's zipper down, reaching in and pulling him free of his trousers. She definitely wouldn't be brushing the tips of her wicked fingers across his cock, arousing him until he hardened into her hand.

This was incredibly dangerous. If someone dropped a fork and bent over to get it, they'd get an eyeful.

But Nick didn't give a damn. Maybe he and Izzie couldn't be the "normal" couple the neighborhood would like to see. Somehow, though, this was *better*. Having an erotic secret… and acting on that secret in public where they could be exposed, it was mind-blowing.

It made him hot. It made him desperate.

It made him finish his dinner quickly and declare himself so tired he had to call it a night.

And thankfully, Izzie found an excuse of her own, followed him out the door, and led him to her place for another long night of the wildest sex he'd ever had.

9

"HOW ARE YOU FEELING, Rose? All better?" Holding the back door of Leather and Lace open for her early Saturday evening, Harry watched her closely, as if worried she wasn't up to dancing tonight.

Izzie had to stop for a moment to wonder why. Then she remembered. *Crap.* She'd called in sick the previous Sunday night. Probably really leaving him in the lurch.

"I'm fine, Harry," she said as she walked past him into the building, watching him shut and lock the door behind her. Security had improved around here ever since Nick had been hired. "I am so sorry about last Sunday night."

Harry waved an unconcerned hand. "Hey, don't worry about it, something wicked had to be going around for three of you to get knocked on your butts."

"*Three* of us?"

Harry nodded. "Leah got sick Saturday night."

"I remember."

"She came back in Sunday evening, was here for two hours, got sick all over again and had to leave. So did Jackie."

Jackie was Leah's dressing roommate. Whatever was going around had obviously nailed both of them.

Izzie was about to open her mouth to confess that she really had not been sick—just cowardly. But before she could do it, the back door was unlocked from the outside and opened again. She knew before she even saw him that Nick had arrived.

She recognized his warm, masculine scent. And her nipples got hard. Oh, yeah, it was definitely Nick.

His gaze immediately went to her, hot and appreciative. She'd had to leave his bed early this morning to go to work at the bakery. But right before she'd gone, he'd whispered how much he looked forward to seeing her tonight in her dressing room…which now, he'd made sure last weekend, had a lock.

She'd shivered all day, thinking of that first night he'd been in there, when he'd seen her naked reflection. *Mmm.*

"Nick," Harry said with a nod. He looked back and forth between the two of them. "No more mask, Rose?"

Smiling, she shook her head. "I've decided I trust him."

Nick returned the smile, the two of them sharing a silent intimacy that excluded Harry, though he stood right beside them. Finally, though, Nick broke the stare and addressed their boss. "Everything looking okay so far?"

Harry nodded. "Been kind of a quiet week. Last night was the slowest Friday we've had in a while." Glancing at Izzie, he added, "But I bet the crowd will be roaring back to see you."

"Are you short-staffed again?" she asked, wondering if Harry would need her to dance an extra set.

He shook his head. "Everybody's here, sound and healthy."

"What do you mean?" Nick asked, a frown furrowing his brow.

Harry began to explain about the sick dancers, which made Izzie feel guilty again. Especially when he groaned over how hard it had been to tell Delilah, his "retired" wife that she wasn't in shape to go on in their place. Oy. She wouldn't have wanted to see the redhead's expression during that conversation.

Something else she didn't want to do was have to look Nick in the eye and admit she'd called in sick rather than face him last weekend. She figured he knew that much, but didn't particularly feel the need to confirm it.

Excusing herself, she headed to her dressing room. The door wasn't locked, but she immediately noticed the deadbolt, which had not been there the previous weekend.

"You sneaky man," she whispered with a smile as she dropped her purse and keys on the vanity. She could think of several wicked ways Nick could help her kill time between her numbers.

Of course, being the hard-ass guy he was when on the job, she suspected he might resist her. That was okay. Izzie had found she was pretty good at working around his resistance.

Having stood most of the day at work, she wanted to relax before going onstage. Kicking her shoes off her feet, she pulled her chair out from under the makeup vanity and sat down at it.

She immediately heard a cracking sound, but didn't register what it was until the chair broke apart beneath her, sending her crashing to the floor. "Son of a bitch," she snapped as she lay still on the tile. The back of her head had scraped the concrete block wall on the other side as she'd fallen. She rubbed at it, shocked to see a few flecks of fresh blood on her fingertips.

"Izzie? Are you all right? What was that noise?" Nick asked as he burst into the room.

He swung the door open so hard he almost hit her with it. An inch closer and she would have taken a flat piece of oak square in the face.

"Oh, my God." He immediately dropped into a squat beside her. "You're hurt."

"It's okay," she insisted, slowly sitting up.

He put his hand under her arm to help her. "What happened?"

"My chair broke," she admitted, almost embarrassed about it. She'd never fully gotten over that chubby girl terror of breaking a chair in public.

"Is that blood on your fingers?" he asked, his voice so taut it almost snapped.

She lifted it to the back of her head again. "Yeah, I scraped my head on the wall when I fell."

"You need to go to the hospital." He rose and tugged her up, too. "Come on, I'll take you right now."

"No, Nick, I don't. I didn't bang my head, I promise. I just scratched it on the way down."

He frowned, obviously not believing her.

"Check and see for yourself. I swear, it's nothing but a scratch." She turned around, tilting her head back so he could see the spot where the blood had come from.

Nick gently pushed her hair out of the way. Izzie watched him in the mirror, seeing the frantic expression on his handsome face. And the way his jaw clenched as he tenderly examined her.

He was worried about her. Truly afraid for her.

"See?" she asked softly.

"Looks like a scratch," he admitted.

"Good."

"But that doesn't mean you're not hurt anywhere else. God, Izzie, what the hell happened?"

She gestured toward the remains of the chair, in pieces at her feet. "It fell apart as soon as I sat on it." Glaring at him, she added, "No big butt jokes."

He rolled his eyes. "As if." Stepping away, he ran his hands up and down her arms. "You're sure you're not hurt anywhere else?"

She was hurt elsewhere. Her hip was killing her from where she'd banged on the floor. But thankfully, she hadn't landed on her bum knee. "I'm okay."

Nick shook his head, muttering something, then bent down to examine the pieces of the chair. It was a sturdy rolling one that easily slid around when Izzie needed to reach something on the vanity. But it had fallen apart into several pieces.

"This doesn't make any damn sense." His tone was curt, all business now. "How could it just fall apart like that?"

"I have no clue. Maybe it was just defective."

Nick didn't even look up. He was poking around in the pile, picking up a couple of screws and staring at them hard.

"Rose? Nick? Is everything okay? Somebody heard a crash."

Glancing at the door, she saw Harry Black, and, right behind him, one of the bouncers. They both stared wide-eyed from her, down to Nick and the broken chair.

"Are you okay, honey?" Harry asked.

"Can I help you up?" the bouncer, Bernie, her self-appointed watchdog, asked.

"I'm fine. Just a little mishap."

"She could have been badly hurt," Nick barked.

"But I wasn't," she murmured, trying to calm all three down. If Nick was like a protective lion, Harry was like a fatherly teddy bear. And Bernie was like a big grizzly somebody had poked with a stick. They all looked equally upset.

"It's okay, I swear. Just an accident. Now, if you don't mind, Harry, could you find me another chair? I need to get ready to go on." The older man nodded and backed out of the door, taking Bernie with him.

Glancing at Nick, she added, "You need to get to work, too, making sure everything is safe and secure for me to perform."

He slowly rose, his eyes locked on hers. "Are you really worried about something, or are you trying to get rid of me?"

Izzie offered him a cocky grin, put her hand on his chest, and pushed him toward the door. "I'm trying to get rid of you. I have to be onstage in an hour, and with you in here oozing all that hot man stuff, I'm going to be tempted to test that lock and seduce you."

His eyes twinkled. But his frown remained. "You're not going to seduce me into forgetting you could have been hurt."

"And you're not going to bully me into forgetting I have a job to do."

He reached up and cupped her cheek. Izzie couldn't help curling into his hand, loving the roughness of his skin against her own. "I would never bully you into doing anything, Izzie."

They hadn't yet talked about her job. They'd officially been secret lovers for two wild, passion-filled nights, and she hadn't had a chance to even ask him if he was going to have some kind of macho problem with her dancing. Now he'd opened the door for the question.

"Are you going to be all right upstairs, watching me?"

He brushed his thumb over her jaw. "I love watching you."

Nibbling on his finger, she murmured, "I meant, will you be okay watching everyone else watch me?"

His jaw stiffened and his dark eyes flashed. But he didn't pull away. Instead, he drew closer, tipping her head back so sweetly, so tenderly, she knew he was still worried she could be hurt. "Izzie, I can't promise anything because I haven't experienced it yet. But I can tell you this…I know and want the real you…both sides of you. The Rose and the woman you become when you walk out of this place every Sunday night. I'm in this with *both* of you."

Without saying anything more, he bent down and covered her mouth with his, kissing her sweetly and tenderly. Then, with one more brush of his hand on her face, he turned and walked out.

As it turned out, Nick did not have to test himself to see how he'd handle watching Izzie strip for other men. Because before she ever went onstage, Nick was forced to deal with a couple of punks who didn't understand the rules of a place as upscale as this one. One of them had made a move on a waitress, another had lunged at a dancer. Nick and Bernie plucked the guys up and dragged them out the front door, where, high on liquid courage, they'd both tried to put up a fight.

Maybe it was the residual anger he'd felt at seeing the blood on Izzie's fingertips. Or maybe it was the rage that flooded his head at the thought that it could have been Izzie the prick had grabbed, but as soon as the guy threw the first punch, Nick reacted harshly.

He'd had a few fights in his day, both before his military days and during them. And it was painfully easy to take down a drunk. The fight was over almost immediately after it had begun. Bernie dispatched of the drunk's friend just as quickly and the two of them nodded to each other in appreciation for the backup.

"Thanks, man," Bernie said.

"Not a problem."

Bernie shook the bleary patron. "I think this is the same prick who grabbed Rose a month ago."

Nick's jaw went rock-hard. If the man hadn't already been in Bernie's firm grip, he might have found a reason to throw another punch. But he was a fair fighter and wouldn't do something so out of bounds.

Unless the guy got free…then all was fair.

The guy didn't get free, Bernie had a tight grip and had begun chewing him out for harassing Rose. That incident had obviously been a more serious one than Nick had been led to believe, because Bernie hadn't forgotten a moment of it.

Because things had gotten physical, Nick decided to cover

his own ass, as well as the bouncer's and the club's, and called the police. He wanted this thing on record, now, when there were plenty of witnesses who'd seen both the assault on the female workers inside, and the provocation in the parking lot.

It was just his bad luck that Mark heard the call to Leather and Lace and decided to respond. Nick saw his brother get out of his unmarked car and saunter over, smiling widely. "Get in a fight without me?"

"Just doing my job," Nick replied, trying to figure out a way to get Mark to leave without going inside the club. If he was on duty, it wouldn't have been an issue—his brother was too good a cop to go inside a strip club while on duty. But he knew Mark's hours. No way was he working this late on a Saturday. "What are you doing here, anyway?"

"I heard it on the scanner. Noelle was already in bed—that woman goes to sleep by eight every night now. So I thought I'd head on over and see if you were okay."

"You know this guy?" one of the officers asked.

"My baby brother," Mark replied, his dimples flashing.

"By ten minutes," Nick said, shaking his head.

It took about an hour to clear up matters outside. Nick had stayed near the entrance, far from the stage, but he'd gotten reports from the bouncers about what was going on inside. So he knew when Izzie had performed...and when she was finished.

She'd done her first number and wouldn't be back on for at least an hour or two. Long enough to get rid of his brother.

"Come on, let me buy you a beer," Mark said once the last of the police cars pulled away.

"I'm working."

"Okay, then you buy me a beer." Not taking no for an answer, he threw his arm across Nick's shoulder and tugged him into the club. "Come on, I've never been in this place."

"Noelle probably wouldn't like it."

"I'm visiting my twin at work. No harm in that, is there?"

"Depends on whether you visited me blindfolded."

"I'll keep my back to the stage," Mark said. "Seriously, we haven't talked in weeks. I know something's going on with you."

His twin was right. They had been...disconnected. Not just because of what had been going on with Nick and Izzie, but also because his brother was about to become a father. Mark had changed. He had different priorities, talked a different language, looked at the world a different way.

Noelle and their baby were his family now. Oh, sure, he loved the rest of the Santoris, but he'd crossed that threshold from son and brother to husband and father.

Nick was the only one of the Santori siblings who had not.

"Let's sit out here," Mark said, nodding toward a couple of low, round tables in an outer chamber between the lobby and the main lounge area. They were out of view of the stage.

Nick wasn't surprised. Mark was a good husband. Like the rest of their brothers.

"All right." Gesturing to one of the waitresses, he ordered a club soda for himself and a beer for his brother. Returning to the table, he sat down across from his twin. "Can't be away for too long, though."

Mark settled back into the leather chair. "Nice."

"Yeah, it is."

"Good fringe benefits?"

Holding back a smile, Nick just shook his head.

"Hey, I'm married, these days are long gone. Throw me a bone."

"Throw me one," Nick replied before thinking better of it. "Tell me what it's like."

Mark frowned, obviously confused by the question. "It?"

"Marriage. What's it like being tied down, committed?"

Those deep dimples that had charmed girls from the time he was two years old flashed in Mark's cheeks. "It's the best. Noelle's everything I ever wanted."

"Yeah, but how'd you know what you wanted?" Nick muttered as he lifted his drink and downed half of it.

Chuckling, Mark admitted, "I didn't. I think it was more of a case of meeting her, and *knowing* that whatever I eventually did figure out I wanted for my life, she'd be part of it. It was always her. Everything else fell into place around her."

Somehow, that made a lot of sense to Nick. Because even though he'd been thinking of dozens of reasons why he and Izzie couldn't make it work—the primary one being that she didn't *want* it to—he couldn't help hoping it would. Because, as Mark had said, he suspected she was the one. That whatever else happened in his life, whatever direction he went in, whatever he chose, he'd want her to be a part of it.

Surprisingly, his brother didn't press him about why he was asking so many questions. Probably not because he didn't care—or didn't suspect there was a reason behind them. But because he knew Nick well enough to know that pushing for answers usually only made him clam up tighter.

Nick appreciated the courtesy. And realized yet again just how much he'd missed his twin.

"Hey Nick, we got a live one at the bar," a woman said.

Glancing over, Nick saw one of the waitresses, who was rolling her eyes. "Serious?"

"Not yet. But he could be if he's not handled right."

"I'll be there in a minute." Addressing his brother, he added, "Is there a full moon out tonight? The crazies are out."

Mark stood. "Yeah, including me. I must be crazy to be out here with you instead of home in bed with my wife."

Feeling better than he had in the hours since Izzie's accident with the chair, Nick reached out and grabbed his brother for a quick hug. Mark's eyes widened. He was the demonstrative one, not Nick. "What's that for?"

Nick shook his head. "I don't know. Give it to your wife."

"I've got plenty of my own to give," Mark said with a grin. "But thanks just the same."

The rest of the evening went by quickly, with more of the same insanity to deal with. Nick hadn't been kidding—the crazies were out tonight, and a lot of them had decided to show up at the club. The bouncers had had to forcibly eject more guys in this one evening than he'd seen them eject in the past month.

The only positive thing about keeping so busy was that Nick missed the Crimson Rose's final performance of the evening, too. He hadn't even realized she was on until he heard the thunderous applause, whoops and whistles of her audience. But at that point, he'd been outside, doing a sweep of parking lot to make sure none of their uninvited patrons had decided to come back.

Fortunately, they hadn't. But there were still other issues to deal with, like his conversation with Harry about Izzie's broken chair. She had called it an accident…and it might have been one. But he wasn't taking any chances. He and Harry had talked about adding security cameras to the basement area of the club, to hook into the system already covering the upstairs. Izzie's accident had confirmed the idea for both of them.

Just in case.

Saying goodbye to Harry, he headed downstairs, glancing at his watch. It was after two, the club was closed, everyone drifting out. But he knew she'd have waited. She wouldn't have left without seeing him. Partly because she'd want to see his reaction to her act. Partly because she knew he'd kill her if she'd walked out to her car alone.

"Iz?" he asked, knocking lightly on her dressing room door.

She opened it immediately. "Hi." She was nibbling on her bottom lip and her hands were clenched in front of her. Rather than being dressed to go home, she wore just a slinky robe. Thankfully, though, the mask and hairpieces were gone.

"You doing okay?"

She nodded, then looked at him through half-lowered eyelids. "Um, so? What'd you think?"

He reached for her and drew her into his arms. "I didn't see you dance."

"What?"

"Sorry, other stuff was going on."

"I heard there were some problems."

"Yep."

She fisted her hands and put them on her hips. The pose did really nice things, like pulling her short pink robe apart at the neck to reveal the lush, upper curves of her breasts.

"You're telling me you just happened to have to deal with various crises during the exact times I was on stage? And that was simply coincidence?"

She might not believe it, but it was true. At least, he *thought* it was. He guessed he could have done the parking lot sweep a few minutes earlier or later. He hadn't evaluated his decision before. But now, looking back…well, maybe something inside him had made sure he didn't have to see other men looking at the beautiful body of the woman he considered his.

"You're *sure* you're going to be all right with this?" Her chin went up. "I won't be able to handle it if you go all Cro-

Magnon man and try to drag me by the hair back to your cave."

"You woman. Me man," he said, slipping his hands down and parting her robe further. He nuzzled into her neck, breathing in her essence, realizing twenty-four hours had been far too long to go without making love to her. "Me got heap big appetite."

She swatted at his shoulder. But she didn't back up. "You're such a dork."

Nick had *never* been called that, or anything like it, in his entire life. Ass maybe. Jerk. Cold-hearted pig, on one occasion. But never a dork. And it surprised a laugh out of him.

She delighted him. Simply brought every good feeling that existed inside him out into the open.

"God, I love being with you," he muttered, unable to help revealing a little bit of what he was feeling.

"I know, I feel the same way."

She didn't admit that easily, the words had come haltingly out of her mouth. Which made Nick value them that much more.

He moved his mouth down, sampling her collarbone.

"Did you put that lock on my door yourself?" she whispered as she tilted her head farther, silently begging for more.

He nodded, continue to kiss and lick, lower now, to the curves of her breasts, beautifully bare under the robe.

"Let's use it."

"My thoughts exactly," he murmured.

He didn't let her go, he simply reached back and flipped the lock, then dipped down lower to lick his way down her to her pert nipple. Flicking it with his tongue, he waited until she was quivering to cover it with his mouth and suckle her.

"Mmm…more."

Nick stroked her sides, his thumbs meeting near her belly button and scraping lower to tease the top edge of her pretty pink panties. With one last sweet suck on her breast he moved down her, following the path his hands had taken.

Izzie moaned softly, swaying on her feet. Nick kept her steady as he kissed his way down the front of her body. The soft robe brushed his face. So did her soft skin.

"Do you know what I wanted to do to you the first time I came into this room?"

She tangled her hands in his hair as he dropped lower, kneeling on the floor in front of her. "I think I have an idea."

He pressed his face in her belly, licking at that tender bit of skin right above her pelvic bone, slowly pushing her panties down as he dipped lower.

"Did it involve that nice, big, flat surface in front of the mirror?" she asked.

Smart girl. "Uh-huh." Gently holding her hips, he flicked at the panties, watching appreciatively as she shimmied out of them. The robe fell, too. Under the bright light bulbs ringing the mirror, he was able to see every glorious inch of her. But he wanted to see more—didn't want his view blocked even by her pretty brown curls. So he turned her and edged her back until her bottom brushed the edge of the vanity top.

"Wait," he said, suddenly remembering her accident. Wrapping his hand around the edge of the vanity counter, he tugged at it sharply, testing the shelf's sturdiness. It remained firmly in place, well secured into the wall.

"Good," she murmured. Rising on her tiptoes, she slid onto the vanity, parting her legs just the way he wanted her to.

Someone had brought her another chair, and Nick grabbed it, sitting on it directly in front of her. Reaching for her knees, he slowly pushed them apart, watching a pink flush rise through her entire body.

She made no effort to resist. Confident. Sensual. Incredibly seductive. She knew what he wanted and she wanted it, too.

He pushed her legs further, until he could see the glisten of moisture on the sensitive slit between her legs. "Do you have any idea how beautiful you are?" he asked.

It was a rhetorical question. She couldn't possibly know how beautiful she looked to him, wanton and aroused, opening herself up so he could pleasure them both.

He couldn't wait any longer. With a low groan of need, Nick dropped his face to that sweet, warm spot. He lapped at her in one slow, long lick, feeling her thighs quiver beside his face.

Izzie tilted up for him, inviting him further, and he sampled her again. "You taste just as good without the cannoli, Cookie," he mumbled.

She managed a choppy laugh. "Don't call me Cookie."

"Can't help it." He nibbled his way up to catch her erect clit between his lips. He played with it even as he scraped his fingers across her swollen sex. She was drenched and ready to take whatever he wanted to give her. Wanting that warm, wet flesh wrapped around part of him while he continued to savor her with his mouth, he slipped a finger inside her.

"Mmm," she groaned. "More. More of everything."

He complied. Licking harder and sucking deeper, he slid another finger into her, then slowly moved them in and out, timing his strokes to her helpless moans.

With one more swirl of his tongue on her most sensitive spot, Izzie cried out and climaxed. He wanted to be part of that climax, to experience the spasms of her body as she clenched and shook. Standing, he tugged his shirt up and off, then unfastened his belt and pants and pushed them down, out of the way.

When he looked up again, Izzie had slid down to stand before him. He frowned. "I wasn't *nearly* done."

Her eyes sparkled. "Neither was I." Then, with an Eve-like smile on her face, she turned around, facing away from him, until they were both looking in the mirror. She slowly bent forward, putting her hands flat on the vanity, curving that sweet ass back in pure, unspoken invitation.

His pulse roared. "You're sure…"

"Oh, I'm *very* sure," she promised him. She was still smiling, her eyes still glittered in avarice and hunger. "It's *your* turn to take *me,* Nick."

Remembering the way he'd begged her to take him the other night at his place, he nodded in lazy agreement. "Oh, honey, you can't imagine how much I want to take you like this."

Making love to her face to face—watching her incredible eyes widen with pleasure, and her sweet mouth fall open on every long sigh—was amazing. He knew he'd never tire of doing it.

But the idea of taking her like *this*—with raw, hot passion—excited him beyond reason. He'd be able to see her expressions in the mirror, be able to plunge deeper than ever before until he imprinted himself somewhere deep inside her. Deep enough that, perhaps, she might never want to let him go.

"Nick," she begged, "please." She arched again, those long, dancer's legs putting her curvy butt directly in line with his cock. She backed into him, as he moved forward to her.

He held her full hips in both hands, bending a little so he could see her sweet entrance and ease his way into it. She hissed and arched, trying to take him deeper, but powerless. His hands held her firmly, he was setting the pace.

And he planned to go slowly, wanting to savor every second of the experience.

"Give it to me," she begged, watching him with desperation.

He smiled at her in the mirror and thrust forward a tiny bit. Rewarded by her gasp and the flare of her eyes, he pulled out again. This time, she didn't beg for more, she simply licked her lips and watched, trusting him to make it good.

He didn't make it good. He made it amazing. By the time he finally sunk all the way into her tight heat, Izzie was whimpering. And by the time he began to lose his mind and thrust wildly, in and out, over and over, she was practically sobbing.

He thought they were alone in the building. But he couldn't be sure. "Izzie…," he said, slowing to ease out of her, to calm them both a little, "…wait."

"Don't stop."

"I'm not stopping, sweetheart," he said. Then he stopped. She whimpered, watching him, then realized he was turning her around. "I have to kiss you, Iz," he murmured.

She twisted in his arms to face him, twining her arms around his neck and one leg around his waist. Plunging his tongue in her mouth, he tangled it with hers keeping his eyes open so he could stare into her beautiful face. Lifting her back up onto the vanity, he went right back into her, deep and fast, knowing this last stretch would be a quick, pulsing one.

"Sweet heaven, you amaze me," she whispered against his mouth as he filled her again.

"Amazing. Yeah."

Those were the only words he could manage. Wanting to be connected with her everywhere, he kissed her again, wrapped his arms tightly around her body and drew her up against him.

Stroking and thrusting, he rocked into her with every bit of himself, her cries of pleasure echoing sweetly in his ears. And when he finally heard those cries turned into desperate gasps as she climaxed, he let himself go, too, erupting inside her until he was completely empty.

"HEY HOT STUFF, you're looking delicious again today."

Bridget jerked her head up, blinking the columns of numbers out of her brain as someone stepped into her office

Sunday afternoon. She knew it wasn't Dean...he didn't speak to her like that, which was good. She wanted him to notice her, wanted him to realize she was interested in him. But she definitely didn't want a man who'd speak to her so coarsely.

"Oh, hi," she said, seeing one of the salesmen standing in the doorway. The guy, Ted, was a middle-aged divorcé with a phlegmy chuckle. He also had what she and her friends in middle school used to call Roman hands and Russian fingers.

He was grabby. Touchy. But he'd never gone too far beyond pats on her shoulder. She hoped that wasn't about to change.

Ted wore his usual ugly striped sports coat over a dingy dress shirt and a red tie. In other words, he looked a mess. Usually, she saw him as a kind of sad guy whose wife had dumped him. He was smarmy and coarse, but had never given her any reason to be wary of him personally. Now, however, goosebumps had prickled her body and tension throbbed in her temple.

She didn't like the look in his eye.

"You dressing like that just for me, hot stuff?" he asked as he sauntered into the office.

"I think that question would be called sexual harassment," she said as she stared hard at him, hoping he'd take the warning as a threat and get out now, before he'd gone too far.

When he smiled and pushed the door shut behind him, she had a sinking feeling he'd *already* gone too far.

Damn. She should have left an hour ago. It was four o'clock, an hour after the dealership closed on Sundays. And she had to assume everyone else had gone home. Ted hadn't been around since this morning. Judging by the whiff of alcohol she caught wafting off him, she figured he'd gone for a long lunch at a local bar.

Dean, why didn't you show up? She'd thought for sure he'd

be here. He'd worked every weekend since he started. That was the only reason Bridget had come in herself today...to see him!

It had been for nothing. She'd worn another short, sexy skirt that she'd bought at a cute local clothing store last night. That, with the silky sleeveless shell that draped across her curves invitingly would have been enough to get the man's temperature rising. And he hadn't even been here to see it.

Instead, Ted was. *Ick.*

"Girl, you have been hiding your light under a bushel." He stepped closer. "It's closing time. Let's go have some fun."

"No, thank you," she said, her tone icy. She stuffed her paperwork into a drawer. Normally, she'd be more tidy. Today, she was in a hurry. She wanted out of here.

"Aww, come on, sweetie, I know there's no man in your life. You must be lonely. Why don't you let me keep you company?"

She'd rather keep company with a dead skunk. "No, Ted."

Hopefully that firm tone would get the message across and he'd get out of her way and let her leave. But as she stood, Ted stepped between her desk and the door, right in her path. "You know you really want to stay."

"No. I *really* don't."

Trying once again to be like Izzie, she fisted one hand, retrieved her purse, and tried to walk past him.

He grabbed her arm. "Not even a few minutes conversation?"

"Not even that," she insisted, jerking her arm away.

Her angry tone and the heat in her eyes must have finally gotten through. Because Ted went from stupid drunk trying to *score* to angry drunk trying to *control* in one blink of her eyes. Without warning, he put both his hands on her shoulders and pushed her back. Bridget stumbled over her own high-heeled sandals, landing on her butt on the edge of her desk.

"Perfect." Dropping his hands onto her thighs, he crudely pushed her legs apart and forced his way between them.

"Let me go!"

"Not yet, hot stuff."

She reached around on the desk behind her, hoping she'd left her scissors or stapler out, but all she managed to grab was a small desk clock. Wrapping her fingers tightly around it, she swung, but only managed a glancing blow to Ted's shoulder.

His nostrils flared even as his eyes narrowed in anger. "Playing hard to get?"

"Let me go or I'll scream."

"Nobody to hear you, pretty thing," he said, any hint of charm gone from his voice as his true nature emerged.

Before she could say a thing—or think what to say—Bridget heard something that sounded like an angel. But it was no angel.

It was Dean Willis. *Roaring.*

"Get the hell off her you son of a bitch."

Suddenly he was. Ted was lifted off her and tossed to the side of the room. Bridget saw him land hard against the wall and crumple to the floor. He yelped in either fear or pain. Or both.

He had reason to be afraid. Dean was already reaching for him, his face red, his body emanating danger. "You're dead."

Ted's bravado when facing her disappeared under this new threat. Before Dean could even grab him, he'd launched himself to his feet and run out the door, leaving the two of them alone. The whole thing—from Ted's entrance to his speedy departure—had taken place in under three minutes.

Her head was spinning. Breathing hard and shaking a little, she mumbled, "Thank you so much."

Dean swung around to look at her, that blood rage still evident on his face. His blue eyes were like matching chips of ice. He looked as much like a cute, nice-guy car salesman as she looked like Xena the Warrior Princess.

No. This was not gentle, good-natured Dean. This was a dangerous man in a high fury. And her shivers of fear turned to shivers of excitement.

"What the hell happened?"

Still sitting on the desk, she could only shake her head. "He obviously had been drinking. He came back and caught me alone. It's the first time he's ever…I mean, he's a creep, but I never thought he'd…"

"Maybe if you'd wear clothes that didn't scream 'do me' men wouldn't try."

Bridget's jaw dropped and she stared at him in shock. "What did you say to me?"

"Look at you," he snapped, stepping closer. He pointed to her legs, still splayed open on the desk.

Bridget tried to jerk them back together, but Dean stepped between them before she could do it. With absolutely no warning, he plunged his hands into her hair and bent to cover her lips with his. He thrust his tongue in her mouth, tasting her, devouring her. His body was hard against hers, his hips between her thighs, and Bridget couldn't even try to deny the absolute flood of heat that roared through her in response.

She wrapped her arms around his neck, tilting her head to kiss him back just as deeply. And for a long, heady moment, they made crazy, wild love with their mouths.

Then the moment ended. Dean let her go and staggered back a few steps. "Bridget, I'm…"

She put her hand up, palm out, to stop him. Sliding off the desk, she straightened her skirt and said, "Don't. Okay? Just don't say anything. I wanted that. Maybe I *needed* it just so I could wash Ted out of my memory. I didn't exactly jump up there and part my legs—he pushed me."

Dean instinctively swung his head to look at the door, that tense rage returning.

"He's long gone. Thank you for coming in when you did."

He ran both hands through his hair, his anger finally draining away. "I'll take care of him, Bridget."

"Marty will deal with him." She stepped closer, offering him a tremulous smile. Because now there was no doubt that Dean's interest in her was one of more than friendship. That kiss—and his body's hard, instinctive reaction to it—told her he wanted more. Maybe as much as she did. "I guess that makes you my hero, huh?"

Dean stared at her, his eyes softening, the tension easing. Reaching for her, he pulled her into his arms. But this time, he didn't attempt to kiss her. His embrace was pure, sweet comfort. He held her tightly, running his hand up and down her back. "I'm sorry. Sorry for what he did...sorry for what I said."

"It's all right. You were angry." Tilting her head back, she smiled up at him. "I thought it was kinda sexy."

For a second—a brief one—she thought he was going to smile back. To laugh, then lower his mouth to hers and kiss her again, gently this time.

But it didn't happen. Instead, Dean sighed heavily and his mouth drew tight. "I'm also sorry for kissing you. I should never have done that."

"I've been wanting you to..."

He put his hand up to stop her. "Don't. It was a mistake, Bridget. A big one. And it won't be repeated."

She gasped, unable to believe he was rejecting her. *Again.*

"What is your *problem?*" she asked, completely indignant.

He just shook his head. "I don't have a problem. I just

can't...don't want...hell, Bridget, this just can't happen." As if needing to convince himself, as much as her, he reiterated.
"It *won't* happen."

10

W<small>HEN</small> N<small>ICK</small> <small>MANAGED</small> to get through another evening at Leather and Lace *without* watching her dance, Izzie got a little nervous. She didn't want to ask him about it over the next few nights since they were having such an amazing time doing wildly sensual things to one another. But she couldn't help wondering.

On Sunday night, he'd been too *busy* to watch her dance. Or so he'd claimed. He'd conveniently had to go put out another fire in the club every time she was scheduled to go on.

Suspicious. She didn't want to be, but she was.

He'd said he could handle it…but he wasn't acting like he even wanted to try.

It wasn't that she didn't understand. In fact, putting herself in his shoes, she'd have to say she'd probably have a major problem with other women looking at *her* naked man with covetous eyes, thinking of ways they could have that incredible body and handsome face.

Her man. Her man? Oh, God, had he somehow become *her* man?

Sitting in her apartment, she realized that yes, at some point in recent weeks, Nick *had* become her man.

Maybe it had been when he'd made love to her in the back of the van. Or when he'd cared for her after she'd fallen in her dressing room. Maybe it was because of his sexy smile and the intimate way he watched her when he thought no one was looking.

Maybe it was even because of the way she'd felt every single time she'd woken up in his arms.

Those pre-dawn moments. Yeah. They'd probably done it.

Because each time it had happened—whether at his apartment, or hers, she'd had to lie there and watch him sleep. Study the line of his jaw and the curve of his cheek. Wonder how a man could have such a sensuous mouth and still be so damned tough. Note the small scars on his body, and his tattoo, and grieve for the things he must have gone through as a soldier.

Yes. In those moments, her heart had opened up. And she'd let him in just as surely as she'd let him in her body.

There were moments when she allowed herself not to care. To even consider whether they could make this crazy relationship of theirs work. *Maybe a masked wedding…the Crimson Rose and the sexy night watchman.*

That was *so* lame.

But it was no more crazy to think about than the idea of an official union between Izzie Natale and Nick Santori of Taylor Street.

"Would that really be so bad?" she whispered. She'd been telling herself it would, but at moments like this, she had a hard time remembering why.

"I need sugar," she mumbled as she headed for her kitchen, dying for something sweet. She'd been so good at the bakery and tried to resist temptation, so she never brought any of that stuff home. At moments like these, though, she regretted it.

Nick had called a while ago, saying he'd be leaving the pizzeria in an hour and would come by. She glanced at her watch, wondering if she had time to run to the corner market. She was so desperate she'd go for a packet of Ho Hos at this point.

Before she could grab her shoes and dash for something to binge on, her cell phone rang. Glancing at the caller ID and recognizing the New York City number, she immediately began to smile, now knowing another sure-fire way to escape—at least mentally—from her troubles.

"V!" she exclaimed as she answered.

"Girl-*friend!*" was the reply. "It has been for-*evah,* where have you been?"

Plopping down on the sofa, Izzie kicked her feet up and leaned back, so happy to hear a voice from her old life, she wondered if fate had sent Vanessa's call as some kind of mental gift. Vanessa was a good friend from her Rockette days. The striking, long-legged African American woman had been Izzie's roommate on the road and the two of them had hit it off from their very first hotel stay, when they'd both decided to call for room service French fries at two in the morning, despite the matron's orders to go to sleep by eleven o'clock.

"I'm still in Chicago."

"Still doing that bakery thing?" Vanessa asked, sounding completely shocked. "I can't believe you've lasted this long."

"Join the club. I sometimes forget I haven't spent the past seven years with my arms in cookie dough up to my elbows."

"How's your father?

"Getting better every day, already pestering my mother to let him go back to work."

"That's great. And as soon as he does you can quit."

Yes, she could. Why that idea would send a shot of sadness through her, Izzie didn't know. It wasn't as if she liked working at the bakery. Even if she *had* made friends with all the staff, gotten on a first-name basis with their restaurant clients and the regulars who stopped in every day for breakfast.

Well, maybe she did like it. A little. But certainly not enough to want to stay there permanently.

Vanessa laughed softly. "And then you can come home. You still thinking of choreographing, or teaching?"

She had been, though, not as much lately. But she didn't tell Vanessa that.

Fortunately, her friend quickly moved on. "You've got to come back soon. You are so missing out." Launching into an explanation of all the things that had been going on—with the Rockettes, and in her personal life, Vanessa soon had Izzie laughing so hard she had to wipe tears from her eyes. The other woman was a wild one, and the ballsiest female she'd ever known.

The stories were entertaining, particularly when told with Vanessa's flair. But even as she laughed, Izzie couldn't help wondering whether her friend was truly happy. She sounded a little…empty. Lonely. Bored.

Which made Izzie suddenly remember the way she'd been feeling right before she'd hurt her leg.

Very much the same way.

All the things Vanessa had been describing were things Izzie had been doing the past few years in New York. She missed none of them. Honestly, all she really missed were her friends and her apartment. The lifestyle she'd already begun to outgrow even before she'd been forced to leave it.

Going back to it didn't sound very palatable.

She shook off that crazy thought—not go back to her life? Insane. Like she had anything better going on *here?* "So which guy did you shove in the fountain?"

"The French dude. Pierre from Paris. Only, I think his name was probably really Petey from Poughkepsie or something. He wasn't French any more than my dry wheat toast was French this morning." Sighing, her friend added, "Why do men suck so bad?"

"Not all of them," she said before thinking better of it.

Vanessa caught the tone in her voice and leapt on it. "Talk. Who is he? What's he do? When did you start doing him?"

Having had no one to truly confide in since she'd been here…about her feelings, her relationship with Nick, even a bit about her sexy weekend job, she found herself spilling all of it to Vanessa. She must have talked for a solid five minutes without letting her friend get a word in. Finally realizing that, she whispered, "You still there?"

Vanessa murmured, "Oh, honey. This is serious."

Yes. It was. Very serious.

"This Nick, I remember you talking about him."

Izzie was afraid of that. Nick had always been—for her— the dream guy she'd never landed.

Now she'd landed him. She just didn't know if she was going to get to keep him. Or if he even *wanted* her to, considering he hadn't been able to bring himself to watch her dance again at the club.

"He might be a man worth settling down for, Izzie. Giving up your dancing…wait, what the hell did you say is the name of this place you're dancing at?"

She should have known that would interest her friend more than any potential romance. "It's called Leather and Lace."

"Holy shit, girl, you're strippin'."

"Yeah. I'm stripping. And I'm having the time of my life." Well, the stripping wasn't giving her the time of her life. Nick was. But she'd already talked enough about Nick.

Vanessa demanded all the details on Izzie's secret life, not sounding the least judgmental, and asking a bunch of questions. "That sounds like *fun*. You know, I've thought about taking a strip-dance exercise class they offer at my health club, but there's a waiting list."

"You're joking."

"No, honey, I'm not. It is the hottest thing going— there's a three-month long list to get in this class and everybody I know is putting their name on it. If you come back, you need to teach me how and maybe I'll retire and we can start a school somewhere. Teach housewives how to shake their booties."

Izzie laughed softly at that silly idea. Then she thought of the word Vanessa had used. *If.* "What do you mean, *if* I come back? Why wouldn't I come back?"

Vanessa grew very quiet, as if working out what to say. Knowing her friend was street-wise in a way Izzie never had been, she very much wanted to hear it. Anything Vanessa put this much thought into had to be worth hearing.

Finally, her friend murmured, "Why would you come back here when the life you really want is there?"

"You think I want to be a *baker* for the rest of my life?" Izzie protested, shocked that her friend would even suggest it.

"I don't know whether you want to be a baker or a stripper. A pizza-delivery gal or a ballerina. All I know is that whatever you end up wanting to do, it'll be tied up with that man you've loved for half your life."

Izzie's jaw dropped. She flinched so hard the phone fell onto her lap. Scrambling to get it, she heard Vanessa's words echoing in her head. Especially because they'd come so quickly—mere minutes—after Izzie had been tearing herself apart to try to figure out just what she felt for Nick.

She really shouldn't have had to think about it so hard. She knew what she felt for Nick. It was the same thing she'd always felt for him, only deeper now, adult. Sensual. Mature.

Forever.

Vanessa was right. She loved him. Part of her knew she should resent that, since it had been what she'd feared—and why she'd thrown up walls between them when he'd first pursued her. But she already knew she didn't regret it. How could she regret feeling so emotionally alive for the first time in years?

"You still there?" her friend asked when Izzie finally brought the phone back up to her ear.

"I'm still here."

Vanessa chuckled. Then, in a very low voice, she added, "I better be in the wedding."

Then all Izzie heard was the dial tone.

"HEY, LITTLE BROTHER, when are you gonna come talk to the business lawyer with me and Pop?"

Nick stared at Tony, who'd followed him out the front door of Santori's Friday afternoon. He'd been planning to head up the block to Natale's. He had a real taste for cannoli. The fresh kind that could only be found in Izzie's kitchen.

Or in Izzie. But that was another kind of decadent dessert altogether.

"I dunno, Tony, I really haven't thought about it."

His brother frowned. "I don't get it. I thought it was all set. You know how much Pop wants to retire completely."

"Bullshit."

Chuckling, his brother nodded in agreement. "Okay. We know he won't ever get outta that kitchen until they pry his wooden spoon out of his hand for his own funeral. But I know he's hoping to get you settled."

Get Nick settled. It sounded so archaic. And constricting.

"If you're worried about coming in as a financial partner rather than just a working one, I am sure willing to let you buy in with some of that money you said you saved while you were in the service."

Honestly, that had been one of Nick's big concerns. He didn't want anyone covering his way, he liked to pay his fair share. And if he were seriously considering going into business with Tony, he would absolutely insist on those terms. He did have the money, he did have the desire to get involved in a successful business and help it grow.

But that business was not a pizzeria. He knew it in his heart. He just hadn't figured out how to tell the family that yet. "I haven't made any decisions."

Tony met his stare, obviously trying to figure out what was going on in Nick's head. Nick thought about how best to put into words that he didn't want the life his family had mapped out for him. But before either of them could say anything, Nick spotted Izzie walking up the street, coming up behind Tony. Considering his big brother was a mountain of a man, she probably hadn't even seen Nick yet.

The sight of her face brought a stupid smile to his. But he didn't give a damn. At least, not until his brother turned to look over his shoulder at whatever had made him so happy.

"Whoa-ho," Tony said, when he looked back at Nick. "Izzie? It's *Izzie?* Holy shit, Gloria's gonna love this."

"Gloria's not going to know about this," Nick muttered. Izzie was not twenty steps away and if she heard what they were talking about, she'd probably bolt. Then ignore him for the next week until he could work his way around her defenses again.

Damn, but the woman was prickly.

"Why not? Cripes, the family's been wanting you two to hook up forever."

"That's the problem. Izzie isn't the kind of woman who likes to do what's expected of her."

Maybe that's one reason they got along so well. Because

Nick felt exactly the same way about his family. He just hadn't been able to make that clear to them yet.

"Okay, I won't do anything to jinx it. But I don't know how long I'll be able to keep it from Gloria." Tony grinned, shaking his head back and forth. "The woman can get anything out of me with her sexy…"

"Don't want to hear it," Nick smoothly interjected. He continued to watch Izzie, realizing the exact moment when she spotted him. A quick grin flashed across her face. But when she saw who was with him, the grin disappeared.

"Hi, Tony. Nick," she murmured, reaching them. She sounded so cool and calm. As if she hadn't been in a huge tub of warm bubbles and cold champagne with him twelve hours ago, loving each other until the water got cold and the champagne got flat.

God, what a night. Another amazing one in Izzie's arms. He didn't know what he'd ever do without them.

"How's it going, little sister?" Tony asked, giving her a one-armed hug. "Sorry I couldn't make it to lunch at the folks' house Sunday. Work—it kills me." He glanced at Nick and wagged his eyebrows. "If only I had a partner to take up the slack."

Nick managed to suppress a sigh. Then he turned his attention to Izzie. "I was just on my way to the bakery. I'm jonesing for something sweet."

She chuckled. "I was last night, too. I almost dashed out and got a Ho Ho to tide me over until you…" She quickly snapped her mouth shut, remembering Tony was there.

His oldest brother had never been the king of tact. In fact, his wife affectionately called him Lunkhead. Well, *usually* affectionately. Right now, however, Tony managed to pull it off. "Well, it was great seeing you, Iz, but I have to get back to work. Nick, you're gonna swing by the bank after you go up to the bakery and grab us some of Izzie's fabulous cannolis?"

They had plenty of cannolis left in the restaurant, but, he

assumed, it was the best Tony could do on such short notice. "Sure, Tony. You bet."

They both watched Tony go back into the restaurant, with breezy hellos and good wishes to every customer he passed on the way back to the kitchen. When they were alone on the sidewalk, Izzie continued to stare at the glass restaurant door. Finally, she murmured, "He knows, doesn't he?"

Nick nodded. "Yeah."

"How?"

With a helpless shrug, he told her the truth. "He saw the look on my face when I saw you walking toward me just now."

She finally tore her gaze off the door and directed it toward him. Staring into his eyes, she searched for the meaning of what he'd said.

He didn't try to hide it. He was in love with Izzie and his eyes affirmed that, even if his mouth didn't.

He just didn't know if she'd *want* to see the truth there.

He understood why she wouldn't. Putting the reality of their feelings out there meant they had to deal with them. It meant she could accuse him of breaking their "secret lovers" deal and freeze him out of her life again.

It could also mean she'd acknowledge that she was falling for him, too. And that maybe they could make something work between them. Something good. Right.

Permanent.

"I can't handle this, Nick," she whispered, appearing stricken. "He'll tell Gloria."

"Not intentionally."

"And she'll blab to the known universe and the neighborhood will have me married and fat before winter and my parents will be eyeing a perfect little row house for us right up from theirs, getting our future kids on the waiting lists to go to Sacred Heart and St. Raphael's."

She sounded pained, as if the very idea of living that life devastated her. He understood why. Because he didn't want it, either. Any of it. Oh, he wanted Izzie, no doubt about it. But as for how they lived? Well, it wouldn't be like anything anybody on Taylor Street would understand.

But before he could reassure her, Izzie shook her head and started walking. "I can't talk about this now. Not here."

He fell into step beside her. "Tonight."

"I'm going to my parents tonight. My sister Mia's coming into town for the weekend and I had to promise to come for dinner—which I can't do tomorrow or Sunday."

In a normal relationship, she'd ask him to come with her. In a normal relationship, he'd do it.

They weren't normal, of course.

"Call me when you're done and I'll meet you at your place."

She hesitated, glancing at him from the corner of her eye. "I need a little time, Nick. Just a little time. Can we…maybe take a break until tomorrow?"

One night. She wasn't asking for much. But the thought of going without her tonight nearly killed him.

"All right, Izzie." He caught her arm, holding her elbow before she could stalk away. She looked frantically from side to side, as if to see if anyone was watching, but Nick didn't release her. "Don't panic," he ordered her. "Don't see trouble where there is none."

She flashed him a grateful smile, murmured, "I'm mentally kissing you goodbye," then tugged her arm free and walked away.

He mentally kissed her goodbye, too, until she disappeared into the bakery.

SPENDING FRIDAY NIGHT with her family actually turned out to be a very good experience. Izzie had been half-dreading it, since she'd felt like an alien among all of them since the day she'd gotten home. But something about this gathering was different. Maybe because Mia was home and therefore got a lot of the attention. Or because Gloria's boys were there—the grandsons always caused everything else to cease to exist for her parents.

Or maybe it was just because Izzie forced herself to relax. Not having to talk a lot meant she didn't have to watch every word she said. Didn't have to worry about letting something slip regarding her dancing—which they all assumed she'd given up entirely because of her knee.

Not being so on edge actually allowed her to relax and, to her shock, even enjoy herself.

She was still mulling it over the next day, remembering the smile on her father's face as he talked about returning to work soon. When he told her he'd been talking to his brother—who was about to retire—about coming to work with him at the bakery, Izzie began to see a silver lining in the cloud of her life. With another member of the family coming in to the business, the pressure would be off Izzie to stay involved. Maybe she could get back to something like a real life of her own.

Whatever she did—staying in Chicago or going back to New York, continuing to strip or giving it up—loving Nick or letting him get away—she knew she did not want to be a baker for much longer.

Nick tried reaching her a couple of times Saturday but she'd missed his calls. Not intentionally—the first time she'd been in the shower and the second she'd been waiting on customers at the bakery. By the time she had a minute to call him back, he'd been the one who hadn't answered.

Still, not having spoken to him for more than a day—since that tense moment on the street when she'd realized Tony had stumbled onto the truth of their relationship—she was a little nervous. Heading to work at Leather and Lace, she immediately scanned the parking lot for his car, but didn't see it. She was early—probably two hours earlier than she needed to be, and she knew it was because she was hoping he'd be here.

"Hi, Rose," someone said as she came in the back door.

"Hi, Bernie. How's the week been?"

The bouncer shrugged, offering her one of his big, boyish grins. "Knocked a few heads together, wiped up the ground with a drunk or two. You know, the usual."

Laughing, she began to walk past him.

But he stopped her with a hand on her shoulder. He glanced at the big canvas bag she carried, which was filled with some street clothes and supplies. "Can I help you in any way, Rose? Carry that? Get you some dinner?"

She shook her head. "You are so sweet, but no, honestly, I've got it." The guy had been tripping over himself to take care of her since her first night at work. If he'd ever made a move on her, she'd suspect it was because he was interested. But he'd never been anything but a nice—if overprotective—friend.

Still smiling as she walked toward her dressing room, Izzie acknowledged just how comfortable she felt here. The club staff was like a second family already. Bernie and Harry. Leah and Jackie and the other dancers. They were all people she cared about, who seemed to care about her.

She didn't *want* to give this up. Which was another reason she didn't quite know how to deal with Nick's seeming inability to watch her perform. It was as if ever since he'd become her lover, he no longer liked her doing her job.

That was how it *seemed*. But she couldn't be sure. "Maybe he really is just busy," she mumbled, trying to convince herself.

When she reached her dressing room, she put her new key in the new lock and twisted it. Before going inside, however,

Leah stopped her. "Hey, I feel like I'm always picking up your presents!" the grinning girl said. She held up a gold foil wrapped box. "Yum. Have I told you how much I love chocolate?"

Izzie glanced at the box, looked down at her own full hips—at least an inch bigger than they'd been when she moved back from New York—and sighed. "Have I told you how much chocolate sticks to my hips and butt?"

The one plus was that the candies were chocolate-covered cherries. And she wasn't too crazy about them. If they'd been caramels, she'd probably be much more tempted to grab a fistful. As it was, she easily waved them away. "Take them out of my sight, would you?"

Leah clutched the box to her chest. "Woo-hoo! Remind me to watch for the next jewelry box heading your way."

Entering her dressing room, Izzie slowly slipped out of her clothes and put her robe on. She took her time—there was lots of it. Over the next hour, she got ready for her night. The chatter of women's voices from the greenroom couldn't drown out the sound of lots of footsteps walking in the lounge above her head. Customers were already pouring in, performers already on stage judging by the low bass beat she could almost feel reverberating in her chest.

The whole place felt alive and vibrant. Exactly the way *she* felt when she was here. The only other time she felt as good was when she was with Nick. What on earth was she going to do if he couldn't take her working here anymore?

"Don't think about it," she reminded herself as she glanced at her watch. She'd been here over an hour and he still hadn't come in. Which was making her very jittery.

Izzie forced everything else out of her head and finished putting on her makeup. Her audience might not see much of her face, but that didn't mean she didn't cover the stage makeup basics. She was puffing anti-shine powder on her

cheeks when she heard a knock on her door. "Come in."
Almost holding her breath, she let it out with a pleased sigh
when she saw Nick. "Hi."

"Hi yourself," he said. He pushed the door shut behind him,
bent down and kissed her on the mouth. Quick, hard…hot and
sexy. "Been needing that," he said when he finally straightened.

"Me, too.

"Want more later."

She grinned. "Me, too."

"Things are already heating up upstairs, but I wanted to see
you before it got too crazy."

Izzie turned away, slowly lifting the powder puff to her
face again. "Do you think it'll be too *busy* again for you to
be there during my numbers?"

Nick met her eyes in the mirror. "I don't know," he muttered. "I can't promise anything."

He was still hesitant, she heard it in his voice. Nick was
avoiding having to acknowledge how he really felt—was
going to feel—about her stripping. Izzie wanted to cry,
sensing she knew what that answer would be.

He'd hate it. Sure, he'd been fine with her taking her
clothes off when she was a stranger. But now that they were
lovers? Well, if he was like every other male of the species,
he was going to turn into the caveman he'd once jokingly pretended to be and get all overbearing. He'd want her to quit,
he'd be surly and pouty until she did.

There weren't many men who'd be able to take having
their girlfriend strip down to a G-string in front of a bunch of
strangers…why should she expect Nick to be any different?

"I'm doing my best, Iz."

"Okay," she murmured, blinking rapidly against unexpected moisture in her eyes, welling up not because she didn't

understand, she *did*. But because she so feared what this was going to mean when it finally came to a head between them.

"Oh, God, somebody get a bucket!"

Hearing the loud shout from the corridor outside her dressing room, Izzie immediately rose to her feet.

"Catch her!"

Nick flinched. "Wait here while I see what's going on."

She just rolled her eyes. "Yeah, right."

Following him out, she immediately saw a small crowd of a half-dozen dancers gathered around someone who was lying on the floor. Nick pushed through them, and immediately bent down. "Leah, what happened? Are you okay?"

"She's sick," someone said. "Like, all over the floor sick."

Poor Leah. She'd been ill last weekend, and now again. Izzie briefly wondered if the poor kid was hiding an unexpected pregnancy or something. Then, as the crowd parted and she saw Leah's face, she discounted that idea.

The pretty blonde looked like she was in misery. Her face was ghost white, slicked with sweat, and she appeared too weak to even stand on her own. She looked absolutely nothing like the pretty young thing Izzie had run into a little over an hour ago. She had to have been hit with some kind of fast-moving bug.

Nick didn't waste time asking questions. He bent to lift the dancer, easily cradling her in his arms as if she was a child, and carried her into the greenroom down the hall. "Somebody get her a cold cloth."

One of the dancers rushed off to do as Nick said, the rest of them crowded around. Izzie couldn't say whether their avid interest was more on Leah's behalf, or because of the incredible sight Nick made playing hero. His muscular arms bulged and flexed, but he spoke so softly—gently—to Leah as he gently laid her on the lumpy sofa in the greenroom. He even brushed her hair out of her face.

It was enough to make the hardest of women melt. Even the half-dozen strippers surrounding the sofa.

Izzie, of course, wasn't surprised. She knew the tenderness the man was capable of. She also knew the way he'd been raised and imagined he'd have done the same thing if his little sister, Lottie, had been the one lying on that floor.

"What happened?" he asked Leah.

Leah groaned. "It just came over me out of nowhere. I haven't been nauseous or anything, then all of a sudden, boom."

"Have you eaten shellfish today?" someone asked.

"Or some old lunch meat?" asked another.

Leah shook her head, gratefully accepting a wet clump of paper towels her dressing-roommate, Jackie, had brought her. She pressed it to her forehead and replied, "I had a salad for lunch, then nothing until I binged on Rose's chocolates."

Seven heads swung around to stare at Izzie, seven pairs of eyes wide and curious. Maybe even a little accusing.

She opened her mouth to reply, wondering if they thought she'd done something to make Leah ill, but didn't have to. The sick dancer herself spoke up again. "I found them lying on the stoop when I got to work today, with Rose's name on them. She never even opened the box, she just gave them to me."

That seemed to calm everyone down. Everyone except Nick. Because while all the others turned their attention back to Leah, offering to get her some ice or to drive her home, he frowned and stiffened his jaw so much it looked ready to break. "Where are these chocolates?"

"My dressing room."

He looked up and stared at Jackie. "I'll get them," she said, quickly rushing out of the room.

It seemed ridiculous and Izzie didn't for one second believe Leah had been brought down by some kind of poisoned candy…intended for *her.* That was strictly CSI stuff and she absolutely did not believe it. Judging by the look on Nick's face, however, she knew better than to say that. He was going to see for himself no matter *what* she thought.

"Nick, I just heard one of the girls is sick, what's going on?" Harry came rushing in the room, out of breath as if he'd just run down the stairs. The expression of worry on the older man's face had to make all his employees feel better—no one could accuse Harry Black of not appreciating and caring about his dancers. Which probably made him a rarity in this industry…and was probably why few dancers ever quit here for any reason other than to move on to a different career.

Seeing Leah, he hurried over. "Should we call 9-1-1?"

Leah shook her head. "I don't think so. But I do want to lie here for a little while, if that's okay."

"Oh, honey, don't you even think of getting up," another voice said. A woman's. Delilah had heard the news, too, and followed her husband to the green room. She sounded concerned—a rarity for her. "We can cover you tonight and someone can take you home if you want."

The room was getting crowded. But everybody made way for Jackie when she returned with the box of chocolates. "Here you go, Nick." Frowning, she put her hand on his arm and nodded toward the corner of the room.

Nick took the box and followed Jackie. They exchanged a few words, and whatever she said to him made his scowl deepen. He kept the box tightly clutched in his hand and Izzie wondered if he was going to crush it.

Harry joined them, murmuring, "What's wrong?"

Nick's reply was softly spoken, he obviously didn't want everyone else to hear. Jackie, having delivered whatever message it was that had gotten Nick even more fired up, called 9-1-1 after all, then went back to help take care of her friend. All the others hovered over Leah. Someone offered to get her a pillow for her feet, someone else offered a bucket for her head. That broke the ice a little and the group laughed.

Izzie didn't join them. Nick suspected someone had tried to slip her poisoned chocolates. Damned if she was going to stay out of that conversation.

Striding across to the two men, she asked, "Well? Satisfied that I'm not a mad poisoner's target?"

Nick didn't look at her at first. Neither did Harry. They were both staring intently at the open box of chocolates on the makeup table. One of the men had flipped over all the remaining individually slotted pieces in the package, só they were bottom-side up. And in the bottom of each, very easily visible, was a small hole.

Something that wouldn't have happened at the candy factory.

"Oh, hell," Izzie whispered.

It appeared someone had, indeed, tried to poison her.

And when Nick turned to her and said, "Tell me about the roses," she realized it might not have been the first time.

11

WHEN NICK REALIZED there were holes in the bottom of the candy, he saw red. And it wasn't the cherry cordial filling.

He needed to know more—especially after what Jackie had told him about some flowers Izzie had passed to Leah last weekend. But he didn't want to do it here.

"The police are on their way," he muttered to Harry. Then, without a word, he grabbed Izzie's elbow and pulled her out of the room, straight to her private dressing room.

She stumbled to keep up and he realized he might be holding her too tight. But he couldn't let go, couldn't release his grip. He wasn't letting her get more than six inches away from him…or letting anyone else getting within six feet of *her.*

"Nick, calm down," she muttered.

"I'm calm." *Deadly calm.*

"No, you're not. You're volcanic," she said as they walked into her dressing room.

Nick shut and locked the door. The last time he'd locked the door to this room had been at the start of one of the most amazing sexual experiences he'd ever enjoyed. He really wished he was doing it for the same reason now.

He wasn't. He was locking the door to keep Izzie—the woman he now knew he loved—safe from someone who'd tried to hurt her at least twice now. Maybe even more.

Looking down, he saw the new chair sitting in front of Izzie's vanity and the steam built again. He leaned over and smacked it with his palm, sending it crashing against the wall. It did not fall apart.

But that didn't ease his suspicion about the last one.

"Why did you do that?" she asked, her voice calm and even.

Good thing one of them was. "Just making sure our friend didn't sabotage another chair."

Izzie's pretty mouth opened into a perfect *O* as understanding washed over her. That, more than anything, seemed to finally make this situation sink in. She grabbed the edge of the table and sagged against it. "Someone really is trying to hurt me?"

He stepped close and wrapped his arms around her shoulders and tugged her against him. "I think so, babe."

"Why?"

"I have no idea. Why do stalkers do any of the crap they do?"

Tilting her head back to look up at him, she murmured, "*Stalker?* Why would someone wanting to get *close* to me only to do something as dumb as make me sick?"

He had a few ideas. There were a lot of men out there who liked to play hero. Maybe somebody was setting Izzie up to get sick or take a fall just so he could get near her by being the one who came to her aid. Who knew how some dark, twisted minds worked? "Maybe somebody was hoping you'd pass out on stage and he could say he was a doctor and come to your aid."

She blew out an impatient breath. "That's silly."

"But not impossible," he insisted. "Those flowers that came last week…Jackie said they were for you, but that you gave them to Leah?"

Narrowing her eyes, she nodded. "You think they have something to do with this?"

That seemed incredibly obvious to Nick. "You get a couple of anonymous gifts, and the person who ends up with them gets sick."

She quickly figured out where he was going. "Harry said Leah was sick Sunday night…."

"So was Jackie. They share a dressing room and both smelled and touched the flowers when they were putting them in a vase."

Izzie shook her head, obviously not wanting to believe it. He didn't blame her. It couldn't be easy for her to think someone out there had been targeting her.

Because it was absolutely *killing* him to think it.

"And you think there was something on the roses…."

"Could have been insecticide, roach powder, anything. They both got nauseous and dizzy, and went home with horrible headaches."

Nick didn't know a lot about common household pesticide exposure, but he sure knew about its military applications. He'd been trained in dealing with all kinds of chemical attacks and imagined the most basic symptoms would be similar.

Izzie finally slipped out of his arms, her lovely face taut and strained. Her mouth drooped and she shook her head, appearing almost…*hurt*…that someone would be after her.

But the hurt didn't last for long. As she stared toward the replacement chair, her frown deepened and her eyes narrowed. He saw the clenching of her jaw and knew she was working herself into a temper.

"The cowardly bastard." She smacked her hand flat against the tabletop, muttering a few more choice curses. "You find out who did this, Nick."

He liked the return of that fierceness. Izzie wouldn't let

anything keep her down for long—it was one of the things he loved about her. Which he planned to tell her, just as soon as they got around to having that whole "I love you," and "I love you, too," conversation. Which would be soon, if he had his way. Very soon.

"I intend to. We'll start by questioning everyone to see if anybody noticed your anonymous gift-giver hanging around."

Though he didn't say it to her, Nick also intended to carefully watch the staff when he talked to them. It wasn't impossible that someone who worked right here at Leather and Lace was behind the attacks. An obsessed bartender, a jealous dancer who wanted Izzie's headliner spot. Maybe even a bouncer wanting to be her hero. Hell, maybe even Harry wanting to stir up a big news story as publicity for the club. He could see the headline now: *Hottest mystery dancer in Chicago stalked by unknown assailant.*

It was possible. Anything was.

"I'll watch the crowd tonight and see if anybody acts suspiciously, or if I recognize some of the guys who come every night I'm on." Glancing at her watch, she added, "I have to hurry up."

That comment drove everything else out of his mind. Nick shook his head hard. "You're not going on tonight.

She lifted her mask, turning to the mirror. "Of course I am."

Nick met her reflected stare. "Like hell."

"It *can* be like hell in here if you force me to make it that way," she shot back. "Because if you say that again, we're going to be having a major fight."

Nick couldn't believe her. She'd just found out someone had likely tried to poison her and she still wanted to perform. "Izzie, you can't be serious."

"Oh, you bet I am. We're already down one girl with Leah being sick and I left Harry in the lurch last weekend." Her eyes flashing fire, she added, "Besides, *no one's* going to force me off the stage."

Her expression betrayed her sheer determination as much as her words did. And he had to wonder if they had a double meaning.

Because despite everything that had happened this evening, he hadn't forgotten what they had been talking about before Leah got sick. She'd basically asked him if he was going to watch her dance, and he'd hedged on his answer. He hadn't missed the shine in her eyes or the disappointment twisting at her mouth. But he hadn't been able to reassure her, because even Nick didn't know how he was going to react when that moment came.

"It's too dangerous."

"There are four big, burly bouncers upstairs to make sure nothing happens," she insisted. Piercing him with her stare, she added, "Besides, you'll be there to protect me. Or *won't* you? Maybe there'll be something more *important* to deal with."

Nick now knew for sure she was referring to their earlier conversation. And maybe she had a right to.

But being a little slow to want to watch the woman he loved get naked in front of a bunch of other guys had absolutely nothing to do with his concern for her now. "It's not about that."

"Oh, yes, it is." Izzie stalked around the privacy screen. Given that it offered no privacy whatsoever, considering the mirror, that was a statement in itself.

A frank one…that the walls were going up between them.

"And frankly, I'm tired of asking you about it. You can watch or not, but the Crimson Rose is performing tonight."

She yanked her robe off, then, watching him watch her, dropped her bra and panties to the floor.

"Damn it," he muttered, as always unable to take his ravenous eyes off her. She was just so incredibly beautiful. The woman stopped his heart every time he looked at her.

Izzie continued to ignore him, reaching for her G-string

and pulling it on. Then she covered her dark, puckered nipples with those two ridiculous pink petals.

"Don't do this," he ordered through a thick, tight throat. "Not until we know you're safe." When she stepped out from behind the screen and lifted her chin in challenge, he added, "You don't have to go out there."

"It's my job."

"It's something you do part-time for kicks and to rub it in your family and the world that you're not sweet little Isabella Natale anymore," he said, frustrated beyond belief at her stoic refusal to listen to reason.

She appeared stunned by his accusation. "How can you *say* that? My family doesn't even know I'm here."

"I know and that proves my point. You get your *secret* kicks out of it without ever having to face the consequences. You're not being honest to anyone—not even yourself—about why you're doing this and what you really want."

She jerked as if he'd slapped her. Closing his eyes and shaking his head, Nick wondered how he'd let this whole conversation spin so badly out of control so rapidly.

"You certainly are a fine one to talk," she finally said, her tone steely.

"What?"

"You accuse me of that, but you're doing exactly the same thing, Nick Santori. Stringing your family along with this idea that you're going to be singing *O Sole Mio* and slinging pizza dough with Tony and your father. Meanwhile, you hide your nights doing something exciting and dangerous at a place they would never approve of. I call that hypocritical."

He couldn't believe she'd turned things around on him like that. "That's ridiculous."

"So why haven't you told Tony you're not sticking around? Why haven't you told your father about this 'protection' business you're thinking of going into with your Marine buddies?"

Leave it to a woman to use something he'd told her less than a day ago in a fight against him. "That has nothing to do with whether you go out on stage and flaunt yourself in front of someone who wants to *hurt* you." But even as he said it, a small voice in his head whispered that she might be right. At least a little.

Not that he was going to admit that now…not when they still had the issue of her physical safety to work out. So he pushed on. "And I'm not on stage intentionally taking off my clothes to try to turn on a hundred strangers—one of whom might be trying to poison me."

She'd stiffened at the world flaunt. By the time he'd finished speaking, Izzie's face was as red as her mask. "Well, that's it, then, isn't it? We've finally gotten down to it."

"Izzie…."

She put a hand up to stop him. "I knew it would come to this, and now it has. You need to leave. I'm going on stage tonight. By the time I get back, I hope there will be a new lock on my door, for my own protection." Her chin quivered, her full lips shook. But she had one last thing to say. "And you most definitely will not have a key to it."

NICK WASN'T IN the audience. Izzie scanned the crowd for him throughout her performance, wondering if he'd be lurking in the shadows, watching out for her.

He wasn't.

It was over.

Somehow, she managed to not cry as she gyrated to the music. Managed to not show the hungry-looking men in the audience that her heart was broken.

It shouldn't feel this broken, after all, she'd known going

into this crazy, wild relationship with Nick that it would have to end badly. From day one, they'd wanted each other on opposite terms. He'd wanted the cute kid sister of his brother's wife, who worked at the bakery every day. She'd wanted the sultry, sexy bodyguard who guarded *her* naked body every night.

That he'd tried to put his foot down and forbid her from dancing the very *first* moment he had a convenient excuse emphasized that and more.

As she dipped and swayed and thrust and jumped on the stage, four words kept time with the music. They played over and over, keeping the 4:4 beat.

It can not work.

By the time she was finished dancing, Izzie was as much angry as she was heartbroken. Aside from being her lover, Nick was supposed to be the club's bodyguard. And yet when she'd been the most vulnerable—exposed—he'd been nowhere to be seen.

She'd have something to say about that the second she saw him. But that moment came almost immediately—he had been watching her back. Literally. He was standing, dark and predatory, in the wings just off stage. He'd been watching for her to come off…out of a direct line of sight to center stage. So he *hadn't* watched her dance. And he most certainly hadn't experienced watching her dance with the rest of a big, male audience.

Nothing had changed.

"I'll escort you to your dressing room," he said, his jaw as stiff as his shoulders. *"Rose."*

She didn't even respond as she slipped her robe on over her nearly naked body, then sailed past him toward the stairs. She didn't need his help, she didn't need his approval.

Yes, she needed him. But she'd learn to do without him,

just like she'd done without him all those long, lonely teenage years when she'd pined for the man.

Of course, never having had him might have aided her then. Now that she had?

Izzie feared she was never going to get over Nick.

"Ahem." As they reached the bottom of the stairs, Harry stepped out of the greenroom.

"Everything okay?" Nick asked, instantly on alert.

"It's fine," the older man said, but he didn't sound convinced. In fact, his voice was weak, his face a little pale.

Izzie reached out and put a hand on his shoulder. "Harry, what's wrong? Is Leah all right?"

He covered her hand with his. "Yes. Jackie called earlier. Leah's fine." He glanced over his shoulder into the quiet greenroom. He stepped out of the room and eased the door closed. "But I need to talk to both of you. Will you come with me, please?"

Hearing his urgency and seeing his very obvious concern, Izzie immediately went on alert. Something else had happened…maybe someone else was hurt.

"What is it?" Nick asked in a low voice, obviously realizing the same thing.

The man just shook his head, leading them back up the stairs to his small office which was on the other side of the lobby. They took a private, back hallway—a good thing since Izzie still wore just her long, silky robe. Whatever was bothering Harry, it had to be serious because he hadn't even offered to wait while she put some clothes on.

Harry's office was unpretentious and simple. Comfortable. Much like the self-deprecating man who occupied it.

But Harry Black did not look at all comfortable right now. As he gestured them toward the two armchairs across from his desk, his hand shook.

Izzie almost held her breath, watching him sit down behind the desk. Before he said a word, he dropped his head forward and put it in hands. "I can't even look at you when I say this."

Izzie had no idea what the man could be talking about, but beside her, Nick sucked in a sharp breath. "You…"

Their employer immediately looked up, shaking his head. "No. Not me." Moisture appearing in his eyes, he continued. "It was Delilah."

Izzie suddenly got it. Delilah had been the one after her. She'd poisoned the chocolates—and perhaps the roses.

Nick muttered a foul word, but Harry didn't leap to the defense of his wife. She deserved their scorn. No, she hadn't succeeded in hurting Izzie, her target, but she had certainly made Leah miserable.

"Tell us," Nick said, leaning back in the chair and crossing his arms over his chest.

His eyes were narrowed, his expression forbidding. Izzie recognized that tension in his rock-hard body. It was a good thing Delilah Black was not here for a personal confession. A very good thing. Because if Izzie didn't rip her apart, Nick just might have.

"I thought she *wanted* to retire," Harry said. He had a dazed expression, the same one many men wore when trying to understand their wives. Izzie had certainly seen it on her father's face. "She seemed happy helping me with management."

"How long ago did she stop?" Izzie asked, feeling a sharp sense of pity for the man. She sensed Harry needed to build up to telling them the worst of it.

"A few years ago when she turned forty. Right after we got married." Opening his desk drawer, Harry reached in and grabbed a silver flask and a shot glass. He poured himself a drink, raising a brow toward Nick and Izzie to see if they wanted one.

Neither took him up on it. Izzie because she was already feeling queasy at the story Harry was telling them. Nick... well, probably because he was already on a low simmer in the chair next to her. Throwing alcohol on a slow burn could make it erupt.

"And what, she thought if she could get rid of your head-liner, you'd suddenly put her back on stage? That makes no sense," Nick said, disgust dripping from his words.

"Not to you. Not to me," Harry said with a sigh. "But to her." Growing slightly pink in the cheeks, he added, "I, uh, think there might have been a little more to it, though. I guess I talk a lot about you Rose...Izzie," he clarified, calling her by her real name for the first time since he'd hired her. "And I think Dee got a bit jealous, thinking my interest was some-thing other than professional." Almost blushing to the roots of his balding head now, he quickly added, "That wasn't at all true. I'm as proud of you as if you were my own daughter...but Dee didn't get that."

The man had never even looked at her the wrong way. Izzie didn't doubt he was being truthful.

"Was she responsible for the roses?"

Harry nodded, taking another deep sip of his drink. "She put some kind of bug powder on them. And before you ask, yes, she did the chair too. I got her to admit to both of those things, as well as putting some kind of syrup—Ipecac—in the choco-lates."

This time Izzie was the one to call the other woman a bitch under her breath. She simply couldn't help it. Again, Harry didn't make any effort to defend his wife.

"Why'd she come clean?" Izzie asked.

"I suspected as soon as I saw the box of candy. Dee loves that kind. And she came home with some of that syrup a couple of days ago, saying she wanted it on hand in case one of her nieces or nephews came over and swallowed something poisonous."

Nick shifted a little, his arms still cross, his body still rigid. "So you confronted her?"

Harry nodded. "And she confessed. When she saw how sick Leah was, she felt awful."

"Wonder if she'd have felt that way if it had been Izzie lying on the floor," Nick snapped.

He sounded very protective. Which made Izzie feel all warm and gooshy inside, even though she told herself that was stupid.

"I dunno," Harry admitted. "Maybe not."

Gee, it was nice to be liked.

Nick finally sat up and leaned toward the desk. Fixing a firm eye on Harry he said, "Have you called the police?"

The man slowly shook his head. But before Nick could confront him on it, he added, "I went to Leah first and told her everything. She and Jackie decided to press charges, and they made the call to the police themselves."

Nick relaxed. A little.

"I understand why that needed to happen." Tears rose in Harry's gray eyes and oozed a little onto his round cheeks. "But I couldn't be the one to turn my wife in."

Izzie reached over and put her hand on Nick's leg, sensing he was about to make another comment about Delilah. She squeezed his thigh, warning him not to. Harry was suffering enough. He didn't need to be told he was a fool for loving someone so hateful. "I understand," she murmured.

"I hope you do. And I hope you'll understand that I'm going to see her through this. She'll be facing assault charges."

"At the very least," Nick mumbled.

"I know this might make you want to leave, Ro…Izzie. But

I wish you wouldn't." The man smiled weakly. "You're family."

Huh. If poison was the way Delilah treated members of her *family,* Izzie would hate to see what she did to her enemies.

"I know that, too," Izzie said, slowly pulling her hand away from Nick's warm thigh, already missing the contact. Already missing *him.* "You love her. That's what people who love each other do…they support one another, even when they make what other people might see as bad or foolish decisions." Hearing a quiver in her voice as the subject touched much too close to home, Izzie offered Harry a tremulous smile.

Nick she didn't even look at.

"Thank you for telling me, Harry. I'm going to go get ready for my next number." Without another word to either of them, Izzie walked out and went back to work.

And Nick didn't come anywhere near her for the rest of the night.

WHEN BRIDGET WENT back to the dealership on Monday morning, she looked for Ted, wondering if he'd have the nerve to show up.

He didn't. That was good.

Neither did Dean. That wasn't good.

Hopefully Ted had been scared off, either by Dean, or by the ramifications of his own stupid actions.

Hopefully Dean had *not* been scared off and was just stuck in traffic.

Bridget had spent all Sunday night wondering what on earth she was going to say to him—how she was going to climb that wall he'd erected between them after he'd kissed her so passionately in the office. But for nothing. He wasn't there.

She trudged through her day, going through the same song and dance with Marty about the books. She found problems. He waved them off as unimportant. A typical day in the life.

"I am so gonna quit this job," she muttered that afternoon. Soon. Maybe she'd even give her notice today. After all, she'd only stayed to see if something was going to happen between her and Dean Willis. Judging by yesterday, it seemed pretty clear nothing was.

She went so far as to open up a document on her computer to type her resignation letter. She'd give two weeks notice, even though she had no other job lined up. She had enough of a cushion to be unemployed for a while. And if she didn't come up with another bookkeeping job quickly, she'd lay money that Izzie would hire her on at the bakery, just to pay the rent.

But before she'd typed so much as the date, Bridget heard a commotion—shouts, coming from the sales floor. Her first thought was that Ted had come back and was making a scene. But there were several voices, all yelling at once.

She grabbed her purse and threw it under her desk, then wondered if she should crawl under after it…this could be a robbery. But when the door to the office flew open and she saw a uniformed police officer, she didn't.

"Is anyone in here with you?" the officer barked.

"N-no. Just me."

"You need to come with me, ma'am."

Dazed, Bridget followed the officer, seeing all the other employees being herded together by other policemen. All of them were gathered just inside the front door, and Marty was shouting loud enough to break the glass in the windows.

Everyone was talking—demanding answers. Everyone but Bridget. She didn't have to. Because the second she saw Dean Willis—dressed in a perfectly fitted dark blue suit—talking to other dark-suited men right outside the front door, she knew what was going on.

He was no car salesman.

"Sir, you'll have an opportunity to call your attorney soon," one of the officers said, trying to calm Marty down.

It worked for a brief second, until Dean walked through the door. When Marty saw him with the rest of the investigators, he started ranting and struggling against the officer trying to handcuff him. Another one jumped in to help and between them they got the livid man into custody.

Dean looked her way once. His nice blue eyes were frigid. His smile absent. His tousled blond hair was slicked down and parted on the side—conservative, professional. And his clothes were immaculate, right down to his shiny black wing-tip shoes.

He could have been a picture from an FBI agent's handbook come to life.

The rest of the day went by in a whirl. She was questioned endlessly—never by Dean, who stayed away from her—but by his fellow agents. Apparently there had been a reason Marty hadn't wanted Bridget to do a good job with the books. They were never *supposed* to balance out. Because, if the agents were to be believed, Honest Marty's Used Cars had been bringing in and cleaning up a whole lot of dirty money for some pretty bad guys.

And she'd fallen right in the middle of it.

By the end of the day, Bridget was utterly exhausted. Ready to collapse, her throat sore from answering so many questions. She hadn't asked for a lawyer—had cooperated fully, believing that's what an innocent person *should* do. And she'd spent the last four hours in the conference room, going over months' worth of seized bank statements and ledgers with some FBI accountant, watching step by step as they built a case against her boss.

At first, she felt a little sorry for Marty. But not too sorry. Especially when she caught snips of conversation about where the dirty money had come from. In her opinion, anybody who cleaned cash that had been earned off the sale of filthy drugs to kids deserved what he got. She was just sorry the creep had dragged her into the sordidness.

She'd seen Dean only briefly, when she'd been brought to tears by the relentless questions of the accountant. Dean had appeared out of nowhere, appearing behind the other officer's back, barking, "She's not a suspect, she's a witness. Treat her like one." Then, with one long, even look at Bridget, he'd left again to go back to work with the other investigators.

Finally, when it was nearly dark out, Bridget was told she could go home. She'd be called in to help again—and, likely, to testify—but for now, she was free.

Free. Great. She was free to go home, look back on this horrible day—on these past few horrible weeks—and think about what a damned *fool* she'd been.

Dean had *used* her. He'd feigned an interest in her so he could build his money laundering case against Marty. He'd played her like an instrument, obviously seeing the quiet, sweet-faced bookkeeper as an easy mark.

She hated the son of a bitch with a passion she'd never had toward anyone in her life.

That rage carried her down the block as she strode away from the dealership, heading toward her nearby apartment. Usually when she made the walk home, she kept her purse clutched tightly to her side, and constantly scanned for any possible danger. This wasn't a bad part of town—but as a young woman walking alone, she didn't take chances. To-night, however, she practically *dared* anyone to mess with her. She felt capable of doing real violence.

"Bridget, wait, please!" a voice called.

Though she kept walking, she peered over her shoulder to see who'd called her. She almost tripped over her own feet when she realized it was Dean. "Stay away from me," she snapped, picking up her pace.

He picked up his, too, chasing her down until he reached her. "Would you stop? I've been calling you for two blocks."

"Not real quick on the uptake, are you?" she said. "I don't want to talk to you."

"You have to let me explain."

"I don't *have* to do anything," she said, though she did finally stop and face him. "And you don't have to explain, I got it, okay? You were working undercover. I was the easy mark. Of course you'd come after me by any means at your disposal."

"It wasn't like that."

"Like hell."

"Just…calm down and let me explain. I did not mean to hurt you, and I definitely never meant to get personally involved with you."

"You mean that wasn't in the manual?"

"No, it wasn't. But I was worried, I felt sure early on that you were caught in something you didn't know about." He put a hand on her arm. "I was worried about you."

She shrugged his hand of. "Sure you were. I'm sure your concern was the reason you asked me out. And your fears that I was being used by my boss to help hide money was the only reason you kissed the lips off my face yesterday."

He closed his eyes, breathed deeply—as if for control—and tried again. "I lost my detachment where you were concerned."

Those were the first words he'd said that actually made her pause. Because he'd whispered them hoarsely, as if against his will. Like he didn't want to admit to the weakness.

And she believed him.

Not that it made a damn bit of difference. "Well, that's too bad for you then," she said, lifting her chin, amazed that her voice didn't even quiver. "Because I never want to see you again." She began walking again.

"Bridget, I know you're upset now. But I want to make it up to you. Soon, when you've…"

"When I've what?" she asked, swinging around again. "When I've calmed down? Well, keep dreaming, buddy. Because it's not going to happen. *Ever.*"

Dean met her stare, but didn't try to stop her this time when she turned again to start walking. He did, however, have one more thing to say, low, as if making a vow.

"I'm not giving up."

"Well, too bad for you," she snapped back, feeling both proud of herself for being so strong…and sad at having lost something she suspected could have been very special.

"Bridget…."

This time, she didn't turn around. And she didn't have to wonder what Izzie would do.

Bridget knew what *she* wanted to do.

So without a pause, she lifted her hand, flipped him the bird over her shoulder, and kept on walking.

12

IZZIE DIDN'T SEE or hear from Nick for six long days. The longest of her life.

Since she'd walked out of Harry's office Sunday night, Nick had apparently taken her orders to leave her alone seriously, because that's exactly what he'd done. He hadn't tried calling, hadn't popped in to the bakery, hadn't even nonchalantly walked by the shop and pretended not to look in at her.

That's what *she'd* done, at Santori's, but she hadn't seen the man at all.

"Why didn't you fight for me?" she whispered as she drove to the other side of town Saturday evening on her way to work. "Why did you listen to me and leave me alone?"

Why did you tell him to?

Good question. And Izzie was already forgetting the answer, though it had seemed so important Sunday.

Yes, she was still upset that he'd suddenly gone from an approving coworker to a disapproving lover when it came to her dancing. But maybe they could have worked it out. Maybe he wouldn't have reacted so badly to watching her on stage.

Maybe...hell, maybe she loved him enough that she could have quit and never regretted it.

But he hadn't given her the chance.

In the six days since she'd seen him, Izzie was questioning a lot of the choices she'd made. After accusing Nick of living a lie, too, she'd realized that she was tired of living one all the time. So she'd actually begun to share her secret. Only with her sisters and her cousin so far, but it was a start.

And they'd been remarkably supportive. Even Gloria who had, to Izzie's utter shock, admitted that she'd love to see her perform. Honestly, it felt as if a weight had been lifted, and she'd decided then and there to start thinking of how to work her daytime life into her nighttime one. Slowly…a little at a time. But she might just have to find a way to do it.

Because if Nick ever *did* come back after her, she wanted to try to find a way to make all the pieces of both their lives fit.

Performing again…that caused more stress. Izzie couldn't deny a small amount of trepidation when she arrived at Leather and Lace Saturday night. This was her first time back since last Sunday, the night of Delilah's confession—and her arrest. She hadn't talked to Harry since and she was worried about what the older man was going through.

Bernie was waiting at the back door. "Hiya, Rose," he said without a smile. Obviously the mood around here was still dour.

"Hi. Harry around?"

He shook his head. "He hasn't been here much." Shaking his head, he added, "Wish he'd just ditch that witch and get back to work, this club ain't gonna run itself."

Izzie didn't say anything. She honestly didn't want to think about what she'd do in her boss's situation. He was a man who loved his wife…warts and all. Should he be faulted for that? Maybe. But it wasn't her place to judge.

The dressing rooms and greenroom were pretty quiet for a Saturday night, any chatter between the dancers was going on quietly. Just as well. Izzie didn't feel very social. There was only one person she wanted to see…only, she didn't know what on earth she'd say to him when she did.

I miss you. I love you. Please love me as I am and let's work it out.

All of the above.

He never appeared. She didn't see him downstairs, and he certainly didn't come to her dressing room. Izzie went through the motions getting ready, tense and anxious…but for nothing.

By the time she was ready to go on, she was seriously wondering if she'd made a mistake in coming in at all. Her heart was not in it. Not tonight. "The show must go on," she reminded herself as she walked upstairs and took her place backstage.

She'd like to think she gave her audience her all, but as she began removing her rose petals in time to the music, she knew her heart wasn't in it. Her heart was in little pieces, scattered around Nick Santori's feet. Wherever he may be.

Usually, Izzie ignored the audience as she performed—it was part of her "mysterious appeal" as Harry had described it right after she'd started working here. And he'd been right.

Tonight, however, something caught her attention. Rather, some*one*. Normally, all were still when she performed—including the waitresses. But now, someone was walking from the back of the room straight down the center aisle toward the stage.

It was a man. A dark-haired, dark-eyed man.

A *familiar* dark-haired, dark-eyed man.

"Oh, God," she whispered, stumbling a little.

Because it was Nick. A Nick like she'd never seen before.

Though he wore his typical on-the-job tough-guy uniform of black pants and tight black T-shirt, he was carrying a bouquet of roses. A huge bouquet of them. He was also smiling, his eyes locked on her, apparently not caring that she was dancing nearly naked on stage in front of a bunch of strange men.

And for the first time in her entire dancing career, Izzie did something entirely unprofessional. She committed the cardinal sin. She stopped right in the middle of her number.

"Nick," she whispered.

He had reached the edge of the low stage, which was about as high as his mid-thigh and was staring up at her. The look in his eyes…oh, God, that look. He was smiling broadly, adoring her with his gaze.

He not only looked approving, he looked absolutely enraptured. "Hi, Izzie," he said, his voice low, intimate, just for the two of them.

The music slowly faded away into silence. The audience began to murmur. One man yelled something like "Down in front," but he was shouted down by several others who obviously wanted to see what would happen next.

She'd like to know that herself.

"Hi," she whispered. "Uh…what are you doing?"

His smile widened. "Watching you."

"I noticed."

"You're wonderful."

She nibbled her bottom lip. "Thank you."

"I could watch you dance every night and be a happy man."

"Who couldn't?" someone from a nearby table called.

Nick never even glanced over, not distracted. Instead, he lifted the bouquet and offered it to her. Izzie took it, bringing the flowers up to her masked face and sniffing the heady fragrance permeating the red blooms. "They're beautiful."

"I figured roses were your flower."

"Good call." Laughing a little, she asked, "Is there some reason you gave them to me here? And right *now?*"

He nodded. "I wanted you to know how proud I am of you and how much I love seeing you dance. No matter who else is here."

He'd said it. He'd put it into words. Exactly what she needed to hear. "Oh, Nick, really?"

He nodded. "*Really.* I have more to say. But not here." He glanced over his shoulder at all the men leering at them. "Some things were not meant to do in front of an audience." Then he looked back up at her. "And the next thing I want to say to you can't be said when you're wearing that mask on your face."

She shivered, anticipation rolling through her. Oh, how she hoped she knew what it was he wanted to say to her. That it involved talk of a future. And a lot of uses of the word *love*.

"I'll meet you downstairs in two-and-a-half minutes," he said. "I've timed your song…that's how much you have left."

"You're on," she said with a broad smile as she clutched the flowers close to her body and slowly backed away from the edge of the stage. She put the flowers down right in front of the curtain, where she could easily retrieve them.

Nick turned around and walked back the way he'd come. From where Izzie stood, she could see every man in the place turn to watch him go. Most were regulars who had to have recognized him. And probably all of them wanted to know exactly what he'd said to her…and what he meant to her.

That was easy to explain. *Everything.*

Nodding toward the crew member on the side of the stage, Izzie waited for her song to resume. Now she danced joyfully, the way she hadn't in a very long time. And she smiled during every moment of it.

As soon as the last notes of the music played, Izzie grabbed her flowers and darted toward the wings, pausing only long enough to stick her arms in her robe before tearing toward the staircase. She took the cement stairs two at a time, almost stumbling. But even if she had, it would have been okay. Because Nick was waiting at the bottom of them, staring up at her.

He would have caught her. She knew that, from now on, he would be there to catch her.

"Come on," he murmured, taking her hand. He twined her fingers in his, then lifted them to his mouth to press a soft kiss on them. "Let's talk privately."

She followed him, easing against his body, her curves fitting perfectly in his angles, as if they were two pieces of a puzzle. When they reached her dressing room, Nick opened the door and held it for her, then followed her inside.

"Thank you again for the roses," she murmured as she put them on the makeup-strewn counter. They'd already begun filling the room with their heady perfume and she inhaled of it deeply.

"You're welcome." He immediately added, "You were right."

"About?"

"Everything," he admitted evenly, making no effort to hedge or share blame for what had happened between them. Even though Izzie knew she bore some of the responsibility.

"We both…"

"No, Iz, let me finish, please. You were right to accuse me of living the same double life I'd accused you of. *You* had legitimate reasons, with your father's health and your, uh…"

"Being a stripper?"

He grinned. "Yeah. That."

"I told Gloria and Mia."

His eyes widened. "Really? How'd they react?"

"Better than I expected." Much better. But she'd fill him in on that later. "It's a first step, anyway."

"I know. I made that same step. I told my father and Tony that I wasn't interested in the business. And what I am interested in doing."

"Being a bodyguard?"

For the first time since he'd walked up to her during her dance, Nick looked a little hesitant. He glanced to the side, and scrunched his brow. "Well…not exactly."

Immediately on alert, Izzie crossed her arms. "What did you do? Tell me you're not going to be a cop like your brother!"

He shook his head, as if appalled at the idea. "Not a chance. As it turns out, Harry's going to need to take a step back from this place to deal with Delilah's legal situation."

Not a surprise.

"And he asked me if I'd manage it."

Izzie couldn't prevent a shocked gasp. *"What?"*

"There's more."

Still stunned at the very concept, she waited, mouth agape.

"He needs an infusion of cash…I think he anticipates a lot of legal bills. I have money I've been socking away during all the years I bunked with Uncle Sam. So I've just become a part owner of this club."

That was so unexpected, Izzie couldn't help sinking down to her chair in absolute shock. "You're serious?"

"Very serious."

"You're going to work *here.*"

"Uh-huh. You okay with that? Working with your husband?"

"Oh, I'll love…." His words sunk in, banging around in her head. *"What* did you say?"

He smiled. "I thought diamonds would go well with roses."

Izzie remained still, in a stunned silence, as Nick reached into his pocket and pulled out a ring. A gold one. With a big fat diamond on top of it. "I'm going to slide this on your finger, but not until you take that mask off your face."

Dazed, she reached up and unfastened the clasps of her mask, one on each side of her head. The slow-motion feeling of the moment continued as she drew the red velvet away, letting it fall to the floor at her feet.

He reached for her hand, drawing her up to stand in front of him. "I love you, Izzie Natale. I love you, Crimson Rose. And I want you both in my life from this day on," he said, his voice serious and unwavering. His expression was every bit as serious—as proud and determined as she'd ever seen him—as if he placed more value on this moment than he had on any other.

She certainly did. Because this could be the moment when her life changed forever. When, as silly as it sounded, all her secret dreams—the ones she hadn't even acknowledged to herself—might actually start coming true.

"Whether we stay here, or go to New York, whether you work at the bakery or take off your clothes for a living...I'll follow you. I'll lead you. I'll stand beside you." He reached up and cupped her cheek, brushing his fingertips over her skin in a caress so tender it brought tears to her eyes.

"Be with me. Always."

Now the teardrops gushed. Izzie seldom cried, but, at this moment, it was absolutely the only reaction she could manage. "I will, Nick. I love you so much. I've loved you for so long, I can't remember what it felt like to *not* be in love with you."

Reaching for him, she twined her arms around his neck and drew him toward her. She rose on tiptoe, touching her lips to his in a gentle kiss that gradually deepened. Their tongues sliding together in delicate intimacy, their bodies melted together. They shared breaths and promises not yet made but never to be broken, making a bond in that deep, unending, heady kiss that would last forever.

It was the most beautiful kiss of Izzie's life. Because she was kissing a man she'd loved forever...and his amazing mouth had just given the same words to her.

When they finally paused, Nick smiled down at her. "Are you really going to wear my ring?"

She stuck out her hand. "Starting now. Lasting forever."

Once he'd slid it on, she stared at the beautiful, glittering stone and gasped at the beauty of it. "Oh, thank you for waiting for me," she whispered to him.

"Thanks for pulling me on top of you on that table of cookies to let me know how much you wanted me."

Izzie glared at her new fiancée. "I did not pull you on top of me."

"I'd have to say you pulled, Cookie."

Reaching for the sash to her bathrobe and slowly unfastening it, she smiled a wicked, sultry smile. "Nick? You want to see what's beneath this robe?"

His eyes glittered in hunger and need. "Oh, you know I do."

He reached for her, but Izzie put her hand over his, stopping him. "Then I have one piece of advice for you. *Don't* call me Cookie."

Epilogue

Three Months Later

THOUGH THE COLD WINTER air outside buffeted the city with an early blast of winter, inside Leather and Lace, everything remained *hot*. As usual.

The club was packed this Saturday night, every table full, mostly with men, but a few daring women were in the audience, too. Leather and Lace had started earning a reputation as a "couples-friendly" club and more pairs were coming in. Laughing and partying as they entered...quite often whispering and cuddling seductively as they left.

Nick had thought that a fine idea...until tonight when he'd looked up and had seen his brothers Joe and Luke walk in, their wives on their arms. That had given him a momentary heart attack, but once he'd sat and had a drink with the quartet, he'd realized something: Rachel and Meg were excited beyond belief, not at all judgmental and certainly not jealous that their future sister-in-law was about to strip in front of a bunch of men...including their husbands.

He hadn't understood it at first, until his brothers had confessed that their wives—as well as Tony's wife, Gloria, and Nick's sister, Lottie—were all taking the pole-dancing classes Izzie was now teaching at a Chicago dance studio. Mark's pregnant wife was on a waiting list for a future class.

He had to grin every time he thought about it. Now that she'd stopped working at the bakery, Izzie had found herself a full-time job teaching the housewives and professional women of Chicago how to stay healthy while learning to be ultra-sexy.

"I can't wait to see her. I mean, she's done her routine for us at the gym, but to see her here, in front of an audience…oh, sugar, just you watch and see what I'm going to be doing in a couple of months." Rachel leaned close to Luke, curling her arm around his, and whispered something that made his brother cough into his fist.

Okay. This appeared to be a good thing. And obviously Izzie was aware they were coming, so he didn't have to go track down his fiancée—and star performer—and give her a heads-up.

Leaving his family to their drinks, he ran another sweep of the room, touching base with Bernie and the other bouncers. He'd had to hire another bartender to work on weekends and both guys were rushing around pouring shots of high-end liquor and now, making frou-frou drinks for their female patrons.

Harry would be proud, if he'd been here to see it. But the man had come in less and less, leaving the management to Nick.

"Hey, boss, somebody to see you," one of the bouncers said.

Glancing up, Nick saw four men approaching the bar. Even if he hadn't known them, their postures and bearing would have told them they were brothers in a way that only those who'd been *there* would understand.

"Semper fi, man." He nodded to the first, recognizing the black hair and even stare of an old friend…a good man to have at your back when the situation turned rough. Reaching for the extended hand, Nick shook it, saying, "Been a long time, Joel."

The man nodded. He'd gotten out four years ago, just

before Nick had been deployed to Iraq. "I figured I'd come in and see why this was so much better than coming to work with me."

As Nick greeted the rest, another of the men, also an old Marines friend, glanced toward the stage where one of the girls was doing her thing. "I think I'm catching the vision," he mumbled.

"What can I say?" Nick shrugged. "I've settled down, become respectable." His mouth widening in a grin, he added, "And the little woman didn't want me doing anything as risky as working security with you guys."

Joel's big shoulders moved as he chuckled. He had a pretty good sense of humor considering he was one tough son of a bitch.

Nick gestured to one of the hostesses, asking her to get his friends a good table. But before they walked away, he murmured, "Seriously, thanks for offering to let me in. But I'm pretty happy with what I'm doing."

Joel nodded. "Got it. Still, if you ever change your mind..." He reached into the pocket of his black leather jacket and pulled out a crisp, white business card.

Nick read it. Then he looked back at his friend, offering him a short nod. "I'll keep it in mind."

Reaching out with his elbow bent and arm up, Nick grasped the other man's hand again in a brothers-of-the-field handshake, then watched the group head to their table.

He could have been one of them. Hell, he and Joel even *looked* like they were in the same line of work since they were both dressed in black from head to toe. Old habits sure died hard.

But he didn't regret it. He hadn't been lying when he said he liked what he was doing. A lot. Maybe not forever, but for now, working with Izzie doing something nobody had ever expected either of them to do was suiting him just fine.

"What time you got, Bernie?" he asked the bouncer, who stood nearby, on constant, vigilant guard.

"Eight-twenty," the other man said.

Hmm…about forty minutes before the Crimson Rose's first performance of the night.

Forty minutes. That *might* be enough time to tell the woman again how crazy he was about her. And how very glad he was that she'd stayed in Chicago with him.

When he got downstairs, walked into her dressing room, and caught her standing behind her screen wearing nothing but her G-string, however, he reconsidered that idea.

Forty minutes wasn't going to be enough. Not nearly.

"Hey, lover." She smiled at him in the mirror.

He smiled back. "Hey, Cookie."

Never taking his eyes off her beautiful face, Nick reached behind him and closed the door, flipping the lock to keep the world *out*. And to shut them *in* the wild and sultry one he thrived on with the woman he loved more than life.

* * * * *

A note from Leslie:

Wait…you thought that was the end? Well, so did I, but I just can't say goodbye to the Santoris of Chicago! So for all you readers who've loved this family right along with me, I'm offering one more glimpse at this wonderful clan before it's goodbye forever.

Izzie and Nick are getting married in January, and five of Izzie's bridesmaids—Bridget, Leah, Vanessa, Mia and Gloria—are all going to have romantic adventures of their own.

It's five sexy stories in one sexy book…all written by me.

And it'll be capped off by the one Santori story I never got to tell…Gloria and Tony's!

I hope you'll watch for ONE WILD WEDDING NIGHT, launching the new Blaze Encounters miniseries in January, 2008!

For a sneak preview of Marie Ferrarella's
DOCTOR IN THE HOUSE,
coming to NEXT in September,
please turn the page.

He didn't look like an unholy terror.

But maybe that reputation was exaggerated, Bailey Del-Monico thought as she turned in her chair to look toward the doorway.

The man didn't seem scary at all.

Dr. Munro, or Ivan the Terrible, was tall, with an athletic build and wide shoulders. The cheekbones beneath what she estimated to be day-old stubble were prominent. His hair was light brown and just this side of unruly. Munro's hair looked as if he used his fingers for a comb and didn't care who knew it.

The eyes were brown, almost black as they were aimed at her. There was no other word for it. Aimed. As if he was debating whether or not to fire at point-blank range.

Somewhere in the back of her mind, a line from a B movie, "Be afraid—be very afraid…" whispered along the perimeter of her brain. Warning her. Almost against her will, it caused her to brace her shoulders. Bailey had to remind herself to breathe in and out like a normal person.

The chief of staff, Dr. Bennett, had tried his level best to put her at ease and had almost succeeded. But an air of tension had entered with Munro. She wondered if Dr. Bennett was bracing himself as well, bracing for some kind of disaster or explosion.

"Ah, here he is now," Harold Bennett announced need-lessly. The smile on his lips was slightly forced, and the look in his gray, kindly eyes held a warning as he looked at his chief neurosurgeon. "We were just talking about you, Dr. Munro."

"Can't imagine why," Ivan replied dryly.

Harold cleared his throat, as if that would cover the less than friendly tone of voice Ivan had just displayed. "Dr. Munro, this is the young woman I was telling you about yesterday."

Now his eyes dissected her. Bailey felt as if she was under-going a scalpel-less autopsy right then and there. "Ah yes, the Stanford Special."

He made her sound like something that was listed at the top of a third-rate diner menu. There was enough contempt in his voice to offend an entire delegation from the UN.

Summoning the bravado that her parents always claimed had been infused in her since the moment she first drew breath, Bailey put out her hand. "Hello. I'm Dr. Bailey Del-Monico."

Ivan made no effort to take the hand offered to him. Instead, he slid his long, lanky form bonelessly into the chair beside her. He proceeded to move the chair ever so slightly so that there was even more space between them. Ivan faced the chief of staff, but the words he spoke were addressed to her.

"You're a doctor, DelMonico, when I say you're a doctor," he informed her coldly, sparing her only one frosty glance to punctuate the end of his statement.

Harold stifled a sigh. "Dr. Munro is going to take over your education. Dr. Munro—" he fixed Ivan with a steely gaze that had been known to send lesser doctors running for their antacids, but, as always, seemed to have no effect on the chief

neurosurgeon "—I want you to award her every considera-
tion. From now on, Dr. DelMonico is to be your shadow, your
sponge and your assistant." He emphasized the last word as
his eyes locked with Ivan's. "Do I make myself clear?"

For his part, Ivan seemed completely unfazed. He merely
nodded, his eyes and expression unreadable. "Perfectly."

His hand was on the doorknob. Bailey sprang to her feet. Her
chair made a scraping noise as she moved it back and then
quickly joined the neurosurgeon before he could leave the office.

Closing the door behind him, Ivan leaned over and whispered into her ear, "Just so you know, I'm going to be your
worst nightmare."

Bailey DelMonico has finally
gotten her life on track, and is
passionate about her recent career
change. Nothing will stand in the way
of her becoming a doctor…that is,
until she's paired with the sharp-tongued
Dr. Ivan Munro.

Watch the sparks fly in

Doctor in the House

by *USA TODAY* Bestselling Author

Marie Ferrarella

Available September 2007

Intrigued? Read more at
TheNextNovel.com

nocturne™

Look for

NIGHT MISCHIEF

by

NINA BRUHNS

Lady Dawn Maybank's worst nightmare
is realized when she accidentally conjures
a demon of vengeance, Galen McManus. What
she doesn't realize is that Galen plans to teach
her a lesson in love—one she'll never forget....

DARK ENCHANTMENTS

Available October wherever you buy books.

Don't miss the last installment of Dark Enchantments,
SAVING DESTINY by Pat White, available November.

www.eHarlequin.com   SN61772

Silhouette® Desire

**There was only one man for the job—
an impossible-to-resist maverick
she knew she didn't dare fall for.**

MAVERICK
(#1827)

BY *NEW YORK TIMES*
BESTSELLING AUTHOR
JOAN HOHL

"Will You Do It for One Million Dollars?"

Any other time, Tanner Wolfe would have balked at being
hired by a woman. Yet Brianna Stewart was desperate to
engage the infamous bounty hunter. The price was just
high enough to gain Tanner's interest…Brianna's beauty
definitely strong enough to keep it. But he wasn't about
to allow her to tag along on his mission. He worked
alone. Always had. Always would. However, he'd never
confronted a more determined client than Brianna. She
wasn't taking no for an answer—not about anything.

Perhaps a million-dollar bounty was not the only thing
this maverick was about to gain….

Look for MAVERICK

Available October 2007 wherever you buy books.

HARLEQUIN *Romance*

New York Times bestselling author

DIANA PALMER

Handsome, eligible ranch owner Stuart York knew
Ivy Conley was too young for him, so he closed his heart
to her and sent her away—despite the fireworks between
them. Now, years later, Ivy is determined not to be
treated like a little girl anymore…but for some reason,
Stuart is always fighting her battles for her. And safe in
Stuart's arms makes Ivy feel like a woman…his woman.

Winter Roses

Available November.

HARLEQUIN®

COMING NEXT MONTH

#351 IF HE ONLY KNEW... Debbi Rawlins
Men To Do

At Sara Wells's impromptu farewell party, coworker Cody Shea gives her a sizzling and unexpected kiss. Now, he may think this is the end, but given the hidden fantasies Sara's always had about the hot Manhattan litigator, this could be the beginning of a long goodbye....

#352 MY FRONT PAGE SCANDAL Carrie Alexander
The Martini Dares, Bk. 2

Bad boy David Carrera is the catalyst Brooke Winfield needs to release her inner wild child. His daring makes her throw off her conservative upbringing...not to mention her clothes. But will she still feel that way when their sexy exploits become front-page news?

#353 FLYBOY Karen Foley

A secret corporate club that promotes men who get down and dirty on business travel? Once aerospace engineer Sedona Stewart finds out why she isn't being promoted, she's ready to quit. But then she's assigned to work with sexy fighter pilot Angel Torres. And suddenly she's tempted to get a little down and dirty herself....

#354 SHOCK WAVES Colleen Collins
Sex on the Beach, Bk. 2

A makeover isn't exactly what Ellie Rockwell planned for her beach vacation. But losing her goth-girl look lands her a spot on her favorite TV show...and the eye of her teenage crush Bill Romero. Now that they're both adults, there's no end to the fun they can have.

#355 COLD CASE, HOT BODIES Jule McBride
The Wrong Bed

Start with a drop-dead-gorgeous cop and a heroine linked to an old murder case. Add a haunted town house in the Five Points area of New York City, and it equals a supremely sexy game of cat and mouse for Dario Donato and Cassidy Case. But their staying one step ahead of the killer seems less dangerous than the scorching heat between them!

#356 FOR LUST OR MONEY Kate Hoffmann
Million Dollar Secrets, Bk. 4

One minute thirty-five-year-old actress Kelly Castelle is pretty well washed-up. The next she's in a new city with all kinds of prospects—and an incredibly hot guy in her bed. Zach Haas is sexy, adventurous...and twenty-four years old. The affair is everything she's ever dreamed about. Only, dreams aren't meant to last....

www.eHarlequin.com

HBCNM0907